SECOND VERSE

JENNIFER WALKUP

Pub Date: October 2013
Format: Hardcover, $15.95 978-1-935462-86-6
eBook, $7.95 978-1-935462-87-3
Young Adult
Est. Length: 270 pages, Trim: 5-1/2" x 8-1/2"

For more information contact:

Rebecca Grose
Publicist
SoCal Public Relations
socalpublicrelations@yahoo.com
619.460.2179

Distributed by Midpoint Trade Books.
CIP info to come.

LUMINIS BOOKS
Published by Luminis Books
1950 East Greyhound Pass, #18, PMB 280,
Carmel, Indiana, 46033, U.S.A.
Copyright © Jennifer Walkup, 2013

PUBLISHER'S NOTICE
This is a work of fiction. Names, characters, places, and incidents are either the product of the
author's imagination or are used fictitiously. Any resemblance to actual persons, living or dead,
business establishments, events, or locales is entirely coincidental.

Hardcover ISBN: 978-1-935462-86-6
eBook ISBN: 978-1-935462-87-3

Printed in the United States of America

10 9 8 7 6 5 4 3 2 1

SECOND VERSE

JENNIFER WALKUP

LUMINIS BOOKS

For Mom,
First reader, first friend.

Early praise for *Second Verse:*

"Deliciously creepy and hauntingly beautiful, *Second Verse* satisfied my urge for both thrills and romance, all in one exciting package. Just be warned: extreme fear of the dark—and barns—might occur as a result of reading."

—Debra Driza, author of *MILA 2.0*

"A beautifully written story of love and loss that weaves past and present into a haunting tale that will keep you guessing until the final pages."

—Dawn Rae Miller, author of the *Sensitives Trilogy* and *Crushed*

"Part mysterious ghost story and part thriller, *Second Verse's* twists will keep you riveted. The intense connection between Lange and Vaughn is electric. A truly original debut."

—Cindy Pon, author of *Silver Phoenix* and *Fury of the Phoenix*

1

IF I HAVE to listen to one more debate about decapitation versus stabbing, I may just throw up.

Yet here we are again.

"I'm putting my money on an axe murder downtown. Tons of blood," Stace says, propping her feet on an empty cafeteria chair. "I'm talking in your face gore and guts."

Leaning back, Vaughn drums the edge of the table. "The messier the scene, the more popular it is. Remember that year with the beheaded family? That was awesome."

"Ew, guys, seriously?" I say. "While we're eating?" Even though this kind of talk has been buzzing around Preston Academy all month, it still makes me squeamish.

Kelly grins at me. "Wait, let me give my theory real quick before Lange throws up."

"You better make it quick," I say. "Because if you guys keep it up, I may just have to murder one of you for real."

Laughter bursts around the table as Kelly continues, "I'm betting on some type of serial killer situation." She pushes her headband through her fire-red hair. "Something psychological, and still in motion. Like you have to figure out who's next before you find the killer."

"Totally against the rules. The deed has to be done by nine p.m.," Ben says, expression serious. "And trust me," he says to me. "By the time The Hunt rolls around, you'll be completely into it."

"I doubt that." I nibble the edges of my sandwich. "Unless of course, you guys have managed to land me in the psych ward by then, which at this point is a definite possibility."

Stace giggles. "Never say never, Lange."

"Never," I say in a mock serious voice.

I've only been at Preston Academy of Arts since September, but the one thing I learned quickly is that they take this Hunt thing very seriously. Halloween in general seems pretty important to everyone in Shady Springs, but especially this decades-old tradition of The Hunt, a staged murder in town the night before the holiday. The deed in question is some kind of faked-up murder scheme, usually brutal from what I hear, put on by the seniors for us underclassmen to solve. The winner receives bragging rights, a free day off and a parking spot in senior row for a week. I guess if you put enough creative people in one school, things are bound to get weird.

Vaughn leans across the table, widening his beautiful brown eyes. "You're pretty anti-Halloween for someone who agreed to host a séance."

I grin. Tonight's the Friday the 13th séance at my house, my only contribution to the Halloween festivities. After listening to my friends and everyone else in school talk about The Hunt, and after seeing every store on Main Street decked out in Halloween decorations like a spooky haunted village, I'd had the perfect idea for a freak-out of my own. The fact that the 13th fell on a Friday this October was just icing on the cake.

"That's totally different. I'm all for Halloween creepiness, as long as it's not bloody. But this ax-murderer-decapitation-hunting-down-a-killer stuff is kind of sick, no?"

"Rookie," Stace jokes, rolling her eyes.

"Be nice." Ben wags a finger at her.

"Fine, fine. I'm a murder rookie. I'll admit it." I shrug. "Anyway, for tonight, come whenever you guys want. Kelly and I are setting up after school, right?"

Kelly bobs her head. "Yes! Wait till you see what I borrowed from the Costumes department."

"Awesome. My mom'll be in the house all night, but she knows the barn's off limits."

"You scared?" Vaughn raises an eyebrow.

"Nah. It'll be fun."

I was used to living in our huge, two-hundred year old farmhouse. It's the perfect setting for a séance, not just because it's old, but also because of the brutal murder that took place there years ago. And while nothing too creepy has happened in the four months we've lived there, I don't doubt there could be spirits hanging around. I just hope if there are, they aren't angry about the séance.

"Ha! You should see your face. You're white as, well, a ghost." Vaughn elbows Stace and motions to me. "Twenty bucks says Lange passes out before the séance is over."

"Ha, ha. Very funny."

Stace looks at me sideways. "So possibly contacting real ghosts is fine, but fake murders are scary?"

"Something like that." I laugh.

We're still debating the plausibility of ghosts when the bell rings. Ben and Kelly stand first, arm in arm on their way to toss their garbage. Ben, a concert pianist since he could walk, is the straightest-laced guy in the world. Today he's wearing dark jeans and a white button down shirt, and these fancy brown dress shoes, like he works in an office. But that's totally him. Kelly, who dresses like a gypsy most days, is the total opposite. You'd think they had nothing in common. I mean, Kelly has a nose ring. Ben has a side part. But they're such good friends, I thought they were a couple when I first met everyone early in the summer at the Brew Ha Ha coffee house.

"Wait up, guys!" Stace calls, slinging her patchwork backpack over her shoulder. Ben and Kelly pause, lost in conversation and waiting. When Stace leans over to kiss Vaughn's cheek, I sigh into my ham and cheese.

"Bye, you." Stace says to him before turning to me. "See ya, Lange."

"Later." I half wave.

It would be much easier to crush on Vaughn if Stace didn't seem so happy around him. It's practically the only time she smiles. Her blond ponytail swings as she turns the corner with one last wave.

When she's gone, Vaughn slides down the table to sit across from me. We have Creative Hour right after lunch, so we're here for another period. He shrugs into his denim jacket, covering his Zeppelin shirt, which is a bit ratty, even for him.

He looks at me through lashes that all the mascara in the world will never give me. "So, what's happening Languish?"

I roll my eyes at the name abuse. My name, Lange, is weird enough, thanks to my photographer mom's obsession with the famous photographer Dorothea Lange. But I've never really minded. It's different, like me, and gives a label to what I like to think of as non-conformity, but has probably always just been my non fitting in.

But Vaughn is in a constant state of trying to butcher it into something funny.

I smirk. "Like I haven't heard that one. I thought you were supposed to be creative?"

He throws a balled up napkin at me, missing by a mile.

"Ah, an athlete too, I see."

4

"Smartass." He tucks his light brown hair behind his ears, a gesture that always makes me think of things I shouldn't, like kissing, and how my fingers would feel all tangled in his hair.

Hiding my face, I rummage through my bag, in search of my favorite number six charcoal pencil, until my cheeks no longer feel warm. Finally, I open my sketchpad, sighing at the blank page. "I have this huge project for Motion Drawing and no idea where to start."

"That sucks," he says, drumming on the table again. "I've totally lost all inspiration lately too."

Vaughn, a musical prodigy who's given me chills with his renditions on the piano and can pretty much rock anything on his guitar, also writes incredible music. But lately, I've overheard him grumbling to Stace about Advanced Song Writing. Losing his poetry, he's been saying. His lyrics are amazing, so I doubt he's lost it, but whatever. Anxiety like this takes place all the time here. Unlike my last school in New Jersey, or even the really snooty one freshman year up in Boston, students at Preston are serious about their art. I close my sketchbook, watching from the corner of my eye as he pulls a Twinkie from his bag. I mock gag.

"What?" He asks, eating half of it with one bite.

"You do know what's in those things, right?" I doodle on the cover of the sketchbook, lines and shapes that eventually resemble a tree. A winter oak, leafless and cold.

"Oh stop it. You know I'm addicted. And they help me think. What are you, a food snob, now? You drink all those lattes like they're going out of style."

"That's totally different. Twinkies are like cockroaches. Atomic bombs, the apocalypse, whatever, Twinkies will still be here, never breaking down for all eternity. It's fake food, you do know that?" I wrinkle my nose.

He stuffs the rest of it into his mouth and gives me a smirk. "It's delicious." White cream drips from his bottom lip.

"Ew, gross!" Laughing, I grab the leftover stack of napkins and toss them toward him.

"So did you mean what you said before?" He licks his fingers.

I shade the oak's trunk with my charcoal pencil. "Which was...?"

"About the dead hanging around, ghosts and stuff? You believe in it?"

"I never said I did or I didn't." I think about the cool flashes I sometimes get, when I walk across the empty farmland behind our house. Involuntarily, I shiver. "Who wants to think about spirits lurking around us anyway?"

Vaughn looks at the table, his constant drumming providing a backbeat to our conversation. It's kind of falsely soothing, like one of those white noise machines. "Well, I don't think about it all the time or anything, and not ghosts exactly . . . but I do think about what happens. After we die, I mean."

"Well that's morbid." I add a few lonely leaves around the base of the tree. I ignore the thrumming in my chest and wish we could change the subject.

"But still," he says. "Don't you ever wonder?"

"I guess, but I try to focus on the now. To make life and art count for something while I can. You know?" I'm drawing an abandoned swing from the branch when I notice the absence of Vaughn's drumming.

He stares at me like I've spoken another language.

"What?" I duck my head.

"What you just said . . . " He has a thoughtful look on his face, like he's thinking about something totally distant, his eyes burning with emotion I can only wish was for me. "It's deep. Real." He continues to stare, bobbing his head slightly. "It's powerful, really." His eyes widen and he chews on his lower lip.

"Uh, oh. I think I know that look."

He nods. "Yep. You may have just sparked a bit of inspiration. Finally!" He moves fast, lit with sudden energy, rummaging in his bag for a pen and his beat up red notebook.

Me? Inspiration?

Writing like a madman, his pen scratches wildly across the page, pinning his notebook to the table with his left fist. He looks adorable when he's in songwriting mode. Eyebrows drawn together over milk chocolate eyes, hair hanging in waves against sharp cheekbones. And that bottom lip, always caught by his top teeth.

No. This is my friend's guy. Maybe not technically her boyfriend, but still.

Yet, the way he looks at me sometimes. Like just now when he had that burst of inspiration? It can't all be wishful thinking, can it?

I should not be thinking this way. We're just friends.

I clear my throat. "Can you guys bring your guitars tonight? I was thinking we can have a campfire after the séance?"

He rolls his eyes. "Anything else? I can bring my drum set too? Perhaps my baby grand?"

"Like you have a baby grand."

"Someday, Auld Lang Syne, someday." He pushes another lock of hair back.

"Come on." He motions to the front of the cafeteria, where the teacher's aides stare at their laptops, ear buds in, totally oblivious. "Let's go bug Stace upstairs." He sticks the folded notebook in his back pocket. "I want to show her this."

My heart deflates the tiniest bit, but that's silly. Of course we should go see Stace. I should want to see Stace. And I do. Really.

I follow him into the hall, with an inane sense of pride welling again when I notice the extra bounce in his step.

Now, I just need to find *my* inspiration.

7

2

I MAY HAVE gone a little overboard.

I'll admit it.

Even though the séance idea started as my way of contributing to the whole Halloween hoopla around school, once we're setting up, I can't stop myself. Maybe it's the artist in me, maybe it's the general mood around town, or maybe it's just after years of hearing Mom spew about this new-age, let's-be-one-with-the-spirits stuff I feel it's in my blood to be able to do this. Whatever the reason, I go for the all-out creep-factor.

First of all, our house is huge. I don't mean that in a stuck-up, ohmygodimrich sorta way, like the tight asses in Boston used to talk. I mean that my mom bought this centuries-old farmhouse that has three times more rooms than we could ever use. We've lived in more states than I can count on one hand, but this is the first time she's gone all out. A professional photographer and all-around art lover, Mom is drawn to the romantic and historic, and for her, this house was it. And with its violent history, which apparently kept people from buying it for years, but which doesn't seem to bother her at all, she was able to get a great deal. Don't get me wrong, it's got tons of potential, and Mom and I have been painting and tearing and building like crazy. Honestly, the creative endeavor has helped us bury all the stuff we aren't talking about.

I tie black velvet across the chair backs, my fingers sliding over the material like a whisper.

But, romantic as an old house can be, when it's mostly empty it has a definite creepiness. Add to the fact that we have about three acres of land, half of which is woods, not to mention a huge, looming barn, two additional horse stables and multiple sheds—all empty—you have a lot to work with if you want to freak yourself out.

Which is exactly what I plan to do to my friends.

And then there's the murder. Much as I pretend it doesn't bother me, of course it does. How could it not? Since most of my friends have lived in Shady Springs their whole lives, everyone knows the basic story. A brutal killing of an entire family. It happened in the main house and then the killer hung himself in the barn.

But that's where the details veer off. Considering no one's stories line up, it's easy to dismiss them as rumors. Facts get muddy over time.

Ben says it was a shotgun, that his grandfather's friend told someone who told someone who swore up and down the gunshots rang out across town. That theory isn't very popular, especially since gunshots can't be heard dozens of miles away.

Kelly calls the killer a slasher. Something about knives or swords or an axe. I've even heard scalding water, pitchforks, and poison. There's various bloody details of all theories, of course, and depending on who's telling, it can get graphic. Like that telephone game, the stories get more and more convoluted as they're passed down. Besides, people always get carried away. I for one, like not knowing the specifics. Makes it easier to live here not knowing just how gruesome it was.

I drape a swathe of black gauze over the table I've set up in the middle of the barn.

There's another thing everyone agrees on: the hanging. The murderer found dangling from the barn's rafters. Days later, already rotting.

So the story goes.

Hence the scene of the séance. I figure why not have it in the scariest place I can. Everyone is scared of my barn. Even smartass Vaughn gets a straight face when we talk about the murders. The energy in here is eerie on the sunniest days. If there's anywhere we'll contact a spirit, it'll be here.

I stand back to admire my work. Five chairs around the small round table, all draped with gauze and velvet. Pillar candles lined up in the center. For some reason, Mom had boxes and boxes of votive candles and holders, and I've placed those all around the barn, on every still surface. I've even zigzagged some across the thin layer of hay that covers the floor. In the doorways, the same gauze hangs, filtering the light with its shroud-like material. It drapes the barn with an unnatural dimness that's somehow chilling. In each of the old animal stalls, with the decades of decay most apparent there, the wooden slats splintered and dry-rotted, I've stuck Kelly's *papier-mâché* creations—perfectly detailed severed arms and grasping fingers. They're sickening. It's gross, but I've dribbled fake blood down the wood, pooling it in front of each stall in a sticky heap of hay.

It's perfect.

Blood. That's the other detail about the murders everyone agrees has to be true. Blood all over the house. But that seems like the kind of detail that would get added to any scary story. What's creepier than blood-stained walls? Floors and tiles splattered with it and a dead family strewn around the rooms, like cut up rag dolls?

I shudder.

I drag the empty supply boxes into the furthest stall, piling them next to a stack of wood pallets. I ball the rest of the gauze in my hands. I'd wanted to hang some from the rafters, but I don't feel like climbing that high.

The book Mom gave me said lighting a séance is one of the most important elements. It sets the mood. Everyone has to be open and serious if we want it to work.

A low groan fills the space above me. It sounds positively human. Warmth buzzes through me, numbing me and throwing me off balance. I stumble, shaking off the heavy sense of *déjà vu*. I back quickly out of the barn, looking up into the second story rafters as if I expect to see someone dangling. My hands tremble as I let the gauze fall in front of the doorway again, my breath coming in ragged bursts like I've been sprinting.

I crash into something and hands come out of nowhere, grabbing me. I let out a high pitched scream, warbling like a bad horror-movie actress.

Kelly laughs and drops her hands to her sides. "You all right?"

I shake my head. Out in the daylight, I feel like a moron. "Yeah, I'm fine. I freaked myself out in there, I guess." My laugh comes out like a strangled bark. "Tonight is going to be awesome if I'm creeping myself out this much in the daylight."

"I found more candles." She holds up two white tapers and an ancient-looking pair of candlesticks.

"Nice," I say, taking them from her just as the wind whips my hair around my face. They're heavy.

"Where'd you get these?"

She shrugs, nodding to the house. "Your mom. She said she found them in the attic."

"Of course," I say, smiling. Mom not only gave me the idea for the séance, she pretty much helped me find all the creepy stuff to use for it.

I glance up at the fourth-story window. The light's on. Mom's been cleaning out the attic for weeks now. There's lifetimes worth of stuff up there, dating back to who knows when. She's been photographing most of it for some project.

I look down at the candlesticks again, testing their weight. Some kind of metal. Pewter, maybe. They must be five pounds each. They're gorgeous, with a brushed finish and scrolling designs, thin near the top, then widening into leaves around the base. On their felt bottoms the letter G has been scratched into one and V into the other.

"You sure you're okay?" Kelly says gently, her freckled cheeks lifting with her smile.

"Yes! These are perfect. This is gonna be awesome."

"Lange!" Mom's voice drifts across the yard. She leans against the back porch railing, balancing a heavy box and waving me over. When I get there, she pushes the box toward me.

"I found this upstairs. More candles." She pulls her blond-gray hair off her face and smiles. "Thought they may help set your scene."

"Cool, thanks." Inside are at least two dozen more votives. I place the heavy candlesticks on top of them and take the box from her. "This is great."

"Have fun," she says. "And remember, if you do contact someone—"

"I know, I know. Respect them and they'll respect us." I roll my eyes, but my fingers tremble beneath the box. I've never felt the barn quite like it feels today.

Back at the barn, Kelly and I duck around the gauze doorway. Trying to keep my attention off the rafters, I rearrange the pillars on the table, making room for the candlesticks in the center. We step back with our arms folded and smile.

"Ben is gonna shit." She giggles. "It's perfect."

"You think?"

"Oh yeah. Don't tell him I told you, but he's a big baby. Gets scared super easy." She grins. "I've seen him nearly jump out of his skin from the slightest noise after watching any horror movie, especially if it involves ghosts."

I line up the votives. "Good. Hopefully my small contribution to the Shady Springs Halloween obsession will be a success. You think Stace and Vaughn'll be scared, too?"

"Ah, who knows? You know them. They're so extreme about everything. Vaughn'll probably be trying to channel John Lennon or something."

I can definitely imagine him doing exactly that. But even though I'm smiling, something about her comment makes me uneasy.

"Well, this was a perfect touch." I hand her the remaining ball of gauze.

"I figured it would be. Everything is creepier when cloaked and flowing." She tucks the material under her arm. "Plus, Mrs. Sand loved the idea of helping us out. She gets into this stuff." Kelly's creative outlet is fashion design, and she's one of the department chair's favorite students. She walks over to the severed hands and rearranges a few of the fingers.

She frowns. "Not sure these are realistic enough."

"They are more than realistic." I shudder, unable to take my eyes off them. I motion to the main house. "Come on, let's go get the food ready, before everyone gets here. We'll light all these before it gets too dark."

We step back into the yard, where dusk now bathes the grass in shadows. But I turn back one more time, push the makeshift curtain aside, and look up at the rafters just to make sure nothing is there.

WHEN NIGHT HAS fallen and the candles have been lit, the barn looks better than I could have imagined. It's less creepy in the way of gore, despite the mangled *papier-mâché* limbs and fake blood, and more serenely eerie with the hundreds of candles. There's an energy throbbing in the middle of it all, but that could just be my adrenaline. As we all settle in around the table, something stirs in me, soft as a breeze. It's probably the setting and mood we've created that makes me extra heady and superstitious, but even Vaughn looks serious as he settles into the seat next to mine.

"Okay," I say in a low voice, my eyes cast down at the table and my neatly folded hands. Although I don't feel like myself, I'm not acting. It's like I'm removed, standing at the back of the barn, watching myself perform this ritual. I'd been worried that we'd all be giggling and making a joke out of it, but everything about the scene is serious.

Almost without thinking about it, my body goes into motion, arms flowing effortlessly, hands smoothing the cloth and arranging candles as if I've done this before. I breathe deeply and try to let out all my energy, like Mom said. It feels completely natural.

I invert a hurricane glass on the table. Once it's upside down, I hold my hands up before reaching for Kelly on my left and Vaughn on my right. The motion invites the others to join in, and soon we're all connected, holding hands around the table. I make eye contact with each of them: First wide-eyed Kelly, who looks solemn and serene. If I didn't already know she was a devout Atheist, I would swear she was praying. Next to her is Ben, who coughs and shifts his blue eyes to Kelly every few seconds. He fidgets in his seat. We make eye contact and I nod, offering positive energy to tell him it will be okay. His body relaxes.

Stace is next, her pretty face emotionless with the noncommittal look she always wears. I nod to her, again trying to pass my energy to each of my friends, to force the collective concentration. The intensity that burns in her eyes when she and Vaughn talk poetry and guitar chords flickers on her face, in the tightening of her lips and her narrowed eyes. Candlelight bounces off her.

14

Finally, my eyes meet Vaughn's, which somehow dart without moving, as if he's offering me a secret. Or maybe searching for one in mine. I dig deep into that look, trying to understand what he's looking for. But I can't because it's back, as sudden as before.

That rolling sense of unease. *Have I done this before?*

"Okay," I say with an exhale. I close my eyes and try to summon strength from the group. Outside, the wind screeches in the birch trees. Branches knock against the side of the barn, the wooden planks rattling like old windows.

When I open my eyes, everyone is staring at the table with solemn expressions.

I reach deep inside myself, digging for the right emotions. First, I conjure images of death. Funerals I've been to. The old graveyard my friends and I use to cut through on the way home from school in Jersey, when I used to flit at the edge of the cemetery, pretending I didn't feel the cool touch of the spirits reaching for me. An entire family murdered in this house. A man hanging in this very barn. After that I reach for grief. I don't have to dig far for that. The wounds are raw, still new enough to feel fresh.

I will not cry.

It's like a stream of gasoline has been lit with a single match. The connection, like a tied knot, pulls tight in me and I'm suddenly confident. I can do this.

"We are here to summon your spirit." My voice is nearly a whisper. It's silent outside, not a hint of wind anywhere now. Even the barn is quiet. It's as if none of us is even breathing. That feeling inside me stirs again, light curtains swishing in my stomach, soon churning faster, a whirlwind of tumbling fear and anticipation. I hold tight to the grief, hoping it will bring us a spirit.

Listening to the feeling for a moment, I try to remember what I've read about opening oneself to spirit visitation. As much as I'd wanted this to be for fun, it feels more real than I could have imagined.

"If you are here, please respond by using your power to move the glass on our table."

Breathing deeply, I focus on my heart. It races at a frightening speed.

I stare at the glass, wanting it to move, but terrified of it moving. Everyone holds their breath and I'm afraid to even look around the table.

Silence fills the space like an overinflated balloon.

"Use your power to move the glass. If you're here, show us your power. Use your strength. Show us your power." I repeat variations of the same phrase. Still hoping. Still scared.

Deep in my chest I feel something, like a deadbolt being unlocked. It's a subtle feeling that I almost don't notice. But then, like a door, a space swings open inside me. Inviting.

"Show yourself," I whisper.

Underneath the table, something skitters across the floor, creating a slight breeze across my feet. Everything in me tightens and I force myself to take even breaths. The breeze travels up my legs. Around the table, everyone tenses. They feel it too.

We stare at the glass, but it doesn't move. A scratching noise from the underside of the table, like fingernails on wood, makes me sit straighter. Sweat drips down my neck. Across the table, Stace shifts in her seat, eyes widening. She nods to me, giving me the confidence to continue. The scratching gets louder. Faster, almost frantic, like someone scratching from the inside of a coffin.

"We feel your presence," I say.

The scratching fades slowly and a thick energy fills the air. The breeze travels across my shoulders, down my arms. I shiver.

Beside me, Kelly shivers, then Ben, then Stace, and finally, Vaughn. It's passing across us. Kelly's hand trembles in mine.

A bright light bounces just outside my peripheral and everyone's heads turn toward it.

I tighten my grip on both Kelly and Vaughn's hands. Kelly's grasp loosens, her fingers hanging limply in mine, but Vaughn squeezes back hard, pinning my fingers like a vice. A sudden flush of energy comes from him, like I've been plugged into something electric.

A voice hisses through the barn at an alarmingly loud decibel. *"Sellllll. Herrrr. Sweeeeney."*

The heavy attic candlesticks topple over on the table. Collectively, there's a sharp intake of breath, and then everyone seems to deflate, arms and hands falling to their sides. Vaughn's lingers in mine for longer than the others and I can't shake the feeling of something electric, like live wires. When his hand tightens on mine again, the sensation swells. I hold my breath and so does he. The moment we let go, the doors at the east end of the barn bang open, loud as a gunshot. A hurricane-strength gust rushes through the barn, extinguishing all the candlelight.

I feel hollow inside, as if it's rushed through me too.

Sweat drips down the back of my neck while I listen to my friends' ragged breathing. In the dim moonlight that shines in from the now-open doors, I can just barely make out each of their shadows.

No one speaks. No one moves.

"Wow," Kelly finally says, her normally sunny voice like the darkest, murkiest part of a lake.

"What did that mean?" I barely manage to get the words out.

"Yeah, did you feel that under the table?" Stace's voice is even, though she speaks in a whisper. "And across our arms?"

"Those things are heavy." Ben says in a shaky voice, nodding to the candlesticks. "That was no accident."

I shake my head. "No. Not the candlesticks. Not whatever moved through here. The voice."

A metallic shiver passes through me, like my blood is being drained.

Even in the near-darkness, I see Kelly's profile turn to me. "What voice?"

There's no way I'm the only one who heard it.

My pulse jumps, chasing my erratic thoughts. The door inside, the one I've somehow unlocked, bangs against my ribcage.

"I heard it too," Vaughn whispers, so quiet I can barely hear him. "Loud and clear."

3

EVERYONE'S QUIET WHILE we break down the séance. We move silently, packing away candles and tablecloths and fake blood. Once we've removed every stitch of proof that it happened, we all breathe easier, though everyone keeps their eyes off the barn.

"So," Kelly says, dragging the chairs into the yard. "Are we still doing the campfire?"

"Huh?" I blink. Everyone stares at me.

Sell. Her. Sweeney.

"Campfire?" Ben prompts me, his eyes so wide the white of them glows in the darkness.

"Oh sure. We can do it over here." My words tumble over each other as we move further into the yard, far away from the barn. "I have a CD player somewhere."

"Twenty-first century, Lange. I brought my iPod and dock," Vaughn says, so close to me that I jump. But his voice is quiet, his typical joking tone hidden beneath something chillingly somber.

"I thought we were going to play?" Stace nods to her guitar. "I know *I* could use the distraction."

"Yeah, of course. That sounds like the best idea." I force a smile and try to ignore the layer of sweat on my back and in my hair.

Kelly and Ben carry the rest of the boxes onto the porch while Vaughn and Stace get their guitars. I stumble more than once as I drag the chairs into a circle around the fire pit. On the metal hearth of the structure, I stack the wood into a teepee shape and carefully roll newspaper to stuff beneath it.

Just focus on the tasks, Lange. Don't think about the barn. Or the voice.

"Lighter fluid would help," Stace says, staring at the pile of wood while she tunes her guitar. "Weren't you ever a Girl Scout or did they not have those in Jersey?" She laughs, joking with me like always about living in Jersey, but it falls flat tonight. We're all still freaked.

"Never done this," I say. "Guess it shows."

Shaking her head, she smiles, plucking away at the strings while she starts to hum a song. Vaughn, carrying his guitar by the neck, sits on a chair behind me. I attempt to strike the first match on the box, but my fingers shake and it goes out almost immediately. I try again with even less luck, barely even getting the match lit.

"Damn it." I growl.

"Let me help." Vaughn's somehow inched up next to me again. Gives me a chill.

"Thanks, I'm a total spaz." I force a laugh as I pass him the box. But our fingers brush and there's another faint spark. His eyes glitter in the dark.

"Lange!"

I jump, blinking back to reality. Kelly waves to me from the porch, where she and Ben lean over the banister.

"Wake up out there! Marshmallows and cider? Inside?" She points to the back door.

I nod, unable to speak, still trying to will my body back to the moment.

The fire roars in front of us and through it, I watch Stace play. Her soft song provides a background to the crack of the fire. Her voice is soothing.

"That sounds nice. What is it?"

"Purgatory," she says. "What else?"

Ah, of course. Purgatory. Her favorite band, the local indie group everyone loves.

"Sorry." I smile. "Non-musical, here."

She closes her eyes, getting into the song. Vaughn, still sitting in the chair behind me, picks up his guitar.

He leans forward. "We need to talk," he whispers.

I pretend I don't hear him and roll up more newspaper to put in the fire. When Stace finishes her song, I clap. She smiles with a small nod as she waves Vaughn over. They play together, their melodies and voices melding perfectly.

"Score!" Ben says from the porch, holding up a bag of marshmallows and a jug of store-bought cider. He and Kelly come down the steps and hand out the supplies.

We drink cider and roast marshmallows. We sing songs. And we pretend the séance didn't happen, or maybe that it was no more than a ghost story gone out of control.

I wish.

Sell. Her. Sweeney.

I watch the flames dance and flicker, watch them change from red to orange to blue. The wood cracks and crumbles. Burns. I tune out the conversation, thinking only of the emptiness inside me, the current that moved through me in the barn.

And the one that came from Vaughn.

Just the thought makes me buzz inside and when I look up, I find him staring. A blazing look that rivals the fire's dancing flames. I look away, but we've caught each other. And I know this wasn't just a ghost story to him, even if it was to the others.

He heard it too. Loud and clear, he said.

But I want to believe it didn't happen. I want so bad to laugh and sing and eat marshmallows as if nothing has changed inside me.

I'll ignore it, for now. And I'll ignore him, too. I'll get things back to normal even if it means pretending I don't recognize that look in his eyes. And the dread creeping through me that mirrors it.

4

THERE'S WAY MORE blood than there should be. It rolls down my arm in warm rivulets.

"Shit!" I gather my bloody fingers with my other hand, pressing tightly.

Mom comes rushing in, nearly tripping over the open box I've been working through. By the time she gets here, I'm at the sink, watching the red drops fall and blossom against the cracked, white porcelain.

"What happened?" Her eyes dart to the box and back to my hand.

"There must be something broken in there. Damn." I spread my fingers to inspect the damage. In the dim light of the third floor bathroom, there's too much blood to make out how deep it is.

She turns the cold water knob, but other than the loud squeak of rubbing metal, nothing comes out.

"Here." She rips a clean paper towel from a roll and I soak up the blood on my fingers first, applying pressure. Carefully, I wipe down my arm while I try again to examine the damage. Mom leans over me for a closer look. The dim bulb, flickering as usual from the windy night, shines weakly on my hand, showing two deep-ish cuts across my ring and middle fingers. I press the flesh around them. They're sore, but only a trickle of new blood emerges. And at least it's my left hand.

"Looks like you'll live," she says, pushing her hair out of her eyes. "You need a bandage?"

I shake my head. It already almost stopped.

"In that case," she nods around the bathroom, "Let's find the culprit before one of us cuts ourselves again."

I gape at the mess I've made. Blood runs on the floor in a jagged line from the edge of the claw foot tub to the sink. I peer over the tub's side and see I've managed to drip some down the inside, too.

"Oh crap, I'm sorry."

She looks up from where she's digging through the box. Her eyes narrow on the mess, but she quickly composes herself with a deep breath. "I'll just clean it later," she mumbles.

I feel bad. She's been setting up this shoot for the last few weeks and I've bled down the middle of it. She's arranged all sorts of her attic finds in the tub, old glass bottles, jars, and sea glass in various shapes, colors and sizes, all on top a vintage faded tablecloth she pulled out of the ruins. A few drops of my blood have dripped across the edge of the pale blue cloth.

I can't take my eyes off the crimson blotches, trying to ignore the way they seem to spread and morph on the fabric. A flash like a photographer's bulb lights in my mind, travels through me like a spark. A clench of unease, a taste of fear. A word floats in the air like the aftermath of lightening. *Abyss.*

And then it's gone.

I shake my head, forcing down the ominous fear pumping through me.

"Here it is!" Mom pulls a piece of green glass from the bottom of the box. It makes me think of geometry class. It's an isosceles triangle. She holds it up and, sure enough, blood drips off the edge.

Even though it's my blood, it still makes me shiver, my stomach coiling tightly.

Inside, I feel the click of unlocking again.

Nothing's been normal since Friday night's séance. It's only been four days, but nothing feels right.

Mom stands, dropping the glass into the makeshift garbage box in the hallway. I have to force myself not to look at it. She dusts her hands on her jeans. "Now, where was I?"

I nod toward the stairs, trying to keep my thoughts on her attic excavations, but I don't succeed. *Don't look at the garbage. Don't look at the box. Or the cloth. Or the tub.*

Ignore the blood.

What is wrong with me?

Mom leans against the doorframe, hand on hip. "You never did finish telling me what happened the other night in the barn."

Finish? I never told her anything at all about the séance.

"That's because nothing happened," I say.

She looks at me sideways, squinting as if she's trying to figure me out.

"What?" I snap, afraid she *will* figure me out in that uncanny way she has sometimes. Or, even worse, slip into that brainwashed looking gaze where she starts talking about being one with the spirits and nature.

The phone rings from down the hall.

Thankfully.

"All right, all right, I give up," she says, holding up her hands. She nods down the hall. "Can you get that?" she asks, already halfway up the attic stairs. "I think I left it on the landing of the south stairs. Or in my studio. I can't remember. I'm expecting a call from one of the photo organizers of the New York convention. Come get me if it's them?"

"Sure," I say, glad for the excuse to get out of here. I dash down the hall, the closed doors of the third floor bedrooms rushing by as I sprint. I check the tiny bedroom off Mom's room first, the one she uses as a studio. My eyes quickly take in the still life photos hanging on the wire that crosses the space, and the cluttered desk. No phone here. It rings again, from further down the hall.

"Hello?" I'm out of breath by the time I finally reach it.

"You are aware of the fact that there's an airport that shares your name, right?"

I sigh into the receiver and wish for the millionth time that my mom had invested in caller id. Maybe it was time to join the 21st century. I make my way down the stairs. "Hey Vaughn. What's up?"

Like I don't know. A few days' worth of ducking into stairways and eating lunch in the bathroom couldn't go on forever.

"Where were you at lunch today? And in creative period? Way to ditch your friends all week." His laugh is hollow. Vaughn's not a guy who fakes it. Dancing around the subject has got to be killing him.

"I was meeting with Mr. Murphy about my Transformations project for Motion. I'm so behind." I fake a yawn and try to stretch my voice into boredom. "I'm working on it now. I should go, actually." I step into my room and turn on the light. The curtains billow with wind from the open windows, the screens rattling with it.

"Right. How's this? If I had to guess, I'd say you don't even have your sketchpad out of your bag, let alone open."

I glance at my backpack, thrown haphazardly across my desk, with my sketchpad peeking out from beneath the books inside.

"Come on, Lange. We *need* to talk about what happened." He sounds so defeated, I can't even get mad, and he's using that hard-to-refuse voice that practically purrs.

My first instinct is to say nothing happened, but we both know that's not true.

Not even close.

Sure, everyone was kind of freaked out, and they're even more convinced my house, or at least the barn, is haunted. But that weird sensation I felt? No one knows about that. Except maybe Vaughn. I don't know. I'm not sure what he felt, if the energy that flowed between us went both ways. I know we both heard the voice. Those chilling words that have etched themselves into my brain over and over again.

Sell. Her. Sweeney.

"Fine. What do you want me to say?" I sink to my bed and let my head fall against the pillow.

"Let's start with the fact that you have a ghost that obviously wants to tell us something."

I try to keep my voice even. "Oh come on. There's no ghost. We all just got carried away. It was the history of this place. And the candles, and the Friday the 13th thing. It's just a mind trick we played on ourselves."

He's silent.

"Lange."

Lying on my side, I stare at myself in the window.

"Let's put it this way," he says in a shaky voice. "Up until a few nights ago, things were normal. I wasn't hearing voices."

"Wait, you heard it again?" I sit up and stare at my wide-eyed reflection in the rippled glass.

"Oh, so you admit you heard it."

Ugh.

"Hear me out," he says. "But don't think I'm crazy."

I listen, pressing my thumb against my cut fingers and flinching at the pain.

"I think something happened."

"We've established that, genius." But I know he's not just talking about the voice or the candles.

"Will you listen? It's something else. Something, I don't know... inside? Do you know what I mean?" His voice fizzles.

27

I know how hard this is for him. I should tell him what I feel, what I felt that night, and upstairs a few minutes ago. But that would only feed it, keep it going. If I ignore it, it will go away.

He sighs, frustrated. "Okay, I'll try this another way. Something strange is happening and for some reason, I think you'll understand. Can I just come over? I've got something to show you. It will explain it better than I can. Please?"

I'm thrown off by his request, and he's using that velvety voice again.

"Fine," I say, despite my best judgment.

The only question left is what to do when he gets here. Do I talk, or do I keep pretending nothing is going on?

5

HE SHOWS UP minutes after we hang up. Hearing his car on the gravel, I bound down the north stairs and into the kitchen to open the back door. With his guitar slung over his back, and his hair all disheveled, he looks very rebel without a cause on my porch, his fist raised to knock. I smile and slip outside as he lets his hand fall.

"Hey." I stuff my hands into my pockets and let the back door fall silently into its jamb.

"Hey." He returns my smile, but it doesn't light him the way happiness usually does. There's no joking. No massacre of my name, no smirking.

"What's up?" I don't know what else to say as we settle onto the porch swing. I twist my hands in my lap, afraid that if they had their way, they'd be reaching for him again, trying for that strange, electrifying connection.

He lowers his guitar to the wide-planked floor and stares across my yard. "Um. This probably sounds weird, but can we go to the barn?" He looks into the dark, toward the barn, all serious like he's watching his own funeral.

"That's probably not a great idea."

He turns to look at me, eyes wide and brimming with such passion I don't know whether to be terrified or flattered.

"Lange, I—" He shakes his head, eyes down.

I wait, but he says nothing else.

Finally, I clear my throat. "You said you had something to show me?"

His face brightens briefly when he picks up his guitar. "Yeah, when I left here the other night, something happened. It was weird, like something clicked into place... Like I'd found something I hadn't exactly known I was missing." He shakes his head again. "I know it sounds nuts, but I became almost compulsive all weekend. Writing." He pats the body of the guitar. "The thing is . . . " he lowers his voice, glancing into the dark again. "I don't remember writing much. I mean, I *remember* writing, but when it was finally done, and I played it through, I don't remember the composition. It's familiar, and it's mine, but it's like someone else wrote it. *Through me.*"

I shift on the bench, ignoring the tingling sensation blossoming in my chest. Things hadn't exactly been normal for me either, but I don't know what to say to that. I don't want to understand him. Not when it comes to this.

"Vaughn..."

"I know. Crazy, right? You think I'm crazy." He looks at his shoes.

"No—I don't, I—"

"Well I feel crazy. I can't stop thinking about it. That night." His eyes are vibrant now, lit with energy and excitement.

I look away, trying to think of something else. Anything else. Because he's right, I want more than anything to find out what we felt that night in the barn. I want the answers too, to figure out what those strange words mean. I want to touch his hand and feel those sparks of connection again.

The wind whistles high in the trees, but it's Vaughn who makes me tremble.

"Anyway. I wrote this. It's only the beginning so far, but . . . " He strums his guitar, settling into his playing stance, knee up, guitar balanced. He holds the pick between his teeth while he tunes the knobs, stopping to push his hair behind his ears. Before he even starts, my skin tingles with anticipation.

The melody envelops me, slips over me like a second skin. Like an arm that pulls me close. He looks down, nodding along and watching his fingers as they find the chords. But then he looks up and his eyes find mine.

My breath catches and stays in my chest as Vaughn starts to sing.

Shades are grey, are what you see,
But if you look you will find me,
In the space where stardust lies,
In the dreams of lullabies
The water in the ocean rolls,
with restless waves, but truth be told
it will never silence me.
Forever you will come to me.
Back again. Here I am.
Like the wind across your hand,
Your voice is resting in my ear,
You're in my veins, you're crystal clear.
Hold my heart it won't be long.
I will meet you far beyond.
That abyss. Can't be missed. That abyss.

I STUMBLE AS I try and put one foot in front of the other. Vaughn's hand is on my waist, gently guiding me up the stairs. Everything is hazy like I'm walking inside a cloud.

I can hardly stand, spots dancing in my vision until I lie down. In my mind, I see a weird scene, but it's like I'm watching through that same fog. It's Vaughn's song, but his voice isn't quite the same. It hovers just outside my thoughts, like a memory I shouldn't have, working its way through my mind and veins. Seeping into me. As the music fades, another flash appears, a bright light that hangs in the air.

The whole vision evaporates before I can grab hold of the rest of it. I lie in silence, staring at the water stains on my ceiling.

I rub my eyes. "What just happened?"

"You kind of almost passed out on your porch."

"I did?" I rub my eyes. "Wow, that came out of nowhere."

"Is that what you really think?"

An iron fist tightens, low in my stomach. I open my eyes slowly, afraid of what I'll see. Vaughn looks down at me, leaning against my desk with his arms folded. When I don't answer, he turns to look out the window. Toward the barn.

"I've been sick," I lie. "My head's just foggy."

He doesn't answer.

Finally, my mind clears enough to make me intensely aware of Vaughn in my bedroom. I push up on one elbow. "So, welcome to my room, I guess." I croak out the words, looking quickly to make sure there are no bras hanging out of my drawers.

He pulls out my desk chair and sits down with a slight smile. "Thanks. But I think we're past all that, don't you?"

"Just trying to be nice," I mumble as he pulls his guitar onto his lap, balancing it on his knee. I turn halfway on the bed to face him. "You want a drink or something? Twinkie?"

He returns my weak smile with one of his own as he starts to play. I drift in and out of sleep while he strums his guitar, working on that same beautiful melody. I listen, letting the notes burn into me. Stamping the lyrics to my memory. Wishing he'd never stop playing.

Your voice is resting in my ear, You're in my veins, you're crystal clear. Hold my heart it won't be long. I will meet you far beyond.

His face is fierce. Drawn and concentrated. He stops often to look at me, liquid brown eyes flecked with copper. In them is a place I don't quite know yet, a great leap from where we were last week.

It's a dangerous look.

And I bask in it, even though I shouldn't.

6

I CAN'T AVOID Vaughn or my friends forever, so I head to lunch on Wednesday with my brown paper bag and my sketchpad, pretending like everything's normal. I'm somehow late even though I didn't do anything out of the ordinary after class and I curse the fog I've been living in this week.

"Where ya been?" Stace grins as she bites into her pizza. "You're missing a very interesting conversation today."

Cautiously, I pull out my chair. "That sounds suspicious." We tend to get into lots of interesting conversations, but they don't always end well. The last such talk involved listing famous people we'd hook up with. Stace practically ripped Vaughn's head off with every suggestion he made. I'm not in the mood for a repeat.

"Nah, it's nothing bad," Kelly says, waving away my worried expression. "Since we're still in Halloween mode—"

"Less than two weeks to go!" Stace says.

Kell gives her a look before continuing, "*and* after the night of the séance—"

Ben interrupts by humming the *Twilight Zone* theme song. Vaughn smiles, and when no one's looking, he winks at me.

My sandwich crumbles in my grip.

"Anyway." Kelly shoots Ben a shut-up look. "We're talking about the strangest, weirdest things we've ever done."

Wonderful.

"And?" I take another bite of my sandwich and try to act nonchalant. "What do we have so far?"

Stace bursts out laughing. "Total lameness."

Ben huffs, crossing his arms over his chest. "I'm not lame!"

"Riiiight," Stace says, shaking her head. Even Kelly giggles behind her hand.

"What?" I look between the three of them. "What did I miss?"

"Ben and some friends at piano camp. They played 'Bloody Mary' in the mirror to try and freak themselves out."

"Bloody Mary?" I chew thoughtfully, amused by the look of rage on Ben's face.

Vaughn grins. "It's when you go in a dark room and say Bloody Mary a bunch of times in a mirror to try and evoke the angry ghost of Mary who will come out and kill you."

"Child's game," Stace adds with a snicker.

"It's not a child's game! And anyway, it was a few years ago. I was young."

"You were still in high school." Kelly scrunches her features in an *I'm sorry* way and rests a hand on his arm. "But it *can* be scary. I guess."

"It's no worse than yours." He looks pointedly at her, rolling his eyes.

"Do I even want to know?"

"Ouija boards are totally scary!" Kelly says defensively. Everyone laughs.

I giggle along and try my hardest to not look at Vaughn. From the corner of my eye, I watch him laugh and wonder if it feels as fake to him as it does to me.

Especially after last night.

"Fine, what about you, Stace? If you're so tough?" Kelly sticks out her tongue.

"Well," Stace says, piling her lunch on her tray. "I do have one weird thing. But it's kind of different. It's nothing ghost or spirit-related, anyway."

Sounds good to me.

But like a book that's been slammed, Stace closes up. "Nah, it's weird."

"Come on, we're all friends. Spill. It can't be half as bad as Ben's."

"Kell!"

Stace looks at each of us, frowning. "Fine. But keep in mind, I had a weird childhood. I used to have these strange thoughts. For a long time, I thought they were normal, but I guess they weren't."

I shift my hands to my lap.

"And?" Vaughn's voice is gentle. I don't look up because I don't want to see the way he's probably looking at her.

"There was this one time... I don't know. I didn't do it, but almost. Well, not really, but it was just a thought..."

"Out with it already!" Ben says.

She takes a deep breath. "My sisters were in the tub and I was blow drying my hair. I watched them for a while in the mirror. They were marching these plastic dinosaurs up the wall. And I thought, 'wouldn't it be funny if I threw it in.' The blow dryer, I mean. Well not funny, but you know. I was tempted. To do it."

Silence falls like a blanket over us. I stare at my sandwich, the sound of chewing magnified in my ears.

"Anyway, it was stupid. It doesn't even really count for what we're talking about. I don't even know why I told that story." Her words come out in a rush.

I'm not sure why she told that story either, but my skin crawls with her confession. We clear our throats and push around the trash on our trays.

"Stupid kid's stuff, right?" Ben says in a shaky voice.

36

"Yeah, kid's stuff." Kelly's eyes dart to Vaughn and then me, begging us to change the awkward subject. "What about you guys?"

The bell rings and I say a silent prayer of thanks.

"Next time," Vaughn says, shrugging. "I'll have to come up with something good."

I nod and smile while my friends gather their things. They linger, chatting while I stare at a sketch I did in Life Drawing last period. I tune them out and try my best to ignore Stace as she leans to say goodbye to Vaughn.

All the while I replay the question: The strangest thing we've ever done.

Sell. Her. Sweeney.

When they've all left, Vaughn moves down to sit across from me. He wears an ironic smile when he stretches his arms out on the table, resting his hand inches from mine.

"So," he says, nodding to the door. "What's yours?"

"My what?"

He rolls his eyes. "Strangest thing that's ever happened to you?"

I give him a knowing look. I am so not going there right now.

THAT NIGHT, I think about words. The words in my head. The words in Vaughn's song. The voice in the barn. I pace my room, trying to make the connections, staring into the dark outside my window. The barn looms against the night sky, a hulking black mass that dwarfs the trees around it. Tonight, the barn reminds me of a monster, and I can't make sense of anything.

Vaughn thinks the history of this house ties it all together. I know he's probably right, but I'm scared to find out more. I have to live here, to sleep here. The walls are probably crawling with what happened in this place, room after massive empty room of hidden memories and who knows what else. Trodden-on hallways like paths of strange and twisted happenings. And what if, whatever was in the barn that night has slipped into the house, if it's running through the core of the place, wrapping around and into me, causing me and Vaughn to feel and do the things we're doing?

I need to refocus. My fingers itch with the need to create, to draw until I've worked out whatever thoughts and feelings are lodged in my brain. I feel tiny in my room, as if the walls and house are too much to handle. But they press in on me too. Suffocating.

Sitting at my desk, I pull out my sketchpad. I'll draw the house, I'll draw the barn. How it makes me feel, how I see it. Art is always the best medicine.

My hand moves across the paper quietly, leaving lines and arcs in shapes I don't plan. A face, smooth cheeks, soft lines. I work quickly, barely thinking about what I'm doing, almost out of my control. A body materializes below the face, a young girl, her hair hanging in waves. I add braids, a simple dress. Flat, comfortable shoes.

I frown at the page. It's certainly not what I planned. But I look at her again and I smile, tentatively.

It's not complete, but in my mind, I can see where this girl is going.

My Transformations project has finally begun.

7

ON THURSDAY, I get to the cafeteria just as Kelly's telling every-one about *Turn of the Screw*. She's been picked as Head Costumer for the annual Preston winter production. For a junior, this is huge. I'm proud of her, even if I'm distracted.

"Whoa," Ben says as I slide into my seat. "You've got rac-coon eyes."

"It's called eyeliner," I say, fighting the urge to dig in my purse for my compact.

Vaughn raises his eyes, his gaze trailing my face. His grin pulls up on one side and he nods appreciatively, like I've seen him do when he listens to a song he really likes. I hope no one notices my flaming cheeks.

"Seriously, Ben." Kelly says, paper coffee cup poised at her lips. "We need to work on your sense of what's happening in the real world of style." She coughs into her hand. "Penny loafers." Another cough.

Stace snorts. "Oh, she *so* just went there."

"Whatever." Ben rolls his eyes, nudging Stace with his elbow. He looks at me. "So did you hear? Purgatory is performing for Preston. The night of The Hunt."

"Really?" I adjust my sweater, self-conscious about how low cut it is.

"Yeah. Apparently, it's going to be a whole different set up this year."

"Well, all I know is," Stace cackles, glancing at Vaughn pointedly. "I'm planning to completely woo Kent Lee if I can manage it."

Barely suppressing a yawn, Vaughn balls up his napkin, tossing it in the air and catching it again. Purposely ignoring her stare. And sitting way farther from her than usual.

Kelly places a hand across her forehead, pretending to swoon. "Kent Lee is so yummy. Sweet cartwheeling Jesus, did you see him last time they played? Tank top. Tight. Muscles."

Nodding frantically, Stace grins. "Lots of muscles. Those abs, my God, those abs."

Ben rolls his eyes and waves a hand in their direction. "Good luck with that."

I laugh. To hear the two of them talk about the front man for Purgatory, you'd think he was an actual God. He's cute and all, but he's no Vaughn.

Speaking of.

Mischief blazes in his eyes. "How about you, Lange? You impervious to the charms of Bruce Lee?"

"*Kent* Lee," I correct. "And no. Not impervious, exactly. But he's not really my type." I shrug.

"Oh really? What's your type then?" He leans across the table, rubbing his chin. "Is it the music thing? Musicians don't do it for you?" His smile widens and I wish I had a dollar for every shade of red I must turn.

"No, not at all! Musicians are fine. No. Musicians are good. I love musicians!"

Did I really just say that?

Kelly clears her throat, "Yeah, so Kent Lee? I seriously can't wait."

"Huh." Stace's voice has gone completely dull. She glares at all of us, specifically letting her eyes dart back and forth between Vaughn and me. She stands abruptly. "I'm out of here."

She's in the hallway before anyone else moves.

What just happened?

The bell rings and Kelly gives a nervous smile as she and Ben pack up their stuff. "Talk to you guys later."

Once they're gone, I nod to the hallway. "What was that about?"

"She's always pissed about something." He waves a hand. "I'll talk to her later."

Oh.

I exhale and study the table. When he rests his hand on my arm, the electricity from the barn isn't there, but heat rushes between us like brushfire.

He leans over. "Speaking of music and your *thing* for musicians," he smiles wickedly, "you owe me a violin solo."

"Huh? Random, much? I don't play violin." But I *am* thankful for the change of subject.

"Kidding. Well, kinda." His eyes dance. I follow them to where they're staring at my collarbone. My ugly birthmark, which is usually hidden, stands out against my pale skin.

"A violin? Really? I've always thought of it as the shape of Africa. And what are you doing looking down my shirt, anyway?"

He grins. "What can I say? You're kind of on display today. And anyway, it wasn't *down* your shirt, it's like, your collarbone or whatever."

My mouth hangs open.

"Relax. I'm only looking. I'm human, you know." He smiles. "You look good."

Well then.

"Thanks," I mutter, wishing I could crawl under the table.

I look good?

Vaughn drums the edge of the table again, totally at ease. "We're still on for research later right?"

I groan. "Do I have a choice?"

"Nope, not really. Plus, I've already Googled *some* stuff. I bet you have too."

"No, actually. I've totally been avoiding it."

"Why? Like you don't want to know what's happening?"

He's right of course, but still. I'm not sure I'm ready for more information. I shrug. "I just wish this never started. I'd honestly rather know nothing." *And feel nothing.* My mind flips to the voice in the barn and the way my house has been closing in on me. I shudder, imagining what truths we're probably going to find.

He pushes a hand through his hair. "You're horribly stubborn, you know."

"I agreed to go, didn't I?" I nudge his knee with mine and manage a smile. "That's about all the cooperation you're going to get out of me at this point."

8

IN THE LIBRARY, I pick a table way in the back. Except for a college-aged girl a few tables away, who's completely engrossed in a pile of research books, we'll basically be alone. Vaughn arrives minutes after me, straight from the coffee shop next door.

"Caramel, right?" He holds out a coffee cup, complete with the slim cardboard sleeve that tells me it's a latte, a fact that instantly makes my mouth water.

"Thanks," I say, taking it from him. "How did you know I like caramel?"

He takes a swig of his. "It's what you always get, isn't it?"

"Yeah." *But I never knew you noticed.* "Thanks."

"No problem," he says, dragging a laptop onto the table, next to a small stack of books. His face is inches from mine, so close I can make out the individual hairs in his stubble.

His phone buzzes. He presses buttons while I get the computer started.

"All okay?" I ask.

"Just letting my mom know I'll be a little late."

"Impressive," I say. "My mom would never text."

"As if you would?"

"Shut up! I could if I had to."

"You do realize you're ridiculous, right? You're probably the only human being without a cell. You're like someone from another time. Or maybe another planet." He taps his chin thoughtfully.

I snort as I pull out a notebook and a pen, tapping it on the edge of the table. It's time to dive in, but I don't want to. I know an entire family was murdered in my house, and I know something or someone tried to contact us in my barn. And, if I'm being honest, the weird stuff that's still happening, for both of us, has me more than a little freaked out. But even still, I don't want to learn anything else about this sick stuff. It just feels wrong, like we're unleashing a whole lot of hell. I take a deep breath, counting to ten slowly, like my old psychiatrist, Dr. Ramirez, used to tell me to do when I was trying to deal with things.

"Do you need to call your parents or anything?" He holds out the phone.

"No," I snap. "And it's just my mom. No *parents.*"

"Sorry," he mumbles. "I didn't mean to—"

Jesus Lange. What's wrong with you?

"No, I didn't mean it to come out that way. You were just trying to be ni—"

"It's fine. I shouldn't have assumed." He nods to the table. "Let's just do this."

"My dad's dead." The words come out before I realize they're on my lips. It's the first time I've told anyone since we moved to Shady Springs. I've always just said he's not around.

Vaughn stares at the table, reaches out to squeeze my hand. "That sucks," he says. "I'm sorry."

His words are simple, but they wrap around me like a hug and for those few seconds, the void in me is filled.

"Thanks," I whisper. "For just, I don't know, letting me say that."

His thumb moves slowly across my hand, his body shifting toward mine. I want to squeeze back. I want to wrap my hand around his. But I know better.

"Okay, so what's first?" I break free and pull the screen toward me. Despite the lingering trace of Vaughn's touch on my skin, I keep my hand steady and somehow manage to read the words on top of the screen. "Dutch Country History."

Beside me, he sighs.

The picture shows cornfields and in the distance a brown barn with a weathervane on the roof. I raise my eyebrows and look at Vaughn. "Exciting stuff, I see. This is lame."

"Just scroll through. Let's see what we can find."

I sigh. This is boring. What's next? I reach across to see the list of sources he's printed out. Warmth buzzes where our shoulders press.

"Back off, will you?" He laughs, nudging me with his elbow and turning away.

I lunge for the paper, but he dodges me. We go back and forth a few times, like some little kid game of keep-away. Finally, I grab it from him, letting out a whoop of satisfaction that earns me an admonishing look from the girl down the row.

But when I read the words on the list, my smile disappears. I feel a cold flush inside, like someone's turned on a faucet.

Famous and Infamous Pennsylvania Murders

"Come on, Language Barrier," Vaughn jokes, trying to lighten my obvious mood change. "You knew we would start with this. Finding out the details behind the murders is the only thing that makes sense. How long are we going to pretend it's not connected?" He taps away at the keyboard until the site comes up.

I close my eyes and take a deep breath. He's right, but damn, I don't want to do this.

"Fine," I mumble, pulling my notebook toward me, ready to take notes. I click the top of the pen and press it to the page. Red blossoms down the paper, spreading quickly through to the pages beneath.

"What the hell!" I shriek, dropping it on the table. Red drips from the point like . . . "Is that blood?" I whisper.

Vaughn stares at it for a moment, then back at me, eyes wide. "Where did you get that pen?"

"What? I don't know! It's just a regular pen. I had it in my bag all day. It's normally, blue. See." I point to the words on the side of the pen: blue ink.

With his own pen, Vaughn smears the pool of red on my page. It's translucent. "Not *actual* blood," he says slowly.

But still.

"Halloween prank?" He stares at the page, chewing his bottom lip. "It's gotta be, right?"

I shrug. "I guess. Why else would someone do this?" But I'm still shaking. My friends are funny and everything, but they don't really play pranks on each other. Especially not sick ones like this. And everyone knows how weird I get about blood. "But Halloween's not for what?" I pause, "A week and a half? Kind of early for Halloween pranks, no?"

I rip out the pages and ball them together in the middle of the table, burying the pen inside them.

"Whatever," I say. "Let's just get this stupid research over with. Back to *Famous and Infamous Pennsylvania Murders.*"

On the site's homepage is a black and white photo of a small house, light with dark shutters, all the windows broken, the top two boarded up with plywood. It's an early winter scene – dead grass, leafless trees. Even the bushes look forlorn and neglected. It's faded, yellowed like a scene from an old-fashioned movie. Creepy.

I stare at the picture and try to swallow my fear. Vaughn's right, this research is the next logical step. I can ignore it all I want, but it's not ignoring me.

Or us.

I finger the arrow keys, not daring to actually read more. Vaughn watches, humming softly under his breath, like he so often does. It's that song again, from the other night.

Coolness washes over me as if I'm standing in front of an open window.

"All right, all right." I avoid his eyes. "Now or never, I guess."

"Come on," he says, patting the table as I scoot in closer so we can both read the screen. With our bodies touching at our elbows, thighs and knees, it's like we're connected.

It's unnerving.

But not quite as unnerving as the random page he clicks on. There's a picture of a woman and child, obviously an old photograph. Printed over it is the outline of a target as if they are in the scope of a rifle. *Husband Kills Wife and Young Daughter.* Beneath it are a few lines giving the basics of the murder. They barely register: jealous husband with known anger problems uses his shotgun against his defenseless wife and daughter.

"Wow. This is sick." Vaughn shakes his head.

On the next page, four fat middle-aged men glare into the camera looking tough. A headline reads: *Falcone Family Strikes Again.* I scan the few lines beneath it, the words not really sinking in. Blah blah Mafia. Blah blah.

"Okay, this is gross. Who had the joy of putting this site together?" I mumble as he clicks through the pages. But inside I'm racing. I don't want to see this. Page after page is filled with pictures of smiling couples and grinning families, frozen in time before everything was taken from them. We look in silence as he scrolls through the pages, photos of buildings and schools that had been terrorized. Some are just pictures of houses where people had been killed that thankfully have no pictures of the victims.

But then, on the next screen, my nerves finally come undone.

The headline is horrible: *The Chopain Murders of 1934: A Family Sliced and Diced in the Dead of Night.*

Underneath it, a picture: a close up of a barn. Although it's in black and white, the details tell what an old photo it is. The paint looks flawless, the grounds perfectly maintained. Even the trees, the ones that now grow in dense clumps out back, look smaller, less mature.

Beneath the photo, the write up reads: *Marie Chopain and her five children brutally killed in their Shady Springs home in the summer of 1934 by Hank Griffin, friend of the family, who committed suicide shortly after the murders.*

Murders committed in *my* house.

9

"WHERE DID DAD live?" I ask Mom. She's somehow roped me
into spending my Saturday sitting in the dusty attic with her,
sorting through boxes. "Mostly, I mean. When he wasn't with
us?" It's been days since I told Vaughn about my dad, but I can't
stop thinking about him.

She looks up, a startled expression widening her eyes. It's rare
we talk about Dad. I'm not sure I've ever brought him up casually like this, but ever since I read about the Chopain murders, I've
been thinking nonstop about family and what it means to lose
them.

She blinks, licking her lips. "All over, I guess. He was always
up to something new. Never quite anchored. You know." She
turns her attention back to the magazines in the box at her feet.

But I *don't* know. From what I remember, he was in and out
of our lives, as inconsistent as the weather. As confusing as all
the places we lived, all the new schools and the constantly
changing friends. If I dig deep, I can pull out snippets of him;
the clomp of heavy boots, me planting kisses on his red cheeks. I
remember a circus once, when I was very young, screaming in
the face of a clown and Dad hurrying me away, holding me in
his arms, where I traced the serpent tattoo coiled around his
forearm with my little finger.

I silently paw through my own box until I find an old Coke
bottle. "How about this?"

She wrinkles her nose. "Tacky."

I consider it before placing it back in the box. Rustling through old scarves and books, I think about my dad and all the other things I wish I knew. Why did he always leave? And why did he have to die? It's weird, suddenly thinking about him so much. It's like my mind is purposely trying to stay away from what we saw on that website. Even though I'd refused to look at anything else after that one site, the haunting recap of the Chopain murders had burrowed into me. I have to keep it away. My tendency to dwell on things used to be one of my biggest problems before Dr. Ramirez taught me how to redirect my thoughts. Maybe that's all this dad stuff is now.

My mind flips to the family who was brutally murdered in this house. I try to ignore what's becoming the familiar tugging I get in my stomach whenever I think of them, as if knowing their story and living in this house has somehow connected me to them. I hide my shaking hands deep in the box on my lap, wishing for the millionth time I hadn't read those gory details.

"Aha!" Mom roots around in her box with a victorious smirk on her face. From its depths, she pulls out a rose-colored perfume bottle, bulb shaped with scalloped sides. It balances perfectly on her palm when she holds it out to me. "Isn't this pretty? Look at the shape of it. And that color glass. I don't think I've found any this color yet. You know, the pink reminds me of something," she taps her finger on her chin as she looks at the glass matter of factly. "Plus, pink often wards off disconcerting spirits, you know. This is probably a very lucky find."

I stare at the bottle, unable to think straight. My body leans forward slowly, as if I'm a hulking piece of metal and she's holding a strong magnet. My heartbeat is nearly deafening.

"Can I?" I ask, reaching out.

"Can you what?" Confusion twists Mom's features.

I nod to the bottle in her hand, my fingers aching for it, imagining its cool surface, lightweight in my hand, dimpled around the bottom edge.

When I take it from her, gently, as if it's an egg, something shifts in me. I lose sight of the entire room. The light blinks in and out, like clouds drifting in front of the sun. Mom fades like she's underwater. Blurry. Blurrier still, until she's gone. It's dark all around me and I swallow the urge to scream.

I bring the bottle to my nose and although it's empty, the scent lingers. It's vaguely sweet, musky almost, with the hint of the earliest spring flowers. It overwhelms me.

The light fades in again, like I'm in a forest, sun winking through leaves overhead. Then I'm back in the attic, Mom in the distance, staring at me like I've finally lost my mind.

When it goes dark again, I hear his voice. It's Vaughn, words slipping into my ear like something liquid, something smooth. "For you, my dear. For you." There's a lilt to his voice, something that's out of place.

My skin prickles with anticipation as his voice gets closer and when I can almost feel the heat of him near me, I fall in the darkness, the bottle slipping from my hand. Glass shatters on the floor.

There's a flash, the room lit like lightening.

I see him. It's his face, but not. His hair is cropped now, brushed casually to the side, his face is smooth, without the constant scruffy shadow I've gotten used to. His smile is more eager than I know it, filled with hope, somehow. His bone structure is different too. Lower cheekbones, eyes spread further apart. It's really not him, but like with any dream, I somehow just know it is. He has the same dark, piercing eyes.

But this isn't real.

"Find me," he hisses. "Before it's too late."

I taste metal in my mouth, and feel that same sense of unlocking deep inside, that rush of air.

But then he shakes me, hard. I'm a doll in his arms and I can't even fight. Over his shoulder I see a corridor. It's tight like a tunnel, descending down into darkness. I close my eyes.

"Lange!" Mom's voice cuts through the dark. I blink, staring up at the bare bulb hanging from the attic rafters. Her face comes into view above me, my head throbbing as I come out of the dream like I've been drowning.

"Did I fall asleep? What happened?"

Was that real?

"No! You weren't asleep! You were… I don't know. What's going on? What were you feeling?"

What's going on? I'm not sure. Right now the biggest question is why I'm having dream-visions about Vaughn.

And according to that vision, he needs me.

10

FIND ME. BEFORE it's too late.

It sticks with me, what Vaughn said in my dream. Or vision. Or whatever it was.

There's obviously no arguing that something serious is going on. First it was voices. Now it's visions? I can't make sense of any of it.

And the pen prank still has me freaked out too. All my friends denied it, so I know it wasn't them. But who could have gotten into my bag? And if it was a prank, wouldn't someone have owned up to it by now? In Motion Drawing yesterday, I was so tired and distracted by everything, I almost ruined my Transformations project.

I pull it out now. Despite my anxiety, pride unfurls in my chest.

It starts with the original young girl, drawn in the lightest pencil. She's ten, maybe twelve. Her hair hangs in long waves, tied back with twin braids. She looks off the side of the page. You can just make out the thin slope of her nose. Drawn around her is an older girl, about seventeen. She's drawn in heavier lines, so you can barely see the younger girl within. The elder is taller than I'll ever be, and thinner too, her hair darker than her younger self, her chest fuller, mature. She has started to step away from the younger but still has most of the girl within her. She looks out from the paper as if directly at the viewer. Her face is serious, her dark eyes near set over lips that form a slight smile. It's a smile that knows something.

With these two aspects nearly done all that's left to finish is step three. The third figure, as if she'd twirled away from the others, has kicked up streams of dust that encircle the other two girls. She's shorter than the teenager, but she stoops. She looks over her shoulder, looking back at herself as she was. Her head is thrown back as if to laugh, but a tear slides down her cheek instead.

Whatever happened in the barn that night, whatever is still happening, has to be what inspired this project. What made me draw that first girl that night. It had to come from one of them.

Again, my stomach pulls, thinking about them.

The phone rings, bringing me back to the present. I put down my mug of tea. "Hello?"

"Pippi Langstocking?"

I'm emotionally exhausted, but he makes me smile. "What's up Vaughn?

Taking a sip of my tea, I listen to his guitar bang and vibrate as if he's set it down. I picture his fingers, strumming the strings.

"Not much. Was wondering what you're up to. Tonight?"

I grip my mug tighter.

"I've been online all day," he continues. "Plus I got some stuff from the library archives."

Ugh. Of course.

"That's how you chose to spend your Saturday? Library hopping?" I snort. "Lame." But I have to fight the urge to ask what he found.

He doesn't budge, his voice military when he answers. "Come on, Lange."

Tell him about the vision in the attic. Tell him everything.

"The girl in your drawing," he whispers. "Trust me, you *need* to see this."

The tea in my mug ripples and I set it down to steady it. Deep breath. I'm so not ready to dig further into the Chopain murders, but I guess there's no choice. It's like ripping off a band aid. Just get it done.

"All right, fine. Come on over."

I yawn, feeling like I've overdosed on Nyquil. I slide deeper under my covers. My eyes close for a long blink.

"You there?"

I look at the ceiling. "I'm here."

Find me.

"Vaughn?"

"Yeah?"

"Something's very wrong, isn't it?" I whisper with my eyes closed. It's the first time I've said it out loud.

The words feel like a betrayal.

11

WHEN I OPEN my eyes, the moon has risen high enough to throw pale light against the wall at the foot of my bed. I watch the leaf shadows dancing there while my eyes adjust.

"Ah, sleeping beauty awakes." Vaughn's voice comes out of the dark.

"What the hell!" I sit, clutching my blanket to my chest, my eyes searching the dark. I reach for my lamp, but his hand's already there. When he switches it on, the brightness makes me wince. "What are you doing here?"

He holds a folded piece of paper between his fingers. "I was just leaving you a note, since you were peacefully snoring away."

"I don't snore!"

He smiles and pulls out my desk chair, falling into it with a shake of his head. His guitar, which I now notice leaning against the side of my desk, clangs with the movement. "Believe whatever you want."

"Whatever, stalker. Who sneaks into someone's room like that?"

"Your mom let me in. I didn't know you were sleeping."

"Hello, I thought I was snoring?"

He rolls his eyes. "Whatever. You *did* know I was coming over. And I believe this makes the second time I'm here that you're lying around while I do all the work."

My mouth drops open, and I shoot him my best *how dare you* glare. Smirking, he leans back in my chair, the desk lamp throwing dim light across him like a well-lit museum artifact. I can't take my eyes off him: bright eyes, hair hanging just right, jeans worn-in but clean. My stomach stirs and I wonder how awful I look in comparison.

"Fine. Fair enough." I nod to the paper. "So what was in this magical note you were writing?"

He shrugs and folds it, tucking it into his pocket.

I reach for it, and swing my feet to the floor. The headache hammers my brain, the dizziness almost taking me down. I grab the edge of my desk.

"Whoa," he says, resting his hands on my shoulders to steady me. His eyes soften, deep brown melting. "You all right?"

I shrug away and stretch to look at my reflection. I am a certified mess, hair sticking out, clothes wrinkled, not an ounce of makeup. I wince, trying to smooth my runaway hair down.

"Hey don't do that. You look cute all disheveled and messy."

I throw a glare over my shoulder and narrow my eyes. "Sure, pick on the sick girl."

Cute.

"Although..." He kicks at my rug, mischief in his eyes.

"What?" I pull my brush through my hair.

"Well, I was just thinking about that sweater you had on the other day. *That* was hot."

I look down at my yoga pants and tee shirt and laugh sarcastically. "Oh, and what's this? Not fancy enough?" My voice wavers as I try and play off the fact that Vaughn just outright called me hot *and* remembered what I'd been wearing days ago.

He shrugs playfully, meeting my gaze in the mirror. "Who *were* you dressed up for, anyway? You never did say."

I grab a balled up pair of socks from my dresser and throw them at him. He ducks as they bounce off the desk.

"Fine don't tell me."

I roll my eyes, and put on my best haughty voice. "If you came over just to insult me, you can see yourself out."

"Fat chance," he says. "I wanted to show you this stuff." He nods to his backpack. "Not that hanging out with you is such a horrible Saturday night, either."

Doing my best to ignore his compliment, I frown at his bag, filled to the brim with what looks like tons of information.

"That looks like a lot of stuff," I say as he starts to pull stacks of pages out. "Maybe too much."

"Oh I almost forgot," he says, digging in his bag. "I have something for you."

My chest flutters as he searches, his tight grin widening when he pulls out a book and hands it to me.

"They were having a flea market at the library. Books and crafts and stuff. Anyway, it's about famous portrait artists. Their lives and inspirations and stuff. I know portraits are kinda your thing, so—"

"Wow, this is amazing." I open the cover, my finger tracing the table of contents. Some of my favorites: Arcimboldo, Gericault, Raphael. Even Sargent and Velazquez and Van Eyck. And of course Rembrandt and Da Vinci. I flip through the pages, skimming as I jump from one artist to the other.

"So you like it?"

"I love it!" I say, closing the cover as emotion wells in me. "Seriously, it's really sweet of you."

"Well you're always drawing people so I figured you'd like reading about all those old dead guys who were supposedly the best at it." His cheeks pinken, his eyes still on the book.

Dead guys. Ugh.

I sigh, my mind instantly flashing to my vision.

"What's wrong? Is it the book? Did it—"

"No, no. The book is great. It's just . . . Something happened . . . before. I don't know. I was in the attic with my mom and I just felt weird." I wave my hand. "Forget it. It's stupid."

"Wait, what happened?" He's beside me now.

"I don't really know. It was weird."

"Was it the voice again?"

With my eyes closed, I shake my head.

Find Me.

"Come on, what?" He rests his hand on my thigh and the warmth of him reminds me of how close he was in the vision.

"It was you," I say slowly. "But different. Not totally you. I don't know. Maybe it was more of a daydream?" I pull at a thread that's come loose from the band of my shirt.

He stares at the ceiling as if the answers are hidden in the ripples of plaster. He shakes his head. "This shit it getting weirder by the minute."

"Anyway," I say, waving to his backpack. "Let's see what you were all riled up about."

He leans forward for the stack of pages, but he stops halfway, reaching out to tuck my hair behind my ear. His fingers linger just beneath my earlobe, trailing along my cheek before dropping again. His eyes never leave mine.

The spell is broken when he looks away. He scoots back on my bed until he sits against the wall, pulling his bag with him. He gives me one of his sideways, totally-Vaughn grins and holds up his hands. In one is a package of Twinkies and in the other, a stack of computer printouts.

"All right, Langston Hughes," he says. "Let's get started."

It turns out Vaughn did some serious research. I'd be lying if I said I wasn't impressed. I've always known he was dedicated. He's smart and he works his ass off with his music. But I didn't expect him to pull half the town's history out of his bag.

"A lot of them tell the same basic story," he says. "But I printed everything I could find."

First, there's tons of archived newspaper articles with their various accounts of the murders. I don't want to read them all. The little bit I read at the library had been damaging enough. I can't stand the thought of living and eating and sleeping in a place where these horrible things happened.

But if we want to get back to a normal life, we have to figure out how it's all connected and what we're supposed to do with it.

SHADY SPRINGS TIMES

September 1, 1934 — Shady Springs police discovered the bodies of Marie Chopain, 38, Virginia (Ginny) Chopain, 18, Robert Chopain, 17, Helen Chopain, 15, Ruth Chopain, 13 and Margaret (Margie) Chopain, 12 in the Chopain's Shady Springs home on August 31.

Police described the crime scene as "horrific," the victims in various states of mutilation, decapitation and dismemberment.

"At least a day had passed between when they died and when they were found," Francis Byrd of the coroner's office said.

Police report that Hank Griffin, the man behind the brutal murder of Marie Chopain and her five children, hanged himself after stabbing and mutilating his victims.

"The acquaintance of the family was found in the barn shortly after the victims were discovered," Detective Green said and, at this time, the police investigation is conclusive in his involvement in the murders. There was a suicide note at the scene, fully disclosing his guilt.

Mrs. Chopain lived in Shady Springs her entire life, growing up Marie Miller, daughter of Betty and Clark Miller. She married Joseph Chopain in 1913, and then in 1924, he was killed in a hunting accident.

WE READ IN silence. I sit against my headboard, Vaughn against the wall, legs splayed across my bed. I read account after account of it, fighting tears and bile with each article. And though very little changes between them, I feel the need to read them all, just in case there's something we've missed.

But what's the point? What am I looking for?

Sell. Her. Sweeney.

The words that started it all are nowhere to be found, but I feel like I have to keep going. Have to figure it out. The obsessive way we pore over the documents, and the amount of time Vaughn has obviously spent finding them proves we're in the same frame of mind.

The articles go on and on. Town papers, state, national sources that ran the story. Near the bottom of the stack, I read one of them twice.

"Did you read this one?"

He stretches across my bed. "Which one?"

"*The New York Examiner.* 'The Known Killer.'"

"I think so."

I frown at the article. It talks about how many crimes are perpetrated by people known to the victims. Murders, rapes, robberies. The Chopain murders are mentioned, with the killer Hank Griffin being cited as a "very close friend of the family." It fascinates and freaks me out on a whole new level. As if a murder wasn't bad enough, to have it committed by someone you know and trust? It's totally twisted. What kind of sicko had Hank Griffin been? I let the article fall and close my eyes, picturing him lurking in the hallway, in the barn. Someone they knew, someone they trusted.

I shudder.

"Okay, I've had enough." He drops the last of his papers on the floor and rubs his eyes.

"I know." I'm drained too. Although I'd known the basic story of the murders, after immersing myself in it for—I look at my clock—more than two hours, I can hardly stand to be in this room. In this house. It could have been in this very room, where I *sleep*, that someone was murdered. Dismembered. Decapitated.

My breath catches, like it's stuck in my throat, like I'll choke right here in my room.

Vaughn slides beside me, cautiously draping his arm across my shoulders. I settle against him, which somehow feels incredibly natural. I rest my face against his Rolling Stones shirt and think about dead Marie and her five murdered children. Even if it makes me selfish, I don't want to live here, knowing it happened in my house. My mind runs round and round the murder details like demented movie scenes on an endless loop.

I finally force them to stop, noticing the stillness in Vaughn's breath and the way he brushes my hair back with his hands, humming quietly in my ear. His heart beats solidly against my cheek.

What am I doing? Stace is my friend. I shouldn't be doing this.

"Hey," he finally says, gently rubbing his thumb on my cheek.

When I finally get the nerve to look at him, the clear look on his face gives me chills. It's not only his expression, but the solemn, calming atmosphere he's created around us, like a protective bubble.

With the arm he's wrapped around me, he pulls me closer, the other hand stroking my hair. The sound of our breathing mingles like whispers.

This is where I belong.

I listen to it for a while. That thought, our breathing. His pulse, so close I can feel it mirroring my own.

But then I mentally slap myself again. This is so wrong.

I sit up, pulling away from him.

He runs a hand down my back and gives me his warmest smile. "You all right?"

"Just overwhelmed I guess." I straighten the hem of my shirt, then busy my hands with pulling my hair up into a ponytail and letting it drop again. I have to fight the urge to fall back against him. I so don't want him to leave.

"I'm sorry for all this." He nods to the articles and books on the floor, but I wonder if that's all he's apologizing for. When he gets up, he stretches, the line of his body lengthening to expose a sliver of his stomach and the smooth, tight muscles that flex with the lift of his arms.

I look away.

When he starts shoving papers in his bag, I notice the corner of a photograph sticking out from under the pile.

"What's that?" Instinctively, I reach for it.

He backs away, pulling the bag with him.

"Come on, what is it?"

"Fine. But don't freak."

"What?" I say in a sharper voice than I mean to. "Just show me."

But when he pulls out the photo I gasp.

"It says 1934," he says. "Looks like a senior picture. I'm thinking it's the oldest girl. Virginia. Ginny."

I'm aware of his voice, but his words barely register.

The girl in the photo has brown hair, swept up in a loose bun. Her dress is modest with the neckline covering her collarbone, but fitted enough to highlight her slight frame, her bony shoulders. She smiles knowingly at the camera, a crooked smile beneath a thin, sloping nose, the white line of her teeth just visible.

"Lange?"

But his voice seems far away.

My blood is ice. My mind flashes again, as if racing through photo negatives. I don't need to, but I can't help it; I reach for my sketchpad. I lay my drawing on my desk and place the photo beside it, studying the expression on the second girl in my drawing, the taller one with her younger self inside. The same face stares back at me, the expressions nearly identical. It's as if I'd drawn her from this picture.

I look at the girl in the photograph. *Who are you? Why did I draw you?*

Another flash in my mind. I blink, the picture wavering in my vision, bright red splatters across the girl's face.

Warmth runs down my scalp. Blood. I shriek, falling backwards, leaning against the desk chair, barely noticing Vaughn there, holding my elbow. Warm stickiness drips down my neck and back, pools in the front of my bra. I focus on the way it moves on my skin, like leeches, sliding, as I look at the photo, her smile gone now, replaced by a scream, the camera catching her eyes wide with terror, mouth agape.

Help me. Her voice hisses, surrounding me in a tornado of horror. I shiver, covering my eyes until it stops.

"Lange?" Vaughn says softly.

Still shaking, my fingers creep through my hair, touch my back and chest. Dry.

In the photo, Ginny is smiling again.

And it's then that I know, no matter how painful it is, I can't give up the search. The girl in the photo is begging me not to.

ONCE VAUGHN LEAVES, with a promise to call later to make sure I'm okay, I scoop up a pile of scrap paper and some pencils. Sitting against my wall, I start to draw. They're nothing but doodles, shapes and lines that bend and curve into each other. But with each stroke, my mind begins to unravel.

Ginny Chopain, the girl in the photo. In my drawing. My mind dances around it like a butterfly, trying to find a place to land.

There's a commotion downstairs, loud voices in the kitchen. Weird. Mom hardly ever has people over. Especially angry, loud ones.

I tiptoe to my doorway, leaning on the frame with an ear turned to the hallway.

"You want to call someone? Hold on, I'll get Lange."

Huh?

"Thanks. I'm not sure who would do this."

Vaughn?

I push my hair back in a headband and grab a pair of socks from my dresser drawer, pulling them on as I make my way down the steps, moving faster than I should. I stumble on the last three, skidding on my heels into the kitchen.

"What's going on?" I try my best to stay calm.

Never mind my awkward entrance. No one notices. Vaughn is pacing by my back door, cell phone pressed to his ear. Everything about the situation feels odd, like a play with the wrong lighting, where everyone forgets their lines.

"My car," he says, covering the mouthpiece. "Someone slashed my tires."

12

LAST NIGHT, I sat on the porch with Vaughn and waited for the tow truck. He had a spare, but with three tires slashed, one spare wasn't going to do him any good. So we waited, in silence at first, our breath forming small, even clouds in the air.

It made no sense. Everyone likes Vaughn.

"I know this may sound totally paranoid," I said. "But do you think the bloody pen could be related to this? Like someone is out to mess with both of us?"

He nodded, grumbling something about kicking someone's ass.

"Who do you think—"

He cut me off. "No idea. But I *will* find out."

I'd never seen him so determined.

And now, we're having breakfast.

Well, that's the start of it, anyway. We have a whole long day ahead of us.

Vaughn's mom has an old friend whose grandmother was alive at the time of the Chopain murders. She's in her late nineties, and had been friends with the oldest Chopain kids. Unlike me, Vaughn has apparently been talking about our research with his parents. Of course it's easier for him. His mom isn't like my mom, who would most likely waver between jumping on the ghost hunting bandwagon and overanalyzing my mental state. She'd probably freak if she knew I was looking into these murders. She's already been making comments about what happened in the attic, and after way too many years of her questioning my mental stability, sending me to shrinks, and plying me with piles of self-help manuals and spiritual cleansing ideas, the less she knows, the better. Yet Vaughn's mom sets up meetings with old friends of murdered children to help her son's fascination.

I'm not sure which is worse.

And what about meeting this old woman? What could she possibly tell us? Details about her friends who were killed? Do I want to know? Do I want that girl to become even more real to me?

I'm not sure I do.

By the time we're pushing pancakes around our plates and staring out the diner window, I just want to get it over with. By the way Vaughn stirs his coffee endlessly, I gather he feels the same. He leans back against the booth, the glow of the Halloween lights overhead shining orange in his hair. The entire diner has been decked out in Halloween decorations making it resemble a haunted house more than a restaurant.

"I was writing last night," he says without looking at me. "After everything, I was so tired by the time I got home. I climbed into bed, thinking I'd be out. But then that melody started nagging me again and I had to get up and tinker with it."

"And?"

"It's getting there. It's more layered now. Still needs work though." His eyes shine, but his lips curl down in a frown.

"So why the sad face?" I twirl my cup on its saucer.

"Oh, not sad. It's just..." He looks away, shifting in his seat.

"What?"

"Nothing," he says. "Just nerves, I guess. Today and all."

"You better not be hiding something from me." I point with my fork and try for my best serious scowl.

His laugh rumbles. "Oooh, I'm scared. You going to hurt me with pancakes now?"

"Better than the slow Twinkie death you're headed for." I stick out my tongue and duck as he tosses a sugar packet at me.

"Hey kids." Our waitress places our check on the table and starts to clear the plates. "How was everything?"

"Great," Vaughn says, forcing a smile. But he can't hide that nervous look behind his eyes.

"You kids go to Preston?" When we nod she continues, "You must be getting all geared up for The Hunt, huh? I hear it's gonna be good this year. My sister works down at Macky's and she said all the shops downtown are gearing up to make Main Street spookier than a horror film." She laughs as she wipes down the table.

When we slide out of the booth, Vaughn brushes up against the skeleton-bone garland hanging along the wall, nearly pulling it down.

"It looks pretty good in here too," he says, fingering the bones. "You guys are pretty Halloween-ed out yourselves."

She shakes her head, giving us a knowing look. "Well, you know how it is. There ain't nothing like Halloween in Shady Springs. Can't believe it's coming up next week already. Lord, time flies when you get old, I'll tell ya."

I follow Vaughn to the register, my stomach bubbling in anticipation of the day ahead.

"Lange?"

I cringe before I turn around, plastering a fake smile on my face.

"Hey Kelly. What's up?" I'm not sure if my act of nonchalance fools her, but she gives me a soft smile and leans in for a hug.

"Where've you been?" She looks between Vaughn and me and I can see the questions in her eyes. But Kelly won't ask.

"What do you mean? Same places as always." I reach out and touch the magenta silk Gerbera daisies pinned in her hair. "Love these! Very cute."

Her hand goes up automatically. "Thanks. I picked them up at the thrift shop. Oh, that reminds me, I have to show you my designs for *Turn of the Screw.*"

"Sure. How about tomorrow? You doing anything after school?"

Her face brightens. "Really?"

"Why don't you come over?" I'm trying here, really trying. To make things normal, at least on the outside. Vaughn looks down at his shoes, fidgeting with his jacket sleeves again.

"Sure, sounds good." Kelly kicks the toe of Vaughn's boot and smiles. "What's up? Can't say hello?"

With a tight grin, he laughs his laid back laugh. "I'm sorry. I didn't know you were going to let me get a word in."

Kelly laughs, as though she doesn't see through his act, which I have to admit, is pretty good. He seems normal, almost like himself.

"So, what are you guys doing now . . . " She trails off, looking uncomfortable.

Oh right. Us being here together.

"Lange's helping me. With a song." Vaughn leans against the counter, as if he hasn't a care in the world. "I'm writing this new piece."

What? Kelly knows I know nothing about songwriting.

"Oh." She looks slowly between us. "Cool."

"It was based on this photo she had the other day," he continues, biting his lip. "One of her mom's still lifes."

I want to nudge him, to make him stop. The deeper the lie goes, the more difficult it's going to be to keep it straight. Plus, it sounds completely lame.

Kelly nods, but her eyes have shifted. She looks behind me, her face going a bit pale as her mouth lifts into a smile. It's then that I notice the patchwork backpack hanging from her arm. Stace's bag.

Crap.

I turn, but even as I do, I know who I'll find.

"There you are!" Stace says to Kelly. Then she notices me. And then Vaughn. And then back to me again. Her expression slides, settling into something totally blank. Something that says, *Oh. I see.*

A swollen moment of silence is broken by the burst of Kelly's laughter. "How weird right? We're like, all having breakfast at the same place! I didn't even think we were capable of waking up so early on a Sunday."

But it's not enough.

Vaughn bends to kiss Stace's cheek, but it's cold, like you'd kiss a distant aunt or uncle. I keep my eyes trained on the marble floor.

"Hey," he says smoothly. "What's up?"

"What's up? Hmm. What's up is Kelly and I having breakfast before working on *Turn of the Screw* stuff. I'm helping her out. You know, like *friends* do."

No one misses the implication in her voice.

"That's cool."

He looks at me. Stace looks at me.

Please make this moment end.

"And you?" She says to him coolly, her eyes on me. "What's up with you?"

"Oh they're working on a project too!" Kelly says brightly. "Vaughn's writing a song inspired by one of Lange's mom's photos. Isn't that cool?" She's trying too hard. And at the mention of Vaughn writing a song, Stace's eyes narrow.

"Oh really? Sounds great." She turns on her heel and heads in the direction of the tables. Kelly gives me a pained look before turning to follow. She squeezes my arm and mouths, *call me later.*

"Well that was awesome," I say under my breath as Vaughn holds the door open for me. They probably think I'm hooking up with him. Great. Stace hates me. And Kelly, although she seemed sympathetic, will be close behind. *Call me later.* That was an invitation for me to explain myself before she decides to jump on Stace's side and hate us.

Vaughn and me. There is no us.

"It'll be fine." He unlocks the doors of his mom's minivan and I slide into the passenger seat, slumping down and covering my face with my hands.

"How can you be so lax about this?" I ask when he climbs in-to his seat. "Your girlfriend, who happens to be my friend—"

"Whoa! She is *not* my girlfriend. Not even close."

His heated tone stops me from saying anything else, as does the dark expression that's moved across his face. His attention turns to his rearview as he backs out of the parking spot.

Not his girlfriend? Well that's obviously not what she thinks. Not what anyone thinks.

And . . . really? He doesn't consider her *anything?*

"But I thought you guys—"

He keeps his eyes on the road, slowing at the yellow light. "We were sort of together," he says. "A long time ago. We're friends now."

"Oh."

Well that changes things.

"Besides, things are different now." He continues to look at me but I stare straight ahead, studying the face of the red traffic light like it's an original Van Gogh. "Know what I mean?"

I don't know what to say.

"You guys always seem so close," I mumble. "The whole music thing and, you know . . . " My cheeks burn as he turns onto the twisty road that will take us out of town.

He scoffs. "Sure, we're both musicians, but so what? It's not like *she's* the one I'm writing songs about."

I close my eyes and try to ignore the thrumming in my ears. *Hold my heart it won't be long.*

"Vaughn—"

"Come on. You know exactly what I'm talking about."

With my eyes still closed, I answer. "What kind of friend would I be—"

The slap of his palm against the steering wheel makes me jump. When I open my eyes, he's staring at me. "I already told you, there's nothing going on with me and Stace."

"I'm not *that* girl, you know?"

Silence fills the space where our words aren't. The trees pass and I count them silently. I wish for a thick charcoal pencil in my fingers to draw the way I feel. Empty and out of place. I'm so focused on the world inside my head that when he touches my arm, I flinch. I look down at his hand, big-knuckled fingers splayed against my arm. They squeeze gently, trying to get my attention.

"You," he says softly, "could never, ever be a bad person. Don't doubt that."

"Yeah," I mumble. "Tell that to Kelly and Stace."

He sighs heavily and shakes his head, powering up his iPod to fill the silence. When he pulls his hand from my arm, the spot where his fingers were feels suddenly cold.

I want to tell him how I like the way things are. How he's fun and makes me feel like I can laugh, and talk, and be real. How being here with him, in Shady Springs, feels like I'm finally rooted somewhere for the first time in my life. Right now, that's good enough. Why ruin it?

"Besides," I say. "We've got bigger things to face right now. Don't you think?"

He nods without looking at me, but the clench of his jaw tells me this conversation isn't over.

Not by a long shot.

13

WE DRIVE FOR over an hour on the quietest, prettiest roads I've ever seen. The autumn colors roll endlessly on the mountains that surround us.

We listen to random songs on Vaughn's iPod for most of the trip. I don't recognize a lot of them, but when he turns off the highway and the track changes, the lyrics jump out and I listen intently. Something in them reminds me of Vaughn's song. And they feel like they apply distinctly to me.

To us.

I've searched through the darkness, I've walked through that door. I'll be coming back you know, coming back for more.

I run them through my mind on repeat, trying to figure out what they mean, why I'm drawn to them.

I sneak a sideways glance. On the cracked leather steering wheel, Vaughn taps the slow drumbeat and hums along.

I alternate staring at the clouds and him, the relaxed way he leans with one hand on the wheel as he murmurs along to the next song. I sit forward, tinkering with the button on the iPod. A screechy female voice blares from the speakers.

"Ooops. I was trying to turn it down."

He rolls his eyes, smirking as he slides the button that turns it off, unleashing quiet in the car.

Finally, I get the nerve to ask what's been on my mind most of the ride.

"So what do you think? About the murders?"

He gives me a confused look. "What do you mean? That Hank guy did it, right? Confessed it in his suicide note, even."

"But I'm not sure that's where it ends. I feel like there's a reason we're doing all this. Researching this stuff. You know?"

"Obviously. I don't exactly read about brutal murders for fun." He snorts, reaching over to brush the back of my hand with his, as if our hands touching is the most natural thing in the world.

"You've been saying it since the séance. And I agree, it has to be all connected—the voice, the drawing, the visions. The murders. We agree it can't be coincidence, right?"

He nods.

"Okay, so that's what I'm asking. What's next? Our purpose in all this? If someone or some*thing* did move through the barn or us that night, why? What purpose are we serving, digging into all this stuff?

"I don't know," he says, turning onto a narrow driveway that leads up a grassy hill. "I just keep thinking about those words."

Sell. Her. Sweeney.

Coolness washes through me, prickles on my arms. "Me too."

"Honestly?" He wears a sad smile as he shifts the car into park. "I feel like we don't have any other choice than to find out what they mean."

For a moment, we sit in silence, looking up at the small cottage in front of us. It's adorable, painted yellow with pale blue shutters, its porch stretching all the way across the house, yard landscaped with gorgeous mums in all the autumn colors and neatly trimmed bushes on either side of the steps.

"Ready?" He asks, his hand resting on the door handle.

"Sure. But for what?" I eye the house. Despite its innocent exterior, I'm afraid.

"Let's find out."

Outside, it's quiet. There isn't another house in sight. I'm overwhelmed by the space here. Sure, my house has land, but we've got neighbors. Vaughn and I walk up the front steps soundlessly and he opens the screen door. Just as he raises his hand to knock, the floor creaks, and we turn toward the sound.

At the far end of the porch is an old lady who's no bigger than a middle schooler. She sits on a rocking chair with a red afghan tucked tightly across her lap. She smiles at us, a sweet but toothless smile.

"Hi there." I step toward her with a small wave, Vaughn right at my side. I'm flooded with relief when his hand finds mine and squeezes.

"Mrs. McDermott?" Vaughn stoops to make eye contact. "I'm Vaughn, Aileen Broussard's son? She's friends with Eloise."

She looks back and forth between us. Her eyes are milky, the film on them so thick I wonder if she can see us at all. Her hands rattle in her lap as if she's cold. With that distant smile on her face, she beckons us with her fingers to come closer.

A tremble races through me, but I fight to keep it hidden. As if on cue, Vaughn squeezes my hand tighter, linking his fingers with mine. It's enough to calm me. To give me courage.

She looks at Vaughn first, squinting to see him. "You're friends with Eloise? But you're so young! Does she teach you over at that there schoolhouse?"

Vaughn flashes his best winning smile, the one I've always been sure could charm the most miserable soul. "No ma'am. My mother knows your granddaughter. They teach together."

"How is my granddaughter? Never visits me!" She barks out a coughing laugh.

"Oh. Um. Did she mention we were coming? She said she would. If not, I'm so sorry to take up your time and we can just—"

"Oh heck no! She mentioned it. She calls. Each Sunday, like clockwork. I'll give her that, poor old spinster that she is." She smiles, focusing on something over my shoulder. Or maybe not focusing at all. After a few seconds she looks at me, leaning closer, squinting the way she did with Vaughn. But then her eyes widen. And in her huge, blue-eyed stare, I can almost see the woman she was decades ago.

"Ginny?"

"Oh, no ma'am. My name is Lange Crawford. I'm a friend of Vaughn's from school. We came out here because we thought we could talk to you. About Ginny, actually. About all the Chopains."

But she's shaking her head like a child who doesn't want to listen.

Vaughn watches with huge eyes as Mrs. McDermott leans forward and grasps my shoulders. She may be small, but she's got a strong grip, pulling me forward until our noses almost touch.

"Ginny!" Her toothless grin stretches into a wide jack-o-lantern smile. "Ginny Chopain it is you! I never thought I'd see the day! Oh blessed, blessed be. Ginny, my friend. My dear, dear Ginny." She pulls me into such a tight hug. I can feel the rattle of her breaths against my chest.

"Mrs. McDermott," I say, clenching my teeth and trying to wrench free from her grasp. When I finally do, I fall with a thud onto the floorboards.

"We're very sorry, ma'am. We've obviously wasted your time and we shouldn't have bothered you this way." Vaughn talks fast, in a slick-as-a-car salesman voice. He flashes her another of his signature grins while helping me up. I lock my arm with his as if it's a life preserver. When she looks up at him, her eyes widen again.

"Wait, is it you? It can't be. Come closer." She peers up at him, but we've already backed a few steps away from her. "It is, isn't it? You're her Beau. Oh Ginny, how you loved your dear Beau. On and on you always went about him. My Beau this and my Beau that. It was a bit obsessive really. The two of you. Oh I'm so happy you're still together."

Holy crap. She's whacked.

"We have to get going! So sorry to cut the visit short!" I smile as big as I can, and wave wildly.

"Thanks for seeing us!" Vaughn adds, still doing his Ken doll impression.

We're backpedaling to the car, but she's standing now, leaning against the railing. "Everyone was jealous of you, Ginny. Everyone in town."

And maybe I'm crazy too, but I stop when I'm almost at the car. Mrs. McDermott may be crazy and she may be delusional, but she did know Ginny Chopain. Even if she thinks I'm someone else, it can't hurt to listen.

Our hesitation spurs her on. "The men of course admired your beauty, and the women, well, they looked upon you two like the luckiest people in the world. Women love watching real love, you know." She winks one of her milky blue eyes. "Everyone wants to believe a deep, true love exists. And when they see you, they know it does. It makes them hope. But it makes them jealous. That's why you have to watch out for the crazies, you know." She nods knowingly and I step forward. My arm hooked through Vaughn's gives me strength.

"Who are the crazies?" The words feel terrible when they leave my mouth. I'm leading this old woman on in the worst way, pretending the way I am.

"Everyone. I hear them talking. All the girls at Preston. The boys too. Even their mothers talk. They say he's silly, painting your name on the side of a barn, proclaiming his love in a mown field. The way he brings you things, twisting flowers into garlands for your hair. And at that one dance, that Sadie Hawkins senior year. Well, he didn't look anywhere but your eyes. His whole world is invisible when you're around, Ginny. There it is, just look at him now." She motions to our clasped hands. Embarrassment creeps up my neck but I don't move. I don't want to break her train of thought. "But then, he's always been that way, and you deserve it. Every girl does."

She blinks again, looking directly into the afternoon sun.

We're frozen in this ridiculous tableau and I feel like the world's worst actor. I'm as motionless as the hills around me, my heart seeming to be the only thing moving. I shift, leaning deeper against Vaughn. Slipping his arm around my waist, he steers me toward the passenger side of the car.

"Well then," Mrs. McDermott says brightly with a wave, acting like the normal old lady we saw when we first arrived. "Thanks for the visit. And please pass along word for my granddaughter to visit me."

"We will." My voice shakes as I force a smile.

She stays on the porch while we hurry into the car. Vaughn backs slowly down the driveway, leaning down with one last wave through the windshield as we finally pass the crest of the hill. We pull onto the main road and drive in silence.

"That lady was batshit," he finally says.

"No kidding. I've never been mistaken for a dead person before."

"We weren't just mistaken. She was almost convinced. It's like she was in a spell or something. Wait until I tell Mom this. Nice help she was."

"Oh, I don't know. She may be crazy or senile or whatever, but she did give us some information, even if she didn't know who she was talking to."

"I guess. But what did we really learn? That there was some intense love between Ginny and this Beau guy and people were jealous? Hardly seems helpful." He frowns at the road and turns to me. "I'm shot. Want to stop for coffee?"

"I *would* kill for a latte right now."

With a big grin, he slides a hand over mine and pretends to bow. "At your service."

Staring out the window, I squeeze his fingers and try like crazy to push away the memory of Mrs. McDermott's haunting words.

14

SUNLIGHT SPILLS FROM my bedroom into the hall and I'm humming Vaughn's song as I step through my doorway, the steam from my shower following me.

The water in the ocean rolls, with restless waves, but truth be told, it will never silence me. Forever you will come to me.

It's weird being home when everyone's in school. I towel dry my hair and get dressed quickly, shivering from the strong winds that rush through my open windows. I think about Vaughn and wonder what class he's in. After the last two days with him, my life is quiet today. I miss him. It's been nice having someone to talk to. About nothing, and everything.

Like how he listened when I told him about the first time my dad left. About how I waited up all night, and the next night too. How I wrote my dad a letter each night about what I'd done in school, about all the things I'd tell him when he came back. But then he wouldn't come back, or if he did, he never cared what I'd been up to. And then we'd move again and he'd show up and then be gone again. Never caring. Never staying. But I still kept writing the letters, because I wanted to believe he cared. It sounded so stupid now. Lame. But it felt good to get it out, to tell Vaughn. To have someone know that deep down part of who I am. What I've been through.

Speaking of, as I should have seen coming, after Saturday's attic freak-out, Mom's insisting I go see some new shrink she found, despite my objections. After she dragged me through that years ago, making me talk to them and her about my *feelings* every five seconds, I did not want to ever deal with that again. But here I am, home from school with a doctor appointment this afternoon. I can only hope he's more qualified than the last doctor she took me to, when she was at the height of her brainwashed phase, who focused more on centering my spirit and harnessing my energy than actually working through my problems.

I stand at my dresser mirror, fingering the guitar pick Vaughn left behind the other night. I smile at the memory of him playing for me, swaying to the music in my mind. When I open my eyes, the reflection behind me stops me. My room is a complete mess. Papers have been blown across the floor, pens splayed on the desktop. The wind has whipped through the room, curtains twisted up in themselves. Even my sweaters have been tossed from the back of my chair to the floor.

I think of my drawing and panic. And where is Ginny's picture?

Dropping to my knees, I frantically grab each paper, turning them over. Doodles, old drawings, tests and quizzes from school. My wet hair drips on the floor, soaking into the dull wood and saturating the papers.

I push them away from me, searching for the only two that matter, but I can't find them. The wind pulls at my shirt, still soaked from my hair. I stomp over and shut the windows, ignoring how they rattle in their frames, trying to look everywhere at once, the sweat on my forehead at odds with the chill of my hair. A white square of paper under the bed catches my eye and I drop again to my knees. Other than dust and unworn flip flops, I find a handful of projects I started drawing this summer. Stupid things like praying mantis colonies and black and white rainbows.

I sit back on my feet. Where the hell could they be? I peer into the hallway. Nothing there.

Digging the heels of my hands in my eyes, I slowly count to ten. How would a drawing and a photo simply disappear? It's not even possible.

Wait.

Through my open closet door, I see papers on top of my sea of shoes. I crawl over quickly, practically diving into the space. The first one I turn over is an old English quiz. I throw it behind me and it slides across the floor.

The second is my drawing. My dear, precious drawing. I fight the urge to hold it to my chest like a long lost friend. My eyes dart over the figures in the picture. Once I'm sure they're okay, I dig for more pages. I'm halfway in the closet when I see the photo, the corner of Ginny's dark dress. It's all the way in the back, somehow stuck between the baseboard and the floor. I tug, but it doesn't come free. It's really stuck. Bracing against the wall, I pull harder.

Something gives. But it's not the picture.

It's the wall.

BEHIND THE WALL, the darkness seems to go on forever. The space is narrow, maybe three feet across and just as high, and from where I am, I can't see where it ends. I shimmy onto my stomach, pushing shoes and boots to the side. I'm halfway in the space when I notice the smell. It's musty and damp, like a basement. But there's something else too. Something sour, like old milk, crusted over.

And it's freezing. I look over my shoulder. From here, my room looks like a different universe. Bright and airy and colorful.

How far does it go? It's barely wide enough for me, but I inch forward, reaching blindly into the dark. But I touch nothing.

Pushing back, I back out of the closet and tiptoe across the room, hoping Mom won't hear me. She'll really think I'm losing it if she finds me in here. I grab a flashlight from the table in the hall and make my way back to the closet, squirming on my stomach into the tight space.

Ow! What the hell? My finger burns. I turn on the flashlight and see the floor is unfinished plywood, the rough finish responsible for the huge splinter sticking out of my finger. Blood rolls down the fleshy part of my hand, tickling my wrist.

Shining the light, I see the back of the space a few feet ahead, which is weird. I close my eyes. The room next to mine is a spare bedroom. There's a closet that lines up with mine but unless I'm wrong, there shouldn't be this much space between the rooms. But here it is. I can't argue with what's right in front of me. I inch further along, wondering if I should stop. I'm inside the frickin wall, for God's sake. And if Mom and I didn't know this was here, how would anyone ever find me if I get stuck?

Yet something urges me on. Squinting into the dim shaft of light, I scoot forward and reach out for the wall. It feels like packed dirt, but when I test it with my fingers and examine it in the light, it doesn't crumble. Completely packed dirt or some type of cement. How long has this been here? Was there such a thing as cement when this house was built? When I reach forward again, something moves near my hip. I pull into myself, not wanting to know what could possibly be moving in this space.

I look backward. From where I am, with my entire body in the space now, I'd guess it was nearly six feet deep and much narrower in the back. My shoulders touch the side walls, and even wiggling, I can hardly move. The air is thick and stuffy and

I take short bursts of it, realizing how stale it is, how long it's probably been since this place has been opened.

It's like a casket or a mausoleum.

I have to get out of here.

Moving quickly, I snag my shirt on the unfinished wood. I pull my stomach in, using my toes and hips to push myself back. My equilibrium feels off and the space wavers around me like I'm underwater. A scene from my attic vision floods my brain. It's a different dark space, wooden boards laid in a sort of rudimentary ladder against what looks like a sloping wall. It was in that dusty air that Vaughn told me to find him.

Before it was too late.

With trembling hands, I move as quickly as I can, an inchworm on steroids. Splinters dig through my jeans but I keep moving. A slight breeze moves through the space. I whimper, trying not to think about how little sense that makes. I'm finally back in the closet, kneeling in a heap amidst my shoes, when I hear the rustling. Peering into the space, I see a large package, wrapped in plastic and pressed against the side wall. The edge of it flaps in the breeze and I eye it curiously.

"Lange?"

Crap. Mom. From the sound of it, she's just outside my doorway. I pull my head out of the space, gulping air. The sweet air of my closet. Of my room.

Of reality.

I keep an eye on the package as I grip the edge of the hidden door. Just as I'm about to pull it closed, I grab the bundle and slide the door closed, falling back onto my knees.

The blood from my splintered finger smears across the plastic wrap as I turn it in my hands. An ancient, plastic mummy. Inside, it looks like a bunch of envelopes and papers. Great. I probably just creeped myself out to unearth someone's bank statements.

That musty sour smell wafts from the package as I pick at the edges. If I could just see what one of the envelopes is, I'd get a good idea what secrets are hidden in that tunnel. It's gotta be something important, to be hidden that way.

"Lange?" She's in my room.

"Hey Mom! Just looking for my boots." I slide the package under a pile of shoes, where I notice Ginny's picture still lies.

"Are you ready? We're already running late." Big sigh.

I grab the first pair of boots I see, a hideous purple leather pair. I don't even know why I still have these things, but they'll do.

"Sorry," I say breathlessly when I slide back into my room. The air is delicious here. I try not to be obvious about taking it in like it's the last breath I'll take. With my back to her, I pull on my boots quickly and stand, running my hand through my still-damp hair.

"What happened to you?" She stomps over to me, brushing the front of my jeans with her hand. "You're filthy."

"Um, it's dusty in there."

"Is that blood?" She points to the floor in front of the closet and I cringe, hoping the hidden door or the path I cleared to it isn't obvious. I follow her gaze and see a small spot of blood, no bigger than the size of an olive. But it's bright red and starting to seep into the floorboards. My finger throbs from the deep splinter and I hold it up for her to see. *It's okay*, the motion says. *Just a splinter.*

But I don't say anything else because the blood does something to me. It twists my stomach and I gag, my mind flashing again like angry bulbs.

"All right, that's enough," she says. "We're going to the doctor. Now."

❧   ❧   ❧

"So TELL ME again what exactly has been going on?" Kelly lies on my bed surrounded by the reams of material and costume ideas she's brought to show me. When I didn't show up at school, she called to check on me. Since the doctor, some lame guy who just sat there while I talked about my artwork, told Mom I seemed fine and perfectly sane, she said it was okay for Kelly to come over.

So here we are, me balanced precariously on my desk chair, trying to come up with a decent excuse for a.) spending time with Vaughn, b.) pretty much retreating from her in terms of hanging out, phone calls and generally being involved, and c.) trying not to think about the package I pulled out of the secret tunnel in my closet.

I lean back in my chair and stretch. As I've been doing since she got here an hour ago, I fight the urge to look at my clock and try keep my eyes off my slightly-open closet door. My drawing, Ginny's photo, and the package all lie waiting for me and I'm practically crawling the walls to get to them.

"Nothing's been going on. Working on the Motions project has eaten my week. And I've been totally sick with some stomach flu or something."

She snorts and raises her eyebrows. "Totally sick *and* hanging out with Vaughn?"

"Come on, I already told you about that. It's nothing, it's just—"

"I know. The song, the picture. Got it." She makes pouty lips and piles her stuff in the middle of my bed, stopping with her arms full of dark velvet. "I'm not gonna lie. It doesn't sound too believable." Her voice softens, but she doesn't look at me.

When I don't answer, she continues, "Listen. I like you. We're friends. We're all friends. But I've known Stace my entire life, and, well . . . "

Ouch.

"I already told you, nothing's going on with us . . . "

Even I can hear how untrue the words sound. I try not to flinch at the narrowed-eyed expression she gives me.

"You never struck me as the type to hook up with someone's boyfriend."

"But I thought he wasn't her boyfriend."

Her eyes darken. "Please, Lange. Don't make me choose between you. Stace is fragile, you know. She doesn't seem like it, but she is. Don't do this to her."

Oh, Stace is fragile? What about me? Besides, nothing has happened between Vaughn and me. Not really, anyway.

Not yet.

I ignore the voice in my head. It's not like I can explain how complicated this really is.

Kelly looks at me and shakes her head sadly. "Whenever you're ready to talk, I'm here, okay?"

I'm not sure what she sees on my face, but I fake a bright smile. "There's nothing to talk about." I gesture to the dresses draped across my bed. "Now show me again what you're deciding between for the governess's costume."

15

AFTER KELLY FINALLY leaves, and by the time I've eaten soup with Mom, sat through her endless dissection of our astrological charts as a means of explaining my behavior and heightened emotions, I'm nearly bursting with anticipation and I practically run to my room. As quiet as a cat creeping through a graveyard, I close my door and click the lock into place.

And then I barrel for the closet.

I grab all of it. The package, the photo, my drawing. I spread it out on my bed, tucking my feet under me and settling against my pillows.

After carefully unwrapping the package, I remove the bundle inside. At first, it's a bit overwhelming. Various sizes of what looks like cards and letters and who knows what else, some folded, some flat, some in envelopes, even a few small notebooks that are stained with water damage. I try to open one of the books, but the pages are stuck together, so I grab a stack of letters instead.

I take a deep breath, unfold the first one, and start to read.

July 7, 1934
My dearest, dearest love,
There's this overwhelming sense of sadness around the place these days. You've only been gone a week, and I can't believe I have to wait three more to see you. How dare your parents insist your visit be so long? I know, we've got forever ahead of us, but my dear, it's a month apart, which hurts me so.

How is your grandmother feeling? Please send her my love. Make sure to make her tea often and read to her. If you choose the newspaper, be sure you skip the worst stories. No one wants to hear those things, especially old ladies. I'd suggest a novel instead, or perhaps some poetry. I know how you feel about poetry. But believe me, it would make her health improve in no time. Words are powerful, my love.

I must run now as Mother needs my help. We'll be on the porch with the washing, but my thoughts will be with you in New York and with the last night we spent together on that same porch, with the stars. I want to hear your voice, want to hear you sing to me. Even if you're off key, you're mine, and that is worth more than all the gold in The Ten Story Gang, which I know not much of, other than Robert constantly burying his nose in them like they're literature.

Mother's calling again. Take care, my love. And write soon.

Forever, your Ginny

It's unreal. In my mind, I've seen her. I've drawn her and I have her photo. But this letter is her, her voice. It's like I'm hearing her now, too. A second page is folded behind Ginny's letter. I open it and look down at the much messier handwriting.

July 12, 1934

My dear Gin —

You've missed me as much as I've you, and in such a short time? I thought for sure you and your sisters would be gallivanting around the lake by now, swimming with half the town and eating vanilla ice cream at Old Mack's without me. If I'd known it was only my singing you'd miss, however, I would have tried a bit harder. And off key? Well, I resent that! I shall practice up here in the quietest place on Earth and be ready to serenade you when I return.

I've been thinking a lot about what you said to me before I left. About September. And if you're ready and I'm ready, you're right, we should just go for it. Though I do worry about disappointing our families if we do it without them and before they think we should. But, I'm sure you're right. Besides, we're no longer students, finally adults with the world at our finger-tips. The future is ours, Ginny! I can feel the freedom in my bones, way down to my core. I can feel how lucky I am every night when I close my eyes and know that someday soon, I'll see you every morning, noon and night.

My grandmother is much better, thank you. It seems our coming here does serve a great purpose. Mother is tending to her while Father and I mend all that's fallen apart in her old house. Today we nailed down some floorboards and tomorrow will be some window chains that have slipped. She sends best wishes to you as do my mother and father. We all miss you, Gin, but me especially. At night I look from the window here in grandmother's guest room and I count the stars and try to sleep. I remember those nights on your porch, where we counted the stars together. Each one a year of our future, remember? This, I promise. I'm counting the days already, Ginny. Someday soon, we'll count the years.

My eternal love is yours, if you'll have it.

Your Beau

P.S. I've seen Ten Story Gang at the newsstand. Tell Robert to expand his horizons and read something useful.

Wow. Mrs. McDermott was right, those two really were in love. What does it feel like to have someone so completely in love with you at my age? Promising a universe's worth of years?

I refold the pages carefully, wondering as I continue to dig through the pile, how these letters ended up here, together. The next page is thin, like scrap paper, covered with crude drawings of cat faces. There are tons of these, each drawn with different versions of animals. Stick figure dogs and lions with balding manes. On the back of each, in tiny letters is the name Margie Chopain.

Who were you, Ginny Chopain? Who were you who saved your little sister's artwork and wrote love letters to your dearest Beau? And why are you in my life now?

The phone rings, shattering the quiet.

"Hello?"

"Lange?" It's Vaughn, his voice so clipped my heart skips.

"What's wrong?"

"It looks like someone does *not* like us snooping around. Listen to what I got today." Paper crinkles in the background. He clears his throat. "Perhaps losing your tires wasn't enough to keep you from your destination. Next time I'll try harder and perhaps you'll lose more."

For a long moment, there is nothing but silence.

"Where did you find that?"

"In my mailbox. Plain envelope, like an off-white color, with my full name on the cover, Vaughn Broussard. Both the note and envelope are written in a fancy script. Almost like calligraphy."

"Holy shit."

"Right?"

"And you think this is about the murders?"

"What else could it be about?" he asks.

"But why would someone care about us looking into that? It was like a million years ago."

"How should I know? But this is freaky. How does anyone even know? I haven't told anyone."

"Me either."

"And what have we really done? Read some newspaper articles? That's hardly groundbreaking."

How about reading personal letters and crawling into secret tunnels to find the dead's hidden, private secrets? What about visiting the murdered's old, senile friends?

I doodle on the corner of some old scrap paper, the pencil in my hand giving me focus and comfort. In the background, Vaughn's guitar clangs quietly as he settles it onto his knee. We're quiet, each lost in our own way of working through our thoughts.

As I listen to the melody he strums, I consider something else. "Well. Do you think—"

I cut myself off. I shouldn't say it. Hell, I shouldn't even think it.

"What?"

"Well, Kelly was here today."

"And?"

"Well, she was kind of, well not exactly, but sort of . . . I don't know, maybe she wasn't. She just said—"

"Lange. What are you trying to say?"

"Stace!" I push the word out before I have time to over think it. "Kelly warned me about, you know, spending time with you. Getting Stace upset."

Another long, quiet moment.

Finally, he clears his throat. "Nah. She isn't capable of this. Stace can be intense about things, but she wouldn't do this."

Intense. The way he says it makes me uncomfortable.

"Okay," I mumble. "Well you know her better than me, obviously."

Strumming casual chords now, calm notes that are the exact opposite of the tension that gallops through me, Vaughn sighs.

"I'll talk to her. Would that make you feel better?"

"It would, actually."

"She wouldn't do this though. Not slashed tires and threatening notes. But I'll talk to her anyway. If it'll help. For you."

"Thank you."

"But I can't think of a single person who would care." His voice cracks. "Why would someone try to stop us?"

From beneath her letters and personal papers, I pull out Ginny's photo. I stare in her eyes, trying to read her expression. It's a cross between sadness and amusement.

What is your secret? What could you possibly know, more than eighty years after your death, that someone doesn't want us to find out?

A loud creak emerges from my closet and at the same moment, the stained glass butterfly I've hung on the top of my mirror falls, shattering on the dresser top. I screech, my heart pounding against my ribs.

In the mirror, I catch sight of my pale face, my sunken eyes, my lifelessly hanging hair. I look like death and feel it too. And even though we look nothing alike, in my eyes is that same intense, haunted expression Ginny once wore.

The music on the other end of the line abruptly stops. "You okay?"

"Yeah," I say, looking at the letter on my lap. "But I have news too. I also found something today."

"Not a note, too?"

"No, not exactly. Not like yours. But I found some letters. They're Ginny and Beau's."

For the space of two heartbeats, we're silent.

"Read them to me."

16

IT'S LESS THAN a week until The Hunt and it's all they talk about in school. The hallways buzz with it, the classes too. Even the teachers play along, offering to spy on the seniors if we stay on our best behavior in class. Everyone has a blast, guessing what this year will bring, hoping it will top last year's.

After finding the letters and staying up way late reading them to Vaughn and talking to him, I'm a zombie in school. I'm half asleep in English, one of the only "real" classes we're required to take at Preston, when the first bout of sickness rolls in. This one, though, has a source. And his name is Ben.

The first thing that sets me off are the details. He talks to a group of guys in the front of the room and I can't help but overhear.

"We have this theory about a serial killer." By *we*, I assume he means him and Kelly, since she's the one who mentioned it in the first place.

"I'm thinking something bloody, of course, but I mean, really sick. Like sliced off limbs and stuff. Heads," he makes a slicing sound, "totally cut off. And a whole bunch of people, like a family. You know, Dahmer-style."

Despite my best efforts, my head swivels toward the group of them. Everyone's laughing like a sick murder scene is the funniest thing they've ever heard. I want to vomit. I really do. I want to tell them all to shut the hell up. Stuff like that really happens. It's *not* funny.

But then my nausea grows. I swear Ben looks at me sideways before laughing again. "It would be the ultimate. Plus, if there were multiple murders to solve, they would have to heighten the prize, right?"

My hands shake on my desk. I thrust them into my lap and stare at the door. Where is Mrs. Mantoney? What kind of teacher comes this late to class?

He can't be talking about the Chopains, right? He's not that cruel. This has to be a coincidence.

Has to be.

I keep the mantra running in my head, afraid to look up again, tracing invisible pictures on my lap, shapes and designs. Patterns to distract me.

I'm being paranoid, I know. But after the tires and the pen and Vaughn's note, the thinly veiled threats, I'm totally suspicious of everyone. But this is Ben. He's my friend. Why would he mess with me?

The door creaks open and finally, *finally,* Mrs. Mantoney walks in. She drops her briefcase on the desk and smiles. The conversation decreases only slightly as she begins the long ritual of unpacking her bag. Ben turns and gives me a small wave.

Feeling better? He mouths the words, a genuine smile spread across his face.

I nod, my worry lifting slowly, like fog.

The paranoia has got to stop.

I reach into my bag, digging around for my pencil case, but pull back quickly when something bites me. *Ouch. What the hell?* I wince at the pain, bleeding finger in my mouth, and realize I've managed to knock my bag over, spilling everything from the front compartment onto the floor.

I gape at the pile. No art case. No sketchpad. Just five Exacto knives, without their sheaths, one tipped with crimson. The sight of my blood on the blade makes the room waver.

I don't even carry one Exacto knife, let alone five.

I clean up quickly, hoping no one notices.

AND THEN THERE'S lunch.

Kelly comes up to me as soon as I enter the cafeteria. "Got a minute?"

She's breathless. Behind her, I see Stace's patchwork bag on our table, but no one's there. Weird, considering the bell rang a few minutes ago.

"Where is everyone?" I try and push around her.

"Um, listen. Today is *not* a good day. Maybe you shouldn't sit with us."

I stop, stunned.

"I'm not saying forever, but for today, it would be best if you weren't here. At all actually." She looks anxiously behind her and back to me again, eyes full of an apology. "This isn't up to me, but Stace, well. I don't know, Lange. I don't know what to think."

"What—?"

"Her and Vaughn had it out. Things are toast with them. She is not happy. And, well. There's only one person she blames."

Wonderful. "Fantastic. So you're what, disowning me too?"

"It's not that." She sighs. "We're still friends. Today's just rough, okay? I'm trying to play damage control, to smooth things over. Just give me some time. Talk to Vaughn for the details. Like I said, I have no idea what exactly went down."

"So that's it?" I cross my arms and look behind her, where the lunch table still sits empty.

"I'm sorry."

"Whatever." I turn on my heel and head down to the stairwell at the end of the hall. Upset or not, I'm not about to stand around and get rejected by the only friends I have.

I trudge upstairs, making my way to the only place I can think of that's private and quiet, where I can seethe in peace and figure out what to do next. In the back of the library, I flop into a chair at the most remote, hidden table I can find. Then I look into the next alcove. And despite my anger, I smile.

Vaughn raises his eyebrows and looks over each shoulder, jabbing his finger to his chest. "That smile for me?"

When I wave him over, he plods across the aisle with a zombie walk and sinks into a chair.

"What the hell happened?"

He sighs. "Well, I guess you can say things are not so great with Stace and me. She kind of flipped."

"What happened?" I ask again, ignoring the telling betrayal of my increased heartbeat.

Lange, you suck. Reveling in someone else's heartbreak.

"I want to be friends with her, I do. But . . . " He waves his hand. "It's useless drama. She's being her normal irrational self. I tried to talk to her, like I told you I would. I didn't bring up the letter or anything. I just tried to smooth things over between us, with our friendship."

"And?"

"She basically exploded on me." He looks at his hands and I can almost see the internal debate of his next words. "She poured out all these feelings for me. Honestly, I didn't realize she felt the way she does. Not to that extreme."

"Seriously? Are you blind?"

He gives me a sheepish smile. "I don't know, maybe. But that's not the point. There's something else . . . "

"What?" I ask, cringing.

"I told her I don't feel that way about her. I just don't." He looks at me. "She blames you. I'm sorry, Lange. It's not your fault. Regardless of how I feel about you, I've never liked her that way, really. She doesn't see it that way, though."

Regardless of how I feel about you.

I attempt to ignore the hammering in my chest. *What way do you feel about me?*

"Well that explains why Kelly basically kicked me out of the cafeteria a few minutes ago and told me to stay clear for a while."

His eyes widen. "She what?"

"Well not in so many words, but . . . yeah." I stare at the table. "How did things get so out of control?" A shudder passes through me but I swallow and raise my chin. I will not get upset over Stace.

"Hey," he says. "Come here."

I scoot my chair closer. He circles an arm around my shoulders and pulls me against him.

"It'll all work out. Don't even worry about *that* of all things." He mock laughs and I nod. He's right. At this point, we definitely have bigger problems.

"That reminds me," I say, pulling back and holding up my index finger, Band-Aid and all. "Wait until you hear what I found in my bag this morning."

IN MOTIONS, I work on the final touches on Transformations, darkening the face of the third figure, who looks back, stuck in half-shadow with her expression mostly hidden. It's the first time I feel in control all day, bringing my pencil to the page. Creating. An argument erupts at the end of the table. Jake and Anthony, two of the best painters in school, who happen to be brothers, are *always* arguing about something. This time, it's The Hunt.

Of course.

This is seriously going to be the longest week ever.

"I'll bet you a hundred bucks it's downtown. It's *always* downtown."

"I don't know. I heard it doesn't have to be though. Who knows? Could be at a house."

"What house? Like half the school is gonna be running through someone's house! You're a dumbass."

"Well maybe not a house, but maybe not downtown either."

"But all the Halloween festivities are down there. It's where we all end up right? Trust me, that's the first place to look."

"Whatever. You look where you want, I'll look where I want."

I listen to them bicker while I draw, wondering how their family can stand to live with them. They are so annoying.

"Very nice, Lange." Mr. Murphy nods. Standing next to me, with his arms crossed and an impressed, if subtle, grin on his face, he makes me feel good. Proud. Accomplished.

"Thanks." I stop working, tilting my head to the side like him, trying to see it as he does. Obviously it's impossible to be subjective, but I try.

"I had no idea you were doing a self-portrait piece. I really love it."

"Oh, it's not a self-portrait!" I laugh, brushing my hand across the surface of the page. "This was inspired by something else. Definitely not me."

He steps back, surprise turning his smile into confusion. "Oh. I'm sorry. That last figure, the one you've been working on today. It favors you so much. I'm sorry I misinterpreted. Although, if you plan to be one of the greats, that will happen often." He laughs, the smile crinkling the corners of his eyes.

One of the greats. I want to snort. As if that's going to happen.

"Thanks," I say meekly, picking up my pencil again. I start shading the third figure again, adding more darkness to her shadow.

I try to see it with a critical, unbiased eye. The third girl does have dark hair and a slight frame. But her nose is wrong and the chin too. Even the set of her eyes, though partially hidden... they're the total opposite of mine. There's no way this is even close to looking like me.

Crazy Mr. Murphy.

17

AFTER SCHOOL, I look through the pile of Ginny's papers again. I reread the letters and cards, look through the stack of drawings. I pick up one of the small notebooks, a red hardcover with frayed edges on the binding, this one not nearly as water damaged as the others. I'm surprised—and excited—to discover what is handwritten on the first page: *My Journal.*

When I lay across my bed and turn the page, my heart skips.

"Lange?" Mom calls from upstairs.

I sigh without getting up. "Yeah?"

"Can you give me a hand up here for a minute?"

Dropping the book on my pillow, I reach for my fleece. It's freezing up there.

When I get to the top of the stairs I see she's pushed half the boxes to the far end of the room. Against the wall is an enormous mirror. It's at least five feet tall and twice as wide, the glass itself is a bit warped near the bottom of the frame. It looks like it weighs a ton. Mom leans against its gilded edge, breathing heavy.

"There's no way we're getting that downstairs." I watch my reflection as I step closer. It's almost like a trick mirror, making me shorter and taller as I move from one side to the other.

"I know that. It was hard enough to get it this far." She huffs. "I just need you to help me move it over there." She chin nods to the furthest end of the attic. "I want to stand it up, out of my way. I'm not sure how it's survived this long without getting broken."

"Well let's get it done. I'm sort of in the middle of something." I shift it from the wall and am almost toppled by its weight. "Holy crap. This thing is even heavier than it looks."

"Isn't it?" She squats down with her hands cupped around the bottom corner. "Okay, push." She grunts and I lean into the frame, pushing it toward her. With a maximum amount of effort, we finally move it across the room, tilting it just enough to keep it upright.

"Okay?" I move from foot to foot, impatient to get back downstairs.

"What's the rush?" She eyes me suspiciously. "Is it that boy again?"

I roll my eyes. "No. I'm working on my drawing."

Still out of breath, she shrugs and fans her face. "Suit yourself."

Behind her, something moves, disappears behind a box. I barely catch it out of the corner of my eye, but hear a faint giggle like a child playing hide and seek. Goosebumps flash across my skin.

I shiver, wanting nothing more than to get out of the attic. "Let me know if you need any more help."

"You okay?" She raises her brows.

"Yeah, fine. Just thought I saw something. Must be a dust bunny or something."

She shakes her head. "You never know. I myself have felt some strange energies up here from time to time."

I force my shaking hands in my pockets. "Nah. Just my overactive imagination."

"Are you sure? Because after what happened to you the other night up here, if you feel like you need to talk to the doctor again, he can definitely help you work it out, and you know, with the way the moon is nearly full, and it being, of course, October, it's no wonder you're feeling psychologically off balance. I mean, you know we're in touch with the otherworldly more than other people, and sometimes it helps to talk—"

She's getting that dazed look. I have to get out of here.

"I'm fine, Mom. Seriously. I have things to do." I inch toward the stairs.

"Fine," she says with a sigh. "Don't listen to me. What do I know? Hey, I have an idea. You know, I'm going to that photo convention this weekend. On the way back we can stop and see Berta if you think it would help. I don't mind you tagging along."

Oh God. Berta Ramirez. My old *doctor*-slash-spiritual-advisor.

"Um, no. Sorry. I have plans. Here. Last weekend before the Hunt and I told my friends . . . "

She shrugs. "Well, okay. But the offer stands. Anyway, before you go, take this. I found it earlier. Thought you'd like it." She holds out an antique hair comb with a row of beads and a large gilded bird across the top.

"Pretty," I say, trying to ignore the thrumming in my ears. When I take it from her, my fingers feel numb as I trace the sharp edge of the bird's wings. "Thanks."

I'm halfway down the stairs when I hear her. "Huh. What do you know?"

She isn't talking to me, but curiosity gets the best of me and I skip back up the stairs. She's on her knees in front of the mirror, holding what looks like an index card.

"What's that?"

She waves the card in the air. "I guess it's who owned the mirror at some point. It was taped to the back. Too bad there's no year on it. I'd love to know how old this thing is."

Standing to dust herself off, she mumbles, "Actually, I bet it's worth money. We should call one of those antique dealers in town." She drops the card on the box by my feet and I half turn to walk downstairs.

"I'll be in my room," I say, waving over my shoulder even though her attention is already somewhere across the room. But the handwriting on the card catches my eye.

Edith Sellers. Shady Springs, Pennsylvania.

"I'm ordering pizza later," Mom says, her head halfway in a box.

"Sounds good," I mutter. As a last thought, I tuck the card into my pocket and walk down the stairs, anxious to get back to the diary.

18

IT'S INCREDIBLY LATE by the time I get through the first part of the diary. The entries are sporadic at best. Sometimes Ginny writes daily, sometimes every few months. She chronicles everything from the mundane class schedules and what her mother cooked for dinner to the intimate details of her family's life on the farm. But finally, at almost midnight, I get to the juicy part. The place where the letters left off, mere weeks before her murder.

August 12, 1934

Ah, well, my love is back here in Shady Springs, where he belongs. Oh thank the Lord too. I was starting to go a bit loony. His first day back was one of the best we've ever had. We walked around Pike's, just like he said we would. And then back here, we had a picnic lunch out back and no one bothered us, except of course Mr. Whiskers. That love bug of a cat won't leave my side for anything. We lay on a blanket, out behind the barn, and we read all our sappy letters from the last month to each other. We promised to always keep them. I'll store them with this diary, hidden in my secret closet compartment, like I always do. He says we'll use them as proof, someday when our children and grandchildren don't believe that the bald old man and stooped lady had passion, well, we'll show them! Oh, I'm so happy I could burst—just burst!

P.S. Although I don't dare say the words out loud, we've agreed about September. We're going. Mother will be unhappy as she refuses that at 18

I'm ready for any big steps like this, but it's not in her hands. I'm an adult now, after all!

August 16, 1934

Well, boys can be so absolutely, unbelievably silly. What can I say to explain my love showing up on my porch with a fresh apple pie, warm from his mother's oven? But it's your favorite! He said when I insisted he take it right back home. Can you imagine, snatching a pie right from his family's kitchen table? But oh, how I laughed. Your cheeks, he said as we climbed into his truck. You should see how pink they are. That's worth all the trouble of a million pies. And more. You don't steal a pie to make someone's cheeks pink! I tried to argue, but I know him, there is no talking sense when his mind is set. Get ready, he replied, because I'm gonna do a whole lifetime of worse things if it means I'll hear you laugh. And oh well, what could I say? He tickles me, that boy. Right down to my toes.

The shock of what I know is coming for Ginny turns me so inside out I'm raw. Yet I can't help thinking of that old phrase about loving and losing and how I'd give almost anything for just a fraction of what Ginny wrote about in these pages.

I bet Vaughn would understand. I bet it would inspire him.

Vaughn.

Thoughts of him seep into every part of me. There's nothing I'd rather do than be with him. Just sitting across from him in the cafeteria makes me feel like I've fallen into some place I finally belong.

I shake my head and stare at the pictures on my dresser. Mom and me on our old porch in New Jersey, and another one when we lived down at Virginia Beach a few years ago. There's one of my dad. I'm little, probably seven or so. It was taken a few years before he died. It's a Christmas morning picture and the smiles on our faces don't tell the truth. From this picture, you'd think we were a happy father-daughter pair, not a girl and some dad who was never around.

The memory of his death is still strong. It had been some weird, freak-accident—he'd been bear hunting with his friends in northwest New Jersey and his buddy's gun misfired. I was only ten and Mom hounded me for months, worried I hadn't grieved properly. Because I hadn't really grieved at all. How can you grieve for someone you really didn't know in the first place? If I was upset about anything, it's the childhood I never had with him, not over his stupid death, which I was too young to understand, even as I helped her dump his ashes into the ocean, performing one of her weird new age rituals. But still, she'd dragged me to that wacky shrink constantly and she never stopped talking about it, even at home.

The picture blurs in my vision but I blink away the few tears that have gathered there. He's not worth it.

I turn back to the diary in my hands.

In my peripheral, the curtain moves. I reach toward it, expecting the breeze on my arm, but the window is closed. A soft whimper, the faint, barely there sound of children crying carries on the still air.

Tingles race up and down my spine.

The pages flutter in my hand and I stare at them without seeing, straining to hear. It's completely silent. No wind outside, no sounds upstairs, not even the tick of a clock. Definitely no crying. No giggling hide and seek children.

Breathe, Lange.

Back to the diary.

August 20, 1934

I had bad thoughts today. Mother says I listen to too many news reports. But I've heard all about that Texas murderer who they can't catch. Between those two families he killed and that girl in Maryland who may also be his doing, you can never be too careful. That's what I say. Mother wants to see the world as if nothing bad will ever happen. Not me. I don't trust a soul— not a stranger anyway. And now she's calling, so off I go again!

August 25, 1934

There were five dead rabbits in the grass this morning. Right under my window, in a line. Mother blames Jester and his tomcat friends. Ever since Margie started feeding them, it's like we've got more cats than kids here, after all. But cats don't line up their kills that way. Do they?

The tension in her entry makes my skin crawl. This was written five days before her death. Five days. Five rabbits.

I shudder.

It's almost two in the morning, but I can't stop reading. I'll read one more entry. Just one more.

August 25, 1934

I am a bit embarrassed to put this down on paper, but I just can't help it. God forbid anyone ever reads this. Mother would kill me. But today, in the barn, we laid side by side. We had a blanket spread in one of the back stalls and the sun was just right, my hair warm with it, the air thick with late summer. He ran his hands up and down my body. And I let him. I let him touch my bare stomach, let him kiss every inch of my neck. The way he touched me was slow and sweet. I never knew kissing an ear could be an all afternoon event. And the things he whispered. Ah, my life is so complete. I don't see how it could get better. I suspect my life is going to be what dreams are made of. I'm sure it won't always be barn-kisses good, but I know I'll laugh. He can be so silly. In the midst of all this, he eased the collar of my shirt down, exposing my bare skin. My collarbones felt so bare, I had to shiver with the air. But I let him. Oh I'd let him do almost anything, I suppose. And would you believe what he said to me? Well he looked at me with a face as plain as he was gonna kiss his grandmother and he said he was going to take up a new hobby. Of course I didn't have a clue what he meant.

You don't have hobbies, I said! You want to work with people and be a detective and solve all these big, important crimes. And you like to fish, and watch baseball, and be with me and your friends. But what hobbies have you ever had? Well, he said with a solemn face, I think I'll take up the violin. Can you imagine! The violin! I shrieked with laughter so loud he had to cover my mouth with his hand and remind me that we could be overheard. So I quieted some, but kept on laughing until he nudged my shirt down again and kissed me there, one gentle kiss after another. With his finger, he traced my birthmark and said, "if this isn't the exact shape of a violin, I don't know what is. And I, my love, will play this forever." I don't need to say what happened after that because it was a whole lot of lips on lips and I don't kiss and tell, even to my own diary, but can you believe what a silly thing he can be?

My pulse plays double time in my temples.

A violin.

Precisely what Vaughn said to me, that day he saw my birthmark.

A violin.

This can't be coincidence. But I can't force the pieces to line up in any logical way.

I rush to the mirror, pulling down my shirt to stare at the birthmark, the one I always thought of as Africa-shaped, the one Vaughn said looked like a violin. Did Ginny really have a birthmark like this too? Could Beau have really called hers the same thing—a violin?

At my desk, I rifle through my bag until I find my Transformations project and the photo of Ginny. I think of how crazy old Mrs. McDermott thought I was Ginny. We look nothing alike, but still. Why *had* she said that? And Mr. Murphy, saying it was a self-portrait.

I study Transformations. At Ginny as a child and then a young woman. And the third version of her, the shorter girl, spinning away and looking back.

Is that me?

19

I HAVE NO idea what to say to Vaughn. All night I think about it, and all the way to school.

But right now, I have a much bigger problem. Stace is waiting at my locker. I see her as soon as I turn into the dreary, gray hall. It's crowded and I have to push through students milling by lockers, friends talking and laughing, sharing secrets and gossip and theories about The Hunt.

When I step in front of her, she seethes.

"Hey." My heart thuds in my ears. After yesterday's lunch banishment, I've steered clear of all of them. Not that it was hard. After Kelly told me I wasn't welcome, even if she seemed to feel bad about it at the time, she hadn't come to find me. And it's not like she called me last night.

"Hey," Stace says in a flat voice, her eyes totally blank. She settles in against my locker so I can't get to it. Suddenly, I'm scared. I am so non-confrontational.

Not sure what else to do with them, I cross my arms in front of me, feeling like I'm not totally present, like I've retreated to hide in some far away corner of myself. What can I possibly say?

"I just ran into him." She nods down the hall.

It feels so clinical, the calculating way she looks at me, the way she refers to him. "He's in the music room, playing some new song he wrote."

My stomach clenches. It's *the* song, I know it.

She frowns. Somehow her sadness is worse than if she were yelling. "It's the most beautiful thing I've ever heard him play. Ever heard him write."

In my mind, I hear it. The sweet, perfect melody, the stunning words. *Back again, here I am. Like the wind across your hand.*

The lyrics suddenly have even more meaning.

"I hate you." Looking down at the ground, she whispers. "I hate you so much I can't stand it. I've known Vaughn forever and he's never, ever written anything even remotely close to that."

I just stand here, racking my brain for something, anything, to try and make things better.

"Stace, It's not like I have anything to do with what he writes or doesn't—"

"He doesn't know I heard him," she says, shaking her head, finally looking at me. "He didn't know I'd stopped at the door." She looks down the hall, her eyes glistening. "It wasn't just the lyrics, which were so obviously inspired by you. It's the music. The timeless, melancholy hope between the notes. That song felt like forever. I can't compete with that."

"But there's nothing to—"

Her eyes cut to me and there's anger there. Flashing, dangerous anger. "Don't. Don't tell me there's nothing. And I don't want to hear it from him either. Our friendship is over, you and me. Me and him? Done. I don't even want to be in the same room with either of you. As for Kelly and Ben? I have no idea, but you will not lie to my face any more. It's written all over you, even now. You may want to do the right thing, but I think we both know you're past that."

I say nothing. I may be technically innocent, but my feelings are anything but.

The hallway's mostly empty now and the soft sound of the piano drifts down the hall. I barely move, but cock my head to the side, listening. The melody is familiar, but he's fleshed it out a lot.

Her eyes narrow. "You're a terrible person, Lange Crawford. You use people and lie and are the worst friend I've ever had. Just go. Go to him, like you so obviously want to do."

With a look of disgust, she finally steps to the side. I turn, wanting to say something, anything to even try to redeem myself. But the music reaches down the hall again, like fingers beckoning me.

She pushes me against the locker. "Watch your back."

Then finally, she's gone.

I tremble, trying my combination four times before I finally get it open. Tears sting my eyes. I know I won't make it to first period, but I don't care about that. There's only one thing I can think about. I slide my bag onto its hook and make my way to the music room.

Standing outside the door, I listen. He doesn't sing, but he plays that same beautiful melody and it breaks me open inside. I know she's right. That song is mine.

It's ours.

I close my eyes and listen to notes so raw with emotion it's like I'm inside them, floating in them like bubbles. The song is like an entire life, a rise and fall, a coming full circle. Eventually, it stops.

The door creaks open and he's there, rubbing his eyes and smiling a sad smile. My breath catches in my throat. With one hand, he pulls his hair back and holds it there, looking at me as if he's been awake all night.

And waiting.

His hand drops, his hair falling around his face as he moves aside to let me in.

20

"PIANO, HUH?" I trail my fingers along the top of it before sitting beside him on the bench.

He wears a distant smile. "I like to switch it up. Helps me compose."

"It was beautiful." To hide my shaking, I trap my hands between my knees, my arms pressed tightly against me.

"That's not why you're here." His statement is matter of fact, and there's a steady look in his eyes.

"You're going to think I'm crazy," I say, taking a deep breath. With the music room empty, it feels like we're two ants in a huge cave. I speak softly, but still, my voice seems to carry.

"I promise I won't."

"No really, you will. *I* do."

"Try me." His gaze doesn't waver.

"Ginny," I say. "I'm think I'm her. Or I was. Or, I'm not sure how it works." I stare at the floor, unable to look at him. This is the moment of truth. The make it or break it scene in the movie where the girl suddenly becomes the school loony and gets shipped off to the psych ward.

I expect him to laugh. I expect him to run.

What I don't expect is for him to take my fingers in his to stop their trembling. He lifts my chin so that he's looking right into my eyes. I don't expect his to be wide and filled with something familiar that I've never seen.

And I don't expect him to say what he does.

"You are. You're her. Well, in your last life anyway. And I'm the one who's always loved you."

21

I DON'T BELIEVE him.

Except I do.

Because it's like I've been trying to solve the world's most complicated riddle for as long as I can remember, and he's just given me the missing clue.

He laces his fingers in mine and I rest my head on his shoulder. He brushes soft, barely-there kisses across my forehead while I tell him about the diary entry, what Beau said about the birthmark. What Vaughn himself had said to me.

"I always knew," he says, biting his bottom lip. "Something always felt wrong with me. Different. Like, I never felt connected to anything or anyone. Like I was in my own world, couldn't connect to the real one. Did you ever crave a place you've never been? Ever feel nostalgia for a time you shouldn't know? That's how I felt, all the time. It wasn't just not belonging here, it was belonging someplace completely different. *Sometime* different."

I think of my weird visions and the garden where I used to disappear as a kid, that constant search for another place. An escape. And those bizarre feelings that come over me like I've been the same place or done the same exact thing before.

"This is insane," I mumble, squeezing his hand.

"It feels that way sometimes," he agrees, talking fast. "And it's always been like that. Just different, you know? Always trying to figure it out, find myself or something. I don't know, just someplace to belong. At first I thought it was because I'm adopted. But I tracked down my birth family and that just made things more complicated. They weren't even close to the answer I was looking for. Everything sucked for a long time. But I kept searching, doing research."

"How did you know what to look for?"

"I didn't. Not at all. I was basically just guessing. I knew it had to be something . . . different. I felt like I was living in a fantasy world and yet . . . "

I squeeze his hand for him to continue. He stares as his feet.

"And yet the further I got away from what I considered *normal* or reality, the closer I felt to finding my answer."

"When did all this figuring out happen?" I ask.

Tucking his hair behind his ears, he looks at the ceiling. "I'm not sure exactly. I guess sometime last year. It wasn't fast. Mostly lots of reading. Tons."

"Okay, so you've had a year to soak this all in." I try and smile. "So go slow, I've had about thirty six seconds to digest it. Start at the beginning."

"Sure, yeah. Of course. Like I said. I started reading a lot. Websites, books, you know, whatever. I called some people, went on some message boards. There are experts, or people who claim to be experts, anyway. But no one knows exactly how any of it works. It's all faith and belief and there are so many different opinions. So I took it all in and then just let it simmer, I guess. It festered in me, though. It wouldn't leave me alone and the idea felt so comfortable, like an old coat, you know? That's why I really believed I had finally found the truth. That I was back here from another life. That for some reason, I'd tapped into that reality when others don't. And it set me apart from other people. And it felt kind of cool, kind of great, actually, to figure that out. But what could I do about it? Nothing."

Another life.

It sounds weird. But it feels so right.

But still, I'm freaked out. Even if I reached the same conclusion last night, hearing it confirmed by someone else feels crazy.

"So then what?"

He swivels on the bench. He's got both my hands in his, his big fingers laced with mine like a braid.

"You came to Shady Springs," he says, kicking the toe of his sneaker back and forth on the linoleum. "When you moved here and we first met, it was crazy. It was like, I don't know, like an arrow had pierced me, finally pinning me to the spot I belonged."

My breath catches in the cage of my chest. "But we barely knew each other and I thought you were with Stace and, well, I didn't know—"

He shakes his head. "I didn't make sense to me at first. Right from the beginning, there was something about you. The more I got to know you, the cooler you were, the more I wanted to be around you. I was attracted to you. Hell, how could I not be?" He gives me a sheepish grin.

"Vaughn, I—"

"My feelings for you grew like crazy. And then, the night of the séance, it was weird and it was creepy and it scared the shit out of me. But it did something else too. When I held your hand and whatever happened in that barn happened, I don't know." He shakes his head. "It was a moment I'll never forget. Like a missing key slid into a dusty old lock. Click. My world opened."

I blink, stunned into silence.

"So that's it, then? That's what drew you to me? This connection to our previous lives?"

"No! Of course not." There's fire behind the deep brown of his eyes. "Come on, Lange. Haven't you been paying attention? You know I'm crazy about you. About *you*. You now. Here, in this life. Lange Crawford."

I drop my head in my hands. "This is crazy."

119

He slides off the bench and squats in front of me, so he's looking up into my face. "Crazy why? Because I care about you?"

"No, not that, I just—"

"You have no feelings for me?"

I sigh. "Come on. Of course I do. You know that. I haven't felt this way, well, ever."

His grin is like a thousand light bulbs.

"That's not the problem. I'm not freaked out about liking you, Vaughn. But everything else is just crazy right now." I pause, running the strange words through my mind before I say them. "I swear I'm her. Ginny. How is this happening?"

He takes a deep breath and slides back onto the bench. "It's a lot. I know. This rebirth stuff can be really overwhelming."

"Rebirth?"

"Well, that's what Sharon calls it. I'll take you to meet her. She'll explain more than I can and—"

"Whoa. Who's Sharon?" My mind swims.

He shakes his head. "I'm sorry. Let me back up. There's this woman in the city. Sharon. She kind of specializes in this sort of thing. I've seen her a few times."

"Wait, like a fortuneteller?"

"No. Not at all. She actually doesn't know anything about anyone like that, not like in a see your future or past sort of way. She just knows a lot about the way this works." He motions between us. "Coming back. Past lives."

Coming back. Past lives.

I still can't wrap my mind around it.

"The thing is," he pauses, biting his lip. "From what I've learned, this is not the way this usually works. People finding each other again."

"Then how do you know we have?"

"How do I know, just know, or how do I know, like with proof?"

"Could you manage to be any more cryptic? I think I may have a brain cell or two left that you haven't melted yet."

He's quiet while he searches for an explanation. "Okay, well, why do you think you were her? Ginny? You don't *know* for sure, right? You just feel it?"

When he puts it that way it sounds ridiculous. But still . . .

He reads my silence as agreement and rushes on. "Well when you read me those letters between her and Beau, I just felt something. It's probably the exact way you felt when you read those words in the diary. Beau said the same thing to Ginny that I said to you. I know it's just a birthmark, but still. You have to admit it's too perfect to be a coincidence."

He has a good point.

"When you read me their letters, I just knew. It was us in those words."

This isn't happening.

His eyes blaze. "Ever hear a song you swear you've heard before and just connect to it, bam!" He snaps his fingers. "Like that?"

"Like your song?"

His eyes soften. "Well, that doesn't count. That one's half yours, too."

I squeeze his hand.

"Here's the thing." He lowers his voice as if in conspiracy. "On a totally non-scientific level, I can only go with what I feel. What I've felt. If I was gambling, I'd bet it all that I'm right. And for the record, I've been waiting. I wanted to say something, but was sure you'd think I was nuts."

Another light bulb goes off and I raise my eyes to his. "Ah. So those times you were being shadester and holding back. That was it?"

"Well some of them. Other times were just me wanting to do this."

He leans in, closing the space between us. His nose nudges mine, his lips pressing to mine with the faintest pressure. Even with a lingering, barely-there kiss, my pulse races.

"Is this okay?" He whispers.

"More than okay," I answer, trying to pretend I'm not trembling inside.

"How about this?" He brushes my hair back and holds my face in his hands. I lean into him, returning each slow and deliberate kiss with one of my own. I'm dizzy when he pulls back to stare into my eyes. He presses his forehead to mine while we share the air in the small space between us.

He gives me another light kiss, and another on the tip of my nose before pulling back, shaking his head as if composing himself. He smiles shyly from behind hair that's fallen in front of his eyes.

"Well, then. Why didn't you just say so," I joke, breaking the tension.

He laces his fingers tightly in mine, his smile stretching wide across his face. "Where were we?"

I lean in again, but he stops me and kisses the top of my head. "Before that," he says.

"Um, well . . . " I laugh, looking up at him. "I don't really remember. I think we were at the point of you trying to convince me this crazy idea is true."

A defensive shadow crosses his eyes as he pulls away.

I raise a hand. "I'm not saying it's not. Deep down, I don't *think* you're wrong. I honestly, truly deeply believe I am Ginny Chopain. But what if? What if we aren't really Ginny and Beau? It's farfetched to say the least. It's crazy, really."

"Of course it's crazy. And I know you can't just go on feelings, but if we both feel it, then who's to say it's not? Who's to say I haven't been lucky twice? To get to feel this way about you?"

My chest clenches.

"So what's the other part? You said there's proof?"

"Well, it's kind of complicated. Are you open minded for when things get really crazy?"

I nod slowly. "Crazier than this?"

He smiles. "Crazier than this. There is something else. A way to know for sure. If we're here again. And if we were connected in our last life. Apparently there are things we bring with us, through each life. Things we hold onto. Sort of like a blueprint. It's why we may be more in tune with things in life. Like, the more you've lived, the more certain thinking gets ingrained. Say our compassion for people, our understanding of the world. Sharon says that stuff doesn't develop overnight. It's all in our makeup, sure, but over the course of many lives, we grow. Evolve. And some of it, we hang onto. And yes, there's proof."

I sit up straight. This I like. Proof, concrete evidence. Something to tell me I'm not completely out of my mind.

"Go on."

"Well, someone might argue some of it as circumstantial."

"Like what?"

"Like birthmarks and the like." He runs his fingers along my collarbone, causing goose bumps to flash across my skin. "The other thing Sharon told me about is kind of weird, though. And complicated."

When he looks at the floor, I nudge his toe with mine. "And?"

"Did you ever see a picture that looks like it has a ghost in it?"

If my expression is as blank as my mind, it would explain the way his lips turn up at the corners. "I guess not. Okay, let me see if I can explain this right. Sometimes, there are unexplained photographs. People think they get a picture of a ghost. A shadow of someone, maybe even something that looks like a literal ghost, transparent or whatnot. Most of the time, it's probably just something with the exposure or some processing error, but sometimes, it's something else. This isn't a new idea. People have been claiming to have pictures of ghosts for ages. But Sharon and her family, who have been researching people like us for generations, had another take on it, and one they've more or less proven. Thing is, it doesn't always work perfectly."

"Which is?"

"It's a special image that *sometimes* shows up in photos. If it does, what may appear to some as a blur, or to others as an apparition, could actually be the aura or energy of your last life, particularly if it was vibrant or powerful. Sharon says it seems to work best with strong personalities. And purity. The purer your soul, the more likely it is to show up."

I think of all the photos in my house. All my school pictures, all the random snapshots Mom has covering the walls. There's never been any weird image in any of them. Doubt creeps in.

"I know what you're thinking, that you've never seen anything like that. But, that's just it. The developing process is something special, not just common picture development. If that was the case, there'd be fake auras and sprits in everyone's pictures."

"Are there that many of us?"

"Pretty much everyone comes back, Lange."

I let that sink in.

"What else does she say? This Sharon lady?"

"She was skeptical when I told her about you. She said she's only heard of it once or twice, a couple finding each other a second time around. If it's true, well . . . " He looks away, the tips of his ears turning an adorable shade of pink. "Anyway, I know it sounds weird. It's hard to explain. I could show you, I have these pictures in my car . . . " He looks at the clock and shakes his head. "No time. I can't miss second. Besides, there's bound to be teachers out there. I'll bring them to lunch. Library again?"

I nod slowly, feeling very much like I'm on a speeding, runaway train.

"Can I take you somewhere later? After school?"

"Where?" As if I wouldn't go anywhere with him at this point.

"To meet Sharon. She can explain all of this."

"Sure." I wave my hand as if I do this type of thing every day. "And I can read you some of Ginny's diary. It's mostly all about them. *Us?* Wow, this is weird."

"A diary huh?" He raises his eyebrows.

"Yeah, it's totally freaky, actually. I'll bring it with me this afternoon."

IT'S IMPOSSIBLE TO concentrate, of course.

All morning, I stare into nothing and contemplate the past. Having a past life is something I'd never dreamed of considering. Not that I'm religious or anything, but I've never actually thought about existing before this life.

At lunch, I sit at the same back table in the library. I'm hunched over my sketchpad when the room goes dark. Warm hands cover my eyes. I blink, fluttering my lashes against his palms.

"Guess who?" Vaughn whispers near my ear, the scent of him surrounding me.

I smile, pulling his hands away from my face to look up at him. Even upside down, he's adorable.

He drops into the seat beside me, tossing a big envelope on the table between us.

I raise my eyebrows.

"The pictures I was telling you about."

He chews thoughtfully on his sandwich as I turn the envelope over and slide out a thin stack of pictures. The first one looks like a normal snapshot, featuring a middle-aged man and woman on the overlook of a cliff, blue ocean stretched behind them. They press together, laughing, their hair blown all around them. I'm confused and about to ask when I see it. Just behind her elbow, at nearly the edge of the photo, there is what appears to be a smudge. Like the picture has been doctored somehow. It's see-through almost, and in the shape of an arm.

Interesting.

I place it face down and pick up the next picture.

This time I don't have to look twice. It's beyond creepy. The woman in the photo is probably in her thirties. She's sits in a rocking chair, looking out a window. On the side table is a mug, a book and a lamp. Her hand rests on the book, but from the look on her face, she's thinking about something far away.

But her expression is not what's eerie.

Next to her, with her hand on the back of the woman's chair is a younger woman, maybe twenty. She's bent at the knees, looking over the seated woman's shoulder. And she's transparent, like a real ghost. But the woman in the chair doesn't notice. Her look is one of solitude.

My skin prickles and I look over my shoulder, as if I expect my own recycled spirit to be standing there.

Vaughn watches me with a careful expression.

"Okay," I say. "This is freaky."

"Right? The thing is, as much as it looks like a ghost, it's not. People with strong energies hanging around from the last life can show up this clearly. Intense, right?"

"Very."

I close my eyes and reconsider everything. Maybe I'm getting in over my head.

22

WE STOP AT my house before heading down to the city. It's only an hour drive, but it'll mean I'm gone for dinner. Mom's at another meeting for her photo conference, so I scribble a quick note to let her know I have plans.

Vaughn and I head up to my room for the diary. I tuck all of it into my bag; Ginny's notebook, the envelopes of letters, my drawing and the only photo we have of her.

Vaughn leans against the doorway, looking at my closet. "I can't believe all that was in there. Like it was just waiting to be found."

I pull on a heavy wool sweater. "It's pretty creepy actually."

"What's all this?" He leans forward, examining the pile of junk on my dresser. When he picks up the guitar pick, I groan, wishing I could melt into the floor.

"Keeping souvenirs?" He smirks.

"Oh please. I didn't even know you left that here."

He coughs into his hand, humor lighting his eyes. "Of course," he says. "I'm sure you didn't."

My face burns, but his eyes are back to the dresser, his fingers pulling a scrap paper from underneath. His eyes dart back and forth across it. His jaw, clenched in concentration, slowly slides into a smile.

"Don't make fun of me," I say. But Vaughn's smile is gentle. His expression is soft.

"Pretty good memory," he says, nodding. On the paper, I'd written most of his lyrics. I'd scribbled it the first night he sang to me, but I've been adding to it since, trying to remember them all.

"Thanks," I mumble.

"Seriously," he says. "It's cool that you cared about this . . . "

"How could I not?"

"Come on." He holds out his hand. "I told Sharon we'd be there by four."

But when I slide my hand into his, he doesn't step into the hall. His feet stay planted inside my doorway as he pulls me roughly against him.

"Whoa," I say into his chest.

"Hmmm." His lips linger in my hair, his hands buried in it. Tangling. The distinct scent of boy is all around me, his breath skating across my skin.

I bury my face in his soft cotton shirt, running my hands up to his shoulders and down his back again. I shiver with anticipation.

"Lange." His says my name like a statement.

When I look up, he studies me as if I were a rare, original piece of sheet music by his favorite musician. His eyes follow his fingers as they trace the curve of my face. My lips.

My stomach clenches and unclenches, matching the fast pulse in my veins.

Even though his eyes and hands are moving softly against me and even though my heart is practically thundering out of my chest, it's like time is standing still.

With his arm pressed to the wall above me, he leans in.

He presses against me, kissing me gently at first, then parting my lips with his tongue.

"Hmmm," I moan into his mouth. My reaction seems to urge him on and he deepens the kiss, his body pressed against mine. I kiss him back, really kiss him. I can't get enough.

He pulls back, his eyes searching mine before he moves in again with warm, wet kisses, his hot breath against my lips, my cheek. My whole body tingles as I lose my hands in his hair. It's just as soft as it is wild. Just like I imagined it would be.

Slowly, he strokes my face. My neck. He kisses me there, too, leaving soft, wet nibbles along my skin that make me tremble. And back to my lips again.

He presses his forehead to mine. "My God, Lange. I've waited a long time for that." His soft breath tickles my skin.

"Hmmm." I steal another kiss.

I think of Ginny and Beau in the barn and I know exactly what she meant when she described his kisses. His gentle touch. It doesn't matter what Sharon says, or what any weird pictures show. As I lean in my doorway, Jell-O-kneed and kissing Vaughn, I understand. This is the feeling of love.

Everlasting and true.

Ginny was right. I could do this forever.

THINGS ARE DIFFERENT now. It's like I can't get close enough to him in the car, resting my head against his shoulder, keeping our hands clasped as if suctioned. He listens intently when I reread him the letters from Ginny and Beau's summer apart.

He shakes his head. "Those letters are nuts. Not memories exactly. Yet familiar. Like déjà vu."

It's funny, how this has come full circle. When I read them in my room, I fell in love with Ginny and Beau. I couldn't imagine ever having a love like theirs.

Maybe my life is a dream. Both present and past.

Sure feels like it.

"What's that?" He motions to the envelope, where I've tucked the index card from the attic mirror.

"Not sure. Mom found it on this ancient mirror in the attic and I grabbed it."

He eyes it curiously. "What's it say?"

"It must have been the woman who owned the mirror. It says Edith Sellers. Shady Springs, Pennsylvania."

He makes turns through the city streets in silence, face tight with concentration. Suddenly his eyes widen. They're huge when he turns to me, big brown pools that could rival the most beautiful paintings.

"Sellers," he whispers.

What?

"Sellers," he says again, tapping his fingers on the dashboard. "Sell. Her. Sellers."

Sell. Her. Sweeney.

"Holy crap." I stare at the card quivering in my hand. "Edith Sellers."

"Sell Her."

"Could it be?"

"I guess that'll be our next order of business. After this, of course." He pulls up at a curb on a quiet side street.

It takes me a minute to stop reading the name. *Edith Sellers.* My head spins.

"I wonder who she is," I mutter.

He takes a deep breath. In an overwhelmed voice, like we're at the bottom of a very huge and unclimbable mountain, he says, "One thing at a time."

Buildings loom above us as we walk. We make a few turns down sidewalks swarming with the going-home crowd, passing vendors on every corner. They sell pocketbooks, scarves, bootleg CDs. Sharon's building is a squat, brick structure, three stories high, with wide, tall windows. She buzzes us in and we walk up the three flights of stairs.

At her door, Vaughn knocks softly while we wait, hand in hand.

I'm not sure what I expected, but it's not this. Sharon opens the door to an ultra-modern apartment. She's sleek looking – tall and thin and dressed in an impeccable white pants suit and at least three-inch silver heels. She smiles at us, extending her hand to me.

"You must be Lange." Her grasp is firm, yet friendly. Her auburn hair is cut in a bob. She's not beautiful, but she's pretty in a classic way with wide, light eyes and clear skin. She wears a lot of makeup, but even still, she looks good for her age. I'd guess she's in her sixties at least, but with her style, she appears younger. She leads us into her living room, framed mostly with large windows. They look out over the downtown area, where traffic is starting to clog the streets. We're late for our appointment and it's nearing rush hour now.

As if reading my mind, Sharon motions to the clock on the wall behind her. "I'm so sorry I don't have much time to talk. I have another appointment soon."

"Sorry we're late." Vaughn sits back on the sofa, legs outstretched and crossed. "Took us forever."

"It's fine, let's just make the most of what time we do have. What is it I can do for you today?"

"I've filled Lange in on the basics of what you told me, but I'm sure I didn't get it all right." Vaughn says, his hand resting on my thigh.

"No, you did great," I say. "The thing is, there is just so much I'm confused about. I have a few questions and—"

"We were wondering—" He cuts me off then stops. "Oh, sorry. Go ahead."

"No, it's okay. You go on. I don't even know what I'm asking."

Vaughn frowns. "You wanted to ask about the voice, right?"

"Yeah, but didn't you say you wanted to know about the memory thing?"

He shrugs.

"What he's referring to," I say, "is the voice we heard in the barn. Did he tell you about it?"

She nods. "He did."

"Well," I say, "I guess, what we're wondering is . . . "

"Who was it?" Vaughn finishes.

Sharon pauses. "Well, it could be anyone," she says. "Almost all of us are here again, but sometimes, others don't technically move on right away. Sometimes they stay by choice, other times because they're stuck for some reason and can't yet go through the rebirth process. My opinion? I don't believe spirits actually haunt, I don't think they reach out to the living world. Unless they have a reason."

Reason.

"Do you think it was one of them? Her family?" I say the words slowly.

Sharon's face slides into the most gentle smile. "There's no way to know for sure, but considering where you heard it, and that the message led you to discover Ginny's past, I would guess so. But of course we can't really know—"

My skin turns to ice. The ghosts of Ginny's family. In my mind, the voice reverberates with its chilling tone. And then I remember the giggles from the attic, the strange breezes in my room. How many of the Chopains were left in my house? And if they were, why hadn't they moved on?

Vaughn runs his fingers up and down my back. His calm reassurance presses through me.

"So," I say, forcing a smile. "What's next?"

Her eyes dart between us, a slight smile playing on her lips. "Perhaps I can take your photo while we talk?"

Sharon sits on the edge of the couch holding an old-school 35 mm camera with a big lens.

"Vaughn has yet to let me take his picture, but watching the two of you now, I'd really like to capture you on film. Has he told you about my development techniques?"

I shake my head. "Not in detail. But he showed me some of the photos."

She nods. "Great. Keep talking and please, ask away. Just stand over by that white wall if you two don't mind?"

It's slightly awkward, posing in the fancy living room of this woman I hardly know. Vaughn stands behind me, arms around my middle. I settle into him, warmed as though I'm standing beside a fireplace. We smile into the flash.

"It's very technical, but basically, we've found a way to add an additional step to photo processing that helps us see the image beyond the image. My father was the first to discover the idea of capturing the energy of past lives on film. The Travises, a married couple who believed they had met in a previous life, were the first to have their auras accurately shown through development. Of course, back then, cameras weren't what they are today and neither were development options. I use a classic C-41 process, but I double and sometimes triple expose everything and overlap them in a very precise manner in their development times."

Even though I have no idea what she's talking about, I nod. Vaughn squeezes my hand.

"That's cool, but it sounds confusing," I mumble.

Sharon laughs. "It is, but I've been doing it for ages." She motions for us to step apart. We step away from each other, our fingers barely touching, like beads pulled apart on a string. Sharon snaps away.

I clear my throat. "Vaughn says you have been studying this for a while. Has your family always been into reincarnation?"

She waves to our hands, motioning for us to separate further. As she's positioning her lens and taking more pictures, she answers. "Well yes and no. My father studied it extensively, as I have. In his day, there wasn't the technology we have now, but he still managed to philosophize much of what I use today. Only, we refer to it as rebirth instead of reincarnation."

"What's the difference?"

"Semantics basically." She motions us back to the couch, not breaking stride as she packs the camera away. "Reincarnation is a very specific belief system we don't take lightly. But what we do here . . . it's a bit experimental, I guess you could say."

I let her words sink in and am about to ask another question when Vaughn speaks up. "We're wondering about memories. We're kind of confused. When we read Ginny's letters, they're familiar to both of us. I have no doubt about our history. Does that make sense, that we'd feel that connection, even without real memories?"

"That's actually really normal," Sharon says, filling three glasses with water. "Most people never make a connection to their past life. It's only people who are open to it and have a feeling they want to explore, that may make the reconnection, or question that there is one. Those are the types of people that end up finding their way to me." She smiles and hands us each a glass.

"But when we read those letters and think about Ginny and Beau, why do we feel like it's all so familiar?"

"I think you're confusing memories with what you're reading and learning. Your case is different. If you have discovered who you were, reading about your past life will naturally evoke an emotional response in you, especially since you are reading the actual writings of the girl you believe you were in your previous life. Now, from what I understand, Ginny's life ended quite violently?"

Sipping my water, I nod.

"Let me ask you, have you had, in the past, any particular fears or phobias that may relate?"

"I don't follow."

"Well often, psychologists try to get to the bottom of people's phobias. In reality, sometimes they're nothing more than what we bring from our last life. For example – someone who may have an intensely deep fear of guns may have died at the hand of one in his or her past life. I once knew a woman who could not watch the news. She would cry and nearly go catatonic worrying about missing children. I do believe that was how her last life ended. I even once knew a man who was so deathly afraid of water that being near the ocean, a lake, or any open water, even from a distance, would give him panic attacks. Even water towers and aquariums bothered him to the point that he avoided them at all costs. He could have died by drowning."

Wow. Interesting. I suppose it would explain my general freak outs and squeamishness about all things bloody.

"So our memories aren't really memories?" Vaughn asks.

She shakes her head and offers us the distant smile of someone who's had this same conversation a million times. "Highly unlikely. Memories rarely resurface on their own since we are, in fact, different people. But I will tell you that your particular case is very unusual for a few reasons."

"Oh?"

"First, the fact that you are in the same place in this life as your last life is extremely rare. I can't figure out how you've returned to the same exact location. It is more than a little intriguing. Also, the fact that you two found one another again. It's not uncommon for us to find the same souls from life to life, but what is rare is for us to be in the same roles. If the two of you have in fact been a couple in more than one life, together with being in the same location . . . Well, together, they are concerning."

"Concerning?" My voice is tight, barely squeaking out of my dry throat.

She smiles at her glass. "I want to believe it's because your love is strong enough to find itself again. I haven't seen it. My father though, he did believe that could happen. But he was much more of a romantic than I am and as much as I'd like to say that is the only reason, I am cautious. I have seen people reconnect for other reasons too."

"Such as?"

"In my experience, evil can be very powerful."

"Evil?"

"Well it's not all grim reapers and lurking shadows, but yes. The world is very torn with good versus evil, but I suppose that's nothing new, is it?"

We shake our heads weakly.

She looks down at her neatly folded hands and seems to consider her next words. "There are people out there. People like me, but who use their knowledge and experience in the worst ways."

"What do you mean?"

"There's a Society," she says, "They know everything. I really can't get into it. I shouldn't. But please be careful. And if anything strange happens, let me know right away."

The doorbell buzzes and we all look at it like a bomb has gone off. I straighten on the couch, opening my mouth to ask another question, or tell her about the strange stuff that's already happened.

"I'm sorry." She smiles serenely and stands. "My next appointment awaits. You can come back anytime, okay?"

When she pulls me into a tight hug, I'm shaking. The smell of hairspray and a clean, almost antiseptic perfume fills the air between us.

"Watch out," she whispers. "All around you. One thing I've learned is you never know. There are no certainties. In this life or the last. You never know when they're watching." After she hugs Vaughn, she bends to pat the camera case on the table. "I'll be in touch as soon as I get these pictures developed."

On the way downstairs, we don't say much. I'm not sure what Vaughn feels, but I feel off balance, like I've just stepped out of a whirlwind, my thoughts stuttering, not fully connecting in my brain.

"Why do I feel like it's us against the world?" I whisper.

Biting his lower lip, he takes my hand in his and squeezes. "Maybe because it always has been. But I don't see why it has to be."

He holds the door open, the cold night wind biting at us, pulling my hair across my face. I'm thankful I changed into the sweater. A middle aged woman enters the building and I wonder if she's the one who buzzed Sharon's bell.

"You know," I say. "Maybe we should just stop looking back. I know we want to solve this stuff about Ginny and find those stupid words, but all Sharon's evil talk kind of freaked me out. What did that last thing mean? A Society? They know everything and could be watching? I don't even know what she meant, and I'm not sure I want to."

"Yeah," he says. "As much as I want to find those words and as much as I feel like something is pushing us to, I don't care about the past. And that means yesterday, last week or last life." He knocks his shoulder into mine. "If you want to stop, I'm all for it."

"Really?" I hook my arm through his as we cross the street.

"Really," he says. He squints up to the next block where a line of restaurants gleams with glittering lights. "You hungry?"

He bends to kiss me, but stops short, looking over my shoulder. "What the hell?"

I step around him to see what he's looking at. It's dark, but I can make out the shiny slickness on the pavement. The dark stains that I instantly know are red.

I scream.

Because right there, right in front of the passenger side door of Vaughn's car, are five incredibly small, incredibly dead, baby rabbits.

23

MY LUNGS HOLD each breath for ransom. Vaughn sits at my side on the narrow stoop of a boarded up restaurant. He's trying like hell to keep it together, but he's gone white as a January sky, too. He looks up ahead, where the dead rabbits lie, and back to me again. He's waiting for me to speak, but my throat is swollen with fear. Even with my eyes closed, I still see them, their five little bodies. Furry. Bloody.

This is what Ginny saw. What she experienced. Five dead rabbits.

And five days later, she was dead.

Vaughn paces in front of me, questions all over his face. He waits, watching me like I'll crack at any second. And for all I know, he's right.

"Ginny," I whisper. "It's all in the diary. The same thing happened to her."

He squats down in front of me. "I'm not following. I really, really need you to tell me what you know. Now."

My breath hitches again, even though I avoid following his gaze to the scene down the street. I look across the road, where a mother kneels in front of a convenience store, zipping her son's jacket. Behind her, neon signs scream: LOTTERY! CIGARETTES! MILK!

"Tell me this. Can you stay here for like, a minute?" His voice is soft and pulls me back to reality, but everything inside me stops.

"Where are you going?" Why would he leave?

"It's fine. *You're* fine." His face crumples, eyes darting. "Come on, Lange. Just hold it together. One minute. I'm gonna get the car and get you out of here. Away from here. You'll be fine. Trust me. Okay?"

I nod.

"Hey." He lifts my face, forcing me to look in his eyes. "I'm here, okay? I'm here."

And then he's gone.

The mother across the street ties the child's shoes. He kicks every time she almost has them tied and even in the dark I can sense her frustration in the way her head shakes when she talks to him. After two more attempts, she smacks his butt. I look away when he starts to cry.

Then Vaughn's at the curb, and I'm in the front seat, eyes trained on the floor until we're blocks past the bunny carcasses.

"Lange?" Tentative.

"Okay." Deep breath. "I'm sorry. That was just, so, I don't know, unexpected. And disgusting. And sad. And everything else today . . . " I shake my head. "Did anyone know we were coming down here?"

"Uh—no one. Who do you think I would tell about this?" It's then I notice how tightly he's gripping the steering wheel. And how fast he's driving.

"Okay, okay. We both need to chill. Let's go somewhere. Anywhere," I say, pointing to a sign. "Take this exit."

Eventually we hit a fast food drive through and pull into a spot in the back, under the brightest streetlamp, by my insistence.

I pick at my French fries and stare out the window. "Okay, here's the story. In Ginny's diary, she wrote about the same thing happening. She found five dead rabbits under her window. Thing is, the entry was dated five days before her murder."

The air in the car is heavy with my words.

"So you think someone is giving us another message? About Ginny and Beau?"

"Not sure," I say. "It doesn't make sense. She's been dead eighty something years, right? Why would someone care? And more, how would someone know about us coming down here tonight?"

"Unless we were followed." He looks in his rearview. "So what happened next?"

"Next?"

"After the rabbits? What came next in the diary?"

"Next was the violin entry. That's as far as I got."

He motions to my bag. "Well, let's hear it."

But I don't move, can barely think about what happened next in the diary. Because something Vaughn said sparked an idea.

"Beau!" I say. "We don't know what happened to him. We were so caught up in Ginny's death, we never considered him. They had this achingly perfect romance, right? And then she was murdered. So what happened to him? Where is Beau? No one ever said."

"Good point."

"Okay," I say. "First things first, we'll hit the old yearbooks tomorrow and find out his last name. After that, we can look up what happened to him. How did we not think of this yet?" I slap my forehead.

"Maybe because we didn't even know about you and Ginny as of yesterday."

I nod, shoving a few more fries in my mouth and take a big gulp of soda.

"Okay." I reach for the diary, a wave of dread swelling as I open to the last entry I read the night before. "Here goes."

24

I READ TO him on the way home.

August 26

Things are getting stranger than I could have imagined. After the rabbits yesterday, when I made a big screaming mess of myself, Mother told me to stop being dramatic. Can you imagine! I didn't dare tell her about this morning. A few minutes ago, I was out back. I wanted to stand in the spot where the rabbits were. It's weird, I know, but I felt like it was a tribute to them. Well, I didn't expect that in that spot, on the side of the house, just beneath my window, four x's had been drawn, right at my height. They weren't huge, each about the size of my hand. But they were drawn in blood. It was bright red and still wet too. Why I put my finger in it, I'll never know, I just thought it would be dry or paint or, well, I'm not sure what. But it was slippery. It was recent. And then the darn rain came and they were gone. I think today I will tell my love. He'll know what to do. He always does. He'll figure out exactly what kind of person would do this. And why! I'll write later. Have to get to school now.

I hold the diary against my lap with trembling hands. "Blood on the side of her house! How is she so calm about it, writing in her diary? I would freak!"

Vaughn taps the steering wheel and stares at the road ahead. But I can tell his thoughts are somewhere else.

"Go on," he says. "Keep reading."

August 26

Telling him was the best thing I've ever done. Unlike Mother, he didn't tell me to stop being dramatic. He did, however, think we should lay low a bit. With everything else we've been dreaming about. Let's slow down, he said, what's the rush? And he's right. He had a gleam in his eye though, when I cried against him. He soothed me all the right ways, hugs and kisses and promises in my ear. But there was anger in his eyes. Whoever is behind this, I know he'll find out.

I guess I shouldn't worry. I can't help it though. And I shouldn't even say it, shouldn't think it, as he told me today. What if this has something to do with that other stuff? We've been reading about that killer and he's been playing detective, trying to figure things out. But from all the way out here in Shady Springs, who would ever know? Now I fear Mother's right and I am being paranoid. I need to focus elsewhere and ignore the sick prankster.

"Killer? What killer?" Vaughn flips on his signal and switches lanes.

"Don't you remember? She mentioned something, in one of the letters. Some murderer. Damn, I can't remember." I reach for the letters, but Vaughn waves his hand.

"Just read the next entry. What happened to her next?"

I turn the page, the old paper crinkling in my hands.

August 27

Three horse tails. In the yard this morning. No blood, no sign of violence, but still. Three long tails.

I ran to the barn first, flying in and out of the stables. But all our gals and guys were there, looking fine and intact. Thank God.

So what does that mean? Five rabbits, four blood x's and now three tails. Who is playing this prank and is it a countdown? Sure feels like it. But to what?

I close my eyes and let the book fall closed.

Vaughn's hand slides over mine as we come to a stop at a red light. He gnaws on his bottom lip.

"Keep going," he says. "We have to know what comes next."

August 27

Okay. Now, I feel like I'm losing my mind and I'm torn – so torn! When you have a fella like I do, intent on becoming a big shot detective someday, you expect maybe he'd help in a situation like this. But when I told him about the horse tails, he became so quiet. He calmed me down, but he refused to let me call the police. At first I thought he was just being stubborn, but it's something else completely. And I'm scared. The look on his face. And oh, the things he said! I'm not sure what he's gotten mixed up in or who's doing this, but he knows something he's not saying and he pleaded with me tonight. He begged and pleaded and said absolutely no authorities. No police. No Mother. He asked me to trust him and I do. I trust he'll do what he can, but who is this terrible person we're dealing with?

I'm breathless with Ginny's fear, laid out on these pages this way. And my own, running rampant through me like a fever.

"What did you know, Beau? What didn't you tell her?" I murmur as I turn the page.

The next page isn't dated. It's just a few lines, written in handwriting I can barely read, scribbled as though she was shaking when she wrote them.

I DIDN'T THINK it would come to this. I'm finding it so hard to keep my promise of not calling the police. Maybe I'm foolish, and the way he spoke to me tonight, yelling at me for getting upset, acting erratic and crazed when I mentioned the police. Something is going on and he won't tell me, but maybe I don't want to know, especially if it is about those darn Sweeney murders! I just want it behind us. Whatever it is.

"Sweeney murders!" Vaughn swerves. "Sweeney murders?"

Sell. Her. Sweeney.

Sweeny murders.

There it is. The second half of the words that have been haunting us.

First, Edith Sellers. And now this. The Sweeney murders.

I try and untangle the facts. "What does it mean? What does one have to do with the other? And why the hell was Beau acting like that? What did he know? What was he mixed up in?"

Vaughn can only shake his head.

When I turn the page, a blank sheet stares up at me, its emptiness like a slap. I flip quickly, but I already know. The rest of the book is empty.

I'm hollow inside, as empty as these pages.

"That was the last entry," I say. "The last words Ginny ever wrote before she and her family were murdered."

25

I'M GOING TO be way late for school.

I take too long getting dressed, then run around my house and yard looking for red, bloody X's. Once I've checked every single inch on the outside of the house, I hit the first floor hard, searching inside cabinet doors, above fireplaces and along the plank floors. I search the second and third floors thoroughly, opening every bedroom and bathroom door and even looking under the rugs. I've already searched my room, but I do it again, just in case. Desperate really, for some clue I may have missed.

The first bell rings as I walk through the front doors, rushing to English. I'm so happy there were no bloody letters in or on my house, I don't even mind being late.

I slide into my seat and hang my coat on the back of my chair. Still no Mrs. Mantoney, which is really no surprise.

I know I'm being kind of ridiculous. No one says we're going to follow Ginny's path. Or Beau's—whatever it was. And as for the Sweeney murders, well . . . I try not to let it twist too much in my mind. Not until we get the facts. Plus, there's still Edith to find. But we'll do it all today. We'll finally make the connections we've been searching for.

Sell. Her. Sweeney.

I sigh, wondering why every time we decide to walk away from Ginny and Beau's past, something falls into our lap, dragging us back into it. But that's beside the point. There was no blood this morning. No creepiness at my house. We are *not* following the events of a dead girl's diary. Even if that dead girl happens to be me.

"Did you hear?" Ben leans over my desk and I jump, blinking until I'm back in reality.

"Huh?"

"A Hunt clue has been leaked!" His grin is stretched so wide he resembles the joker from the Batman movies. He wiggles his eyebrows and laughs.

"Did you drink too many Frappuccinos or something?"

He ignores my comment, rattling on like Kelly does when she's on a roll. "Apparently they're kicking the night off at the community center downtown, which is when Purgatory will play. First time ever they're doing it this way. It's going to be some type of scavenger hunt."

I yawn. I could use a Frappuccino myself.

"You're coming right?"

"I guess so," I mumble just as Mrs. Mantoney finally comes into the room. When Ben turns away, I let out a breath. Saved by the teacher.

Who has time to think about The Hunt murder when there's a real mystery to figure out?

WHEN THE BELL rings, Kelly's waiting outside our classroom.

"Hey!" She bumps my shoulder with hers. "What's up?"

"Hey yourself." I try to act natural, but it's not easy. After the way we left things last time, everything about us feels awkward now, even the way the three of us push together through the mass of people in the between-classes rush. I'm tempted to ask if she's only my friend when Stace isn't around, but her genuine smile tells me she's sorry.

"So, how's the costumer stuff going?" I pull loose scraps from my notebook's spiral, scanning the hall for Vaughn.

"Pretty good. They're running auditions this week. Once the cast is set I'll really be able to go nuts."

"But of course she's done amazing stuff already," Ben says.

"As if he knows." Kelly giggles. "Anyway, I could show them to you sometime, if you want to meet me during a free period?"

"Sure," I say. Like I have time for this. "I can come during my Motions class tomorrow. I have that extra creative period."

We stop, finally in front of my locker.

"Lange?"

I wait, fingers on my combination lock.

"I think it'll blow over," she says quietly. "Just give her some more time."

Keeping my eyes trained on the floor, I nod. With a last squeeze of my arm, she's gone, pulling Ben behind her.

"Later, Lange!" He calls over his shoulder.

For a second, I almost feel like things are normal. Or a millisecond. Or however long it takes me to open my locker, where I find an envelope taped inside the door, with big scrolling letters, just like Vaughn described on the one in his mailbox.

I don't breathe or think or turn away.

I just stare, the top shelf of my locker tilting in my vision. Wobbling.

Written in those big red letters is one word: Lange.

And inside the envelope, four terrifying photographs.

26

THE ENVELOPE IS heavy, ivory with a textured linen finish, the writing way fancier than any I've ever seen. Tucked inside are four pictures that terrify me, filling me with bottled up screams and a deep sense of horrible things closing in. Yet all morning, I can't stop looking at them.

At lunch, I drop the package with a thud on top of the books Vaughn has spread across the corner library table.

He looks up. "Well hello to you too."

I gesture to it. "Is it the same writing?"

His expression answers for him, mouth pulled tight.

"Open it." My voice trembles.

Disbelief and fear mingle on his face as he flips through the pictures.

"Found them in my locker." I drop into my chair. My stomach, which has been churning all day, really kicks up now.

"How recent is this?" He asks.

I look over my shoulder before leaning closer. "She was wearing that same nightgown this morning. And that smudge on her chin, see it," I point. "It's from her attic excavation last night. I'm almost positive that was there this morning, too. I'm pretty sure these were taken last night."

His eyes dart around the library as if we're being watched.

I put the pictures away, but there's no way to erase the images from my mind. The first photo is of my back door, swinging open in the dark, the kitchen lit only by moonlight, shapes and shadows lurking. The second a picture of the north stairs, leading up to the third floor. It was taken from the second floor landing, the cracked window in the bottom corner of the photo, a shadow stretched along the stairs. The third is a big, bulky hand, wearing a dark leather glove.

And the fourth picture.

That's the one that fills my lungs with liquid steel. It's Mom, asleep in her bed. It's a close up, too. Really close, the gloved hand from photo number three outstretched as if to choke her. On the back, words are printed in the same scrolling script:

I watch. I listen. The slightest move, I'll see.

It's a blatant threat.

Under the table, Vaughn's hand is a dead weight on my thigh. He breathes through his nose, absently drumming the corner of his notebook.

"We obviously can't tell anyone," I say. "At this point, calling the cops would be scarier than not calling them. Whoever wrote this made that clear."

"Obviously. We need another plan." His hands slide over my cold ones like mittens. "I don't want you there. Sleeping there, where someone can get to you."

A chill washes through me, his words reverberating through this life and my last.

"Your mom either. Think how messed up this is. She doesn't even know what's going on, and it's right under her—"

"I can't tell her! Who knows what they'll do."

"I'm not saying you should. I'm just saying. Shit, Lange. I don't know. I wish I could stay with you. Or you could stay with me." He shakes his head, balling his fists in frustration.

"I have an idea. It's not much, but…" I yank a cuticle from my thumb, barely noticing the pain. "We have an alarm system. It's not activated, but it *is* installed. I was thinking of calling the company and seeing how we can set it up. Fast, like today."

"What about your mom?"

"I don't know. I'll make something up that I heard at school about break-ins and tell her how scared I am."

He looks skeptical.

"What? It could work. It *will* work. And it won't be an act. I *am* terrified." Hot tears brim in my eyes.

"It's a start," he says. "But we have to work harder and faster to find out who's messing with us. The sooner we catch them, the sooner this ends." His voice is firm and I want to believe him. I *so* want to believe him. But when Ginny believed Beau, where did it get her?

Whatever. Obsessing isn't going to help us. I pull the pack of stapled sheets from my bag.

"Anyway, here's all the Edith Sellers I found. There are forty-one in the U.S. and thirty-two internationally. And that's if she didn't get married and change her name. Or die."

He shakes a chunky lock of hair from his eyes and gives the pages one of his *can't climb that mountain* looks.

I flip through them. "I'm going to start calling them today. Shady Springs is small enough. If we find an Edith that's heard of it, she's our girl. If not, we'll keep going. I can't make international calls though, so let's hope she's one of these." I skate my finger down the first page.

"Good plan. We'll look for her here too." He waves to the pile of books.

I realize for the first time just how many books and papers he's piled on the table. I pick up the leather-bound volume in front of me, etched with gold letters: PRESTON ACADEMY. "Yearbooks?"

"Yep. From 1930-1934. We find Beau, we can find what happened to him and hopefully, we'll finally get some better answers. I've Googled every combination of Beau and Shady Springs and Beau and Pennsylvania. Hardly any Beaus from the entire state, and none even remotely connected to Shady Springs. But it was a long time ago. There may not be an online record of it. But we'll find him." He pats the yearbooks.

"And Hank Griffin?"

He nods to his laptop, a look of disgust on his face. "We'll see if we can get more on him too."

I nod, looking toward the librarian's desk. "Did she ask why you wanted the yearbooks? I don't want anyone knowing what we're researching. You never know." With shaking hands, I thumb through the yearbook.

"She doesn't know anything." He pries it from me and kisses the palm of my hand.

"They were in my house," I whisper. "In my mother's room!"

He rubs his hand in circles on my back, calming like he's putting me to sleep. But when I twist away from him, I see the creases of worry on his forehead before he can hide them.

"All the more reason for us to focus now," he says. "We have a lot to do and only two periods to do it. Let's get started."

We pore over the yearbooks, finding each of the appropriate Chopain portraits. Ginny is in each of the four books, Robert in the later three and Helen as a freshman in Ginny's senior year. I let my fingers linger on their faces.

It's surreal and weird and draining all at once.

We keep looking. Every class of every year. No Edith Sellers, which I expect. Anyone owning a mirror like that would likely not be a high school student. But, even more importantly, we don't find Beau. Apparently Preston used to be a regular school and they had sports and clubs and all the things normal non-art schools have. Even after the class pictures come up empty, we study every sport and activity. Every single club. But he isn't there.

Utterly defeated, we sit back in our chairs. I don't think either of us expected a dead end on this one.

"What now?" I rub my eyes.

"Well, now that I'm thinking about it . . . Did any of the letters say they went to the same school?"

I rack my brain. "I'm not sure. But, no, now that you mention it, I don't think so."

"Or, did she ever say his age? Maybe we should get some older yearbooks? Maybe he graduated before her?"

I shake my head. "No, I don't think so. The plans for September they were always talking about. I'm pretty sure they had both just graduated that year."

Vaughn stares blankly at the bookcase in front of us, a muscle twitching in his clenched jaw. His eyes widen and he snaps his fingers. "Mrs. McDermott!"

"Huh?"

"Mrs. McDermott. She knew them right? She was Ginny's best friend. She'll know where we can find info on Beau, or at least his last name. Who knows, maybe he went to a different school. In any case, she's our only link to their past. We'll go see her again."

That connection, both of my lives meeting in one central place? It freaks me out. But he's right, she probably does have at least *some* answers.

He lowers his voice. "What if it has to do with what Ginny wrote? He was investigating those murders and acting strange about it." He mouths the word *Sweeney*.

I swallow.

His eyes plead with me. "Today, okay? After school?"

"Fine," I mumble. "Now let's just focus on this."

We change gears, searching in a different direction. Beau may have come up as a dead end, but there's plenty of info about Hank.

Hank Griffin. Up until now, we'd only known his name. It had been in all the newspaper accounts of course, but that was all we'd known. The friend of the family who murdered them all.

But a quick Google search on Hank tells us a lot more. It pulls up all kinds of old articles about the murders. Many of them rehash what we already know, though searching by Hank's name pulls up some new ones. One such article is a profile of him.

"Hmm," Vaughn says, pointing to the screen. I lean in closer to read along, starting with the paragraph where he points.

The killer, who committed suicide immediately after the heinous crime of six murders, was not a total surprise. Although he was well known to the community and quite close to the oldest of the murdered children, he was known to have a "dark side." Sources close to him say he had grown obsessive in the weeks before the murder and talked often of "dark things."

"Quite close with the oldest children? Wait a minute. He was friends with them?" Something dawns on me as I reopen the 1934 yearbook. I flip through the pages quickly, my eyes darting across the names: Gable, Gentry, Gharrity, Gilbert. Griffin! "There, there he is."

Hank Griffin.

He smiles in his senior picture, looking at the camera with a lazy grin. His hair is cropped short, with a casual side part. He's got a baby face, smooth and clean-shaven. His eyes are wide set and appear amused. I wonder what's behind them.

The eyes of a killer.

Digging deep in my memory, I try and recall his face, anything about him. It's pointless, I don't know how to recover past life memories. But I can't help trying. Unless it's my imagination, something stirs in me, something familiar.

"Stop." Vaughn nudges me. "I know what you're thinking. But why would you want to remember anything about this guy?" He studies the yearbook for only a second before slamming it closed.

He's right, but it's like a car accident you can't look away from. You know you shouldn't crane your neck to see the details, but you do. You look. And you're always sorry. That's how I feel about Hank. I need to know who he was, what caused him to kill the Chopains.

Vaughn closes the laptop. "God, reading this stuff makes me sick. Knowing who he was. Who took Ginny from Beau."

Nausea swirls and sputters in my stomach.

When he turns to me, eyes shining, a look of determination hardens his features. "There's only one thing left," he says, pointing to a stack of papers. I consider them warily, as if they might bite me.

Vaughn rips open a package of Twinkies and gives me an ironic smile. "The Sweeney Murders."

Great. More murder, more blood. More horror. Just what we need.

But it'll be worth it in the end if we can put Ginny's past behind her and live the future she never had.

27

AFTER SCHOOL, WE drive in silence to Mrs. McDermott's house. My mind whirls, gory details crowding there like monsters under a bed.

The Sweeney murders, perpetrated by Jackson Sweeney of Florida and his wife, Katherine, went on for several years. The number of deaths attributed to them, both solved and unsolved, isn't fully known. There were two families just outside of Dallas, where the Sweeneys originally lived, along with a couple in Florida, three in Georgia and a single woman in Maryland. These murders, investigated over the course of 1925-1934, were eventually tied to the Sweeneys. When police attempted to capture them, Jackson and Katherine committed suicide in their Texas home before the authorities reached them.

It's beyond sick, and I have no idea how it fits in with Ginny and Beau. But even weirder, something about the details feels sickly familiar. I know they shouldn't. I know Sharon says we have no memories, but I can't shake it, even if it's impossible.

"So Beau was reading about these murders?" Vaughn taps absently on the steering wheel.

"I think so. She said he wanted to be a detective, remember? But what could he have possibly known that the cops didn't? These people were wanted by everyone."

He shakes his head. "And even more, what did it have to do with Ginny? And how does Hank play into it? Or does he? Maybe the two are unrelated?"

"Anything's possible, I guess. Do you think the Sweeneys could've killed the Chopains? Their near-capture suicide was just a month after the Chopains were killed."

He frowns, looking into his rearview to change lanes. "I don't know, but I'm sure the cops looked into it. Wouldn't every murder have been considered as one of theirs back then? Besides, the murders don't line up. The Sweeneys shot their victims in the head, execution style. They were clean and calculated with fast getaways. The Chopains." He pauses. "Well, you know…"

"Stop." I push the bloody images from my mind and focus on the world rushing by outside.

"Sorry. I don't mean to sound cold about it."

"Moot point anyway. Hank was the Chopain killer. The whole murder-suicide thing seems to be the only definite fact in this whole mess." I close my eyes, instantly conjuring Hank's yearbook picture and have to fight the urge to vomit.

Counting my breaths, I consider what's next, but I guess that all depends on what Mrs. McDermott tells us. During Creative Hour, I called at least half the domestic Edith Sellers with no luck. If I have the same luck with the second half, we'll be back to square one with the first part of the séance message. *Sell. Her.*

It's one brick wall after another. A frustrated scream inches up my throat.

When we turn onto Mrs. McDermott's street, my stomach flops. I wipe my sweaty palms on the seat as we drive up her driveway.

But then I'm confused.

Because Mrs. McDermott's house?

It's gone.

28

WE STAND AT the edge of the pit of ash.

All around us, remnants of the house's frame—beams and wood pieces, broken glass, half buried cabinets and ribbons of melted carpet—float like islands in the charred remains.

"What the hell?" Vaughn's voice is uneven.

I squat for a better look. Twisted metal that was probably once a picture frame lies next to a blackened heap of a bed pillow. Broken curtain rods stick out from a fuzzy mound of a stuffed animal, its plastic eyes cracked, most of its fur burned away.

When I look up, Vaughn's face has taken on the now-familiar look of determination.

"Come on," he says, reaching down. "We have to find out what happened."

"How're we gonna do that?"

Gripping my hand tightly, he looks down the road. "Neighbors," he says. "No one knows more than neighbors."

Confused, I walk to the car. The only neighbors Mrs. McDermott had are a car ride away.

"PLACE BURNT CLEAR on down to the ground!" The old man spits over his porch railing into bright red bushes. He stretches, and then rubs his stomach in a way that makes me think he hasn't stood up for quite a while before we knocked on his door.

"How did it start?" Vaughn watches the old man intently.

"They ain't tell us nothing. I runned down there just as soon as I seen the flames. I could see it clear down here and we's at least a mile away. Now, I seen some blazers in my life, but that little house shot up something awful. It was just like when we used to light up our leaves in fall time with gasoline. But bigger!"

Gasoline.

"And? Has anyone given any other details at all?" Vaughn's voice is strained, his fingers twisting in his sleeve. I place a hand on his arm. This isn't easy for me either, but what good are either of us if we lose it?

"No ideas. My son-in-law, he's a workin' down there for the sheriff's department. He told me it was surely arson, but I don't know if I believe him. He's a bragger that way. Kinda a know it all, you know?" He spits again. "You know I knowed that woman a long time. We both lived here since the seventies."

My stomach drops. Even though I didn't want to see her today, I don't want her to be gone. Especially not if it has to do with us. Because right now, and with the word arson floating around, I can't think of any other reason for that fire. I feel as guilty as if I'd struck the match myself.

His watery eyes dart back and forth between us. "The firemans got her out, real fast, I hear, like theys trained to do. But the smoke was too much. She was an old lady, you know. She didn't make it." He wipes his nose with a yellowed handkerchief.

It's like I've been punched in the chest, all the air sucked right out of the atmosphere. When I waver, Vaughn catches me with a quick arm around my waist.

"How you know her?" The man looks at me curiously. "You ain't relations are you?"

"No." Vaughn thrusts his arm out to shake hands. "We're just friends of hers. Trying to find out what happened. Thanks for your time."

"Yeah, thanks." I manage, choking on the details as if I'm inhaling smoke myself.

"I'll be seeing ya then." The man nods.

Once we're in the car, I let out a screech. "It's because of us!"

"We don't know that. Calm down."

"No, it is. You know it is! How can this be coincidence? It's like someone *knew* we'd go to her next. She was going to tell us what happened to Beau. She was going to help us reach the next step in this. She would have! And now she's gone."

"We don't know that." He bites his lip. "Not for sure. Come on, she was old. She could have left the stove on or forgot to blow out a candle. It could have been anything." The flat tone of his voice tells me he doesn't fully believe himself.

"Go back!" It comes to me suddenly.

He slams the brakes, looking at the old man's house and then back to me like I've lost my mind. Maybe I have, but something nags at me.

"To Mrs. McDermott's," I say. "We didn't look around enough. We were in shock. I want to see if we can find anything. It won't take long."

"Okay. But I don't know what you think—"

"Please, just go."

When we get there, I throw my door open and run toward the destruction. With a thick branch, I dig around in the ash. Canning jars, with TOMATOES hand written across the lids, lie in a half-shattered pile. It's awful, clawing through pieces of walls and table legs, and half-knit afghans, as if it hadn't been someone's home. Someone's life.

"What are you looking for?" Vaughn asks.

But I just wave him off. I can't explain what I'm looking for. I'm just looking. My fingers itch, wishing for my sketchpad and pencils, to draw the house the way it had been. To make some sense of it.

Vaughn answers his ringing phone in an annoyed voice, but when I look up, he's completely still, listening with his head bowed.

My stick butts up against something heavy. I push against it, accidentally shoving it further into the rubble. It takes me a minute to pry a wooden beam off the top of it, all while Vaughn listens silently to whoever's on the phone.

Finally, I edge it toward me.

No.

It can't be.

It's an ornate candlestick, covered in dust and ash. But beneath all that is a silver finish. It looks like pewter. I lift it, shaking off the debris.

The design scrolls, wrapping thick leaves around the base and growing dainty as it reaches the top. I hold my breath as I turn it over.

And there it is, on the bottom. The edges are so singed, I can barely make it out. But it's there, on the faded, charred felt. The letter V.

The candlesticks from my attic. From the séance. Here, at Ginny's best friend's house, decades after Ginny's murder. How did it get here?

Did it start the fire?

I fall to my knees in the grass, the silence around me the perfect backdrop to the noisy accusations in my head.

"What's up?" Beside me, Vaughn's out of breath.

I wave the candlestick feebly toward him, staring at it like it's a figment of my imagination. Vaughn's pale, the color of milky tea, his eyes full of questions. But there's urgency in them too.

"Bring it with us," he says. "We have to go."

"We can't take it, it could be evidence. And where're we going now?"

"That was Sharon. She developed our pictures and needs to see us right away."

29

"WHAT DOES THAT even mean?"

"I have no idea!" His eyes dart around the site. "We gotta go now, though. She sounded urgent."

"I can't. I promised my mom I'd be home on time tonight. And I don't want her home alone. Especially before the alarm is set up." I shake my head, trying not to look at the candlestick, which I've dropped on top of the ash. "Can't Sharon tell us over the phone? Call her back."

"No, she said she has to show us whatever it is." He rakes a hand through his hair, his eyes avoiding mine. We look out at the purple and orange streaks of sunset until he finally stands with a sigh. "Fine. Tomorrow, then."

"Come on," I say, hooking my fingers in the front pocket of his hoodie. "You're coming home with me for dinner."

"NICE OF YOU to join us." Mom smiles at Vaughn as she rinses lettuce.

"Thanks for inviting me," he says, a nervous smile plastered to his face. "Where can I wash my hands?"

"Right down there." I point down the hall. "Second door."

"Cool, thanks." With one last flash of a shy grin, he's gone.

Mom looks at me from the corner of her eye. "So I get to officially get to know the mystery boy, huh? The reason you've been MIA lately?"

I stack plates on the table and busy myself folding napkins. "Mystery boy?"

"Don't deny it Lange." She frowns. "There's quite a powerful energy around him, around the two of you together."

My hands shake as I fill the glasses with ice, but I keep my voice even. "He's just a boy, Mom."

"Sure." Mom places the salad bowl on the table. "But I do know a thing or two about love, you know." She bows her head toward mine and whispers. "There's something very strong happening here. It's subtle, but powerful. Your auras are practically bursting with it. Almost like it was simply meant to be."

Meant to be.

I need to change the subject before I blurt out the truth.

"Anyway," I say. "There *is* something I wanted to talk to you about."

"ADT alarms, perhaps?" She clucks her tongue.

Gulp.

"People have been talking at school about break-ins around town. It made me paranoid."

She gives me a skeptical look. "You didn't think you could talk to me *before* calling them?"

"Sure, I could. But, I don't know. People were talking and I got nervous. I knew we had the thing." I motion to the keypad by the back door. "I just figured I'd call and find out how to get it hooked up. Sorry. I really was trying to help."

"Are you going to pay for it? These little costs add up."

"Well, no. But the lady said it's like a dollar a day," I say. "I didn't think our safety had a price."

She rolls her eyes. "That's a little melodramatic, don't you think?"

Melodramatic? She doesn't know the half of it. "Fine, I'm sorry. I should have waited to talk to you. I got spooked. Anyway, is it hooked up? I need the code."

"Not yet. The guy's coming out tomorrow. He has to update the wiring," she says. "Don't worry. We'll be under lock and key tomorrow night." She snorts a laugh and I want to scream. She has no idea how close we are to real danger.

"What's up?" Vaughn slides into his seat.

"Nothing much." Mom pats his hand. "Just trying to reign in Lange's melodrama a bit this evening. Good luck to you, Vaughn." She laughs. He grins along, playing the part of friendly guy meeting Mom and being cordial. But I see the questions in his eyes, and the concern that keeps his smile tight. He may be fooling Mom, but he isn't fooling me.

AFTER DINNER, VAUGHN insists on doing the dishes. The way Mom's mouth drops open is almost comical. I'm not sure she's ever seen a member of the male species wash a dish. My father certainly never did.

I shoo her out of the kitchen. "We got this, Mom, why don't you go hang out and relax or whatever?"

She looks back and forth between us with her arms crossed. "You two." She points to us, one at a time. "No getting into trouble just because there's no adults around. Got it?"

She doesn't need to elaborate. From the heat on my face and the deep crimson on Vaughn's, her point was not missed.

He flashes her one of his winning grins. "Of course not. And thanks again for dinner."

She narrows her eyes, but she's smirking. "I've got my eye on you. Are you a Libra, by chance?"

"Mom!"

"I'm just asking," she says. "I was just thinking from the way he—"

"Okay, enough, Mom. Go relax! We got this!" I make an exaggerated show of pushing her out the door with a forced laugh.

As soon as she's gone, I sigh, wishing I could apologize for how embarrassing she can be. Vaughn wraps his arm around me and pulls me to him, but when I turn my face to his, he doesn't kiss me. His eyes flash with mischief and before I can move, he douses me with water from the sink.

I shriek, pulling away from him, grabbing a placemat from the table for defense. On the counter, I find a rolling pin to use against him.

"Ow!" He grabs his arm where I hit him and tries to block me. I let him take my weapon, bumping his hip with mine.

"You won her over, you know. I can tell she likes you. You had her smiling *and* laughing. Definitely not like my mom at all."

"Well that's good. Because I'm not going anywhere for a while."

"Oh really?"

"Yes," he whispers in my ear. "Starting with tonight. I heard what she said. And as long as that alarm is not turned on, there is no way I'm leaving you here alone."

30

WE LIE ON top of the covers, staring at my ceiling. Mom's on the third floor, walking back and forth above us. We listen to the creak of the attic stairs as she climbs up and down and up again.

"What exactly is she doing up there?" Vaughn absently strums his guitar, which leans against the bed.

"I already told you, it's hard to explain. She's a photographer." I nuzzle further into the nook of his arm. Underneath the faded scent of ash and burnt things, he smells like grass and the Japanese cherry blossom soap my mom keeps stocked in the kitchen. "Then again," I say. "Not much about her makes sense."

"Aw, she doesn't seem that bad." His voice is soft and deep, vibrating against my cheek.

"She's pretty out there, but mostly harmless, I guess. Just embarrassing sometimes." I roll into him, forcing his strumming hand to leave the guitar and circle my torso. His hand is warm against my ribs and I'm acutely aware of how close we are, with just my thin shirt between his hand and my skin. "Anyway," I say, ignoring the screaming way my heart thuds. "What about you? Your family? I know nothing about them. You know all about how I come from all over. What about you?"

"Not exactly sure. I'm adopted, born in upstate New York somewhere. My parents got me as an infant. They're cool. They believe in being upfront, and told me I was adopted as soon as I could understand what that meant. Plus, they're very laid back."

"Obviously. Hence you being here at," I look at the clock, "Eleven o'clock at night."

"I already told you, I'm not leaving." He kisses my forehead for the millionth time tonight.

"Not sure we're pulling that one off." I motion upstairs.

"Figure out a way. After those pictures in your locker, and the thought of someone breaking in here, I can guarantee you I am not leaving you here alone. Besides, your mom likes me, right?"

"Maybe, but she won't like you if she finds you here in the morning."

"Details, details."

"What about your parents? I know they're cool and all, but can you just not come home? Won't they care?"

"Nah, they care. But I can call and tell them something came up. They trust me." He shrugs.

I listen to the floor creak above me. Mom's room is on the third floor. That means someone broke in, crept up not one, but two flights of stairs and into her room to take that photo. The gloved hand that reached out toward her. The shots of the back door and dark staircase.

I try not to, but I picture what they could have done if they wanted. With me sound asleep downstairs.

It makes me wonder if they walked down my hallway too.

I look around my room. Had they been in here? While I was right here, asleep in my bed?

He's right. There's no way I can sleep here alone.

"Fine," I say. "You can stay. But you have to at least move your car out of the driveway."

"No problem." He jumps up, reaching for his keys.

"Whoa—a little over excited, aren't you?"

"Just glad you came to your senses is all. As if you had a choice." He grins before leaning down for a lingering kiss. Stopping at my door, he nods upstairs. "Should I make a show of leaving?"

"May as well. I'll walk you out to *say goodbye.*"

I TRIPLE CHECK all the deadbolts and promise myself I'll check on Mom in the morning.

Sneaking Vaughn back into my room isn't hard. Mom's upstairs when I turn off my bedroom light. I lock the door just in case, but I think we're safe from her finding out. She hardly ever comes down here and I'm banking on her sleeping in as usual tomorrow so we can escape before school, unnoticed.

He sits on the edge of my bed. I watch his silhouette, staring out the window, toward the barn.

Of course.

"You know," I say. "I hate that everything from that night in the barn has taken over and become our life."

"Come on. It's not everything," he says quietly.

I watch his profile, the shadow of his lips when he breathes.

"Well it feels that way," I say. "Lately, it's like that's all there is. Figuring out this crap with Ginny and Beau, and Sellers and the Sweeney murders, and . . . "

"Shhh." His shadow turns toward me. "There's a lot more to us than that. And you know it."

"I guess."

"You guess?" I hear the smile in his voice. "What, you're gonna make me spell out how crazy I am about you?"

"If you really want to." I grin, pulling out a pair of pajamas— boxer shorts and a tank top. "Okay, I'm going to change. Don't look over here."

He laughs. "It's dark, genius."

I change quickly and climb under my covers. "What about you?

"What about me?"

"Um, well, I don't exactly have any guy clothes for you to wear. I've got sweats, but considering you're like a foot taller than me, not sure they'd work. Unless you like that skintight-sweatpants-capris look?"

He snorts, flopping down on the bed. "Nah. I'm good. I'll sleep like this."

"That's crazy. You're wearing jeans. Come on, get comfortable, I don't mind." I nudge him, being playful. But inside, I'm racing.

"You trying to get my pants off, Languini?"

Thank God he can't see my face right now. It's on fire, I swear. "Whatever. Last time I try to be nice. It's not so easy to get a pants-off invite in my bed, you know."

Did I seriously just say that?

"You sure you don't mind?" His voice pitches with surprise and I smile. He's as nervous as I am.

Turning onto my side, away from him, I pretend to yawn. "I think I can handle it. There's this little thing called self-control. I'm pretty good at it."

"Is that so?" He shifts on the bed while I study the darkness, pretending not to analyze every movement. Him pulling off his pants. And then his sweatshirt. I imagine him sliding into bed with me but then I stop imagining it because he's here, under my covers. He pulls me against him, the warmth of his legs tangling with mine, his arms hooked around my stomach. Our bodies bend and press in all the same places, lined up like two halves of the same whole.

And then he's humming to me, singing softly. Our song. Buzzing against my earlobe. Teeth nibbling there, moving down to nip my neck. My shoulder.

Uncontrollable shivers.

And then we're kissing.

And then I'm thinking we aren't going to get much sleep to-night.

31

TO BE ON the safe side, we wake early. After seeing Mom snoring away safely in her bed, I sneak down the street with Vaughn while the sun's still spilling its first rays into the early morning sky. Between us, there's more of a closeness now. His arm around me feels more protective than it did yesterday, his hand on my hip more secure. I've never felt more like he was mine than I do right now, walking along like we've been sewn together. I squeeze his hand, the weight of our lives heavy on me. The weight of everything hanging in the air.

I try to enjoy it, the way his thumb gently moves against mine, the way he smiles at nothing and steals glances at me at the exact same time I look at him.

But there's only one thought in my head. What's going to happen next?

The remaining Edith Sellers were duds. Half of them seemed to have barely heard of Pennsylvania, let alone Shady Springs. Today I plan to look up old death records in town. Depending how old that mirror is, she's probably long gone. But still, there could be a trail there. Some information to help us.

I drop my stuff into his backseat on top of a sea of books and magazines. "Ew. Do you live in your car?"

Laughing, he lets his bag fall on top of the mess, carefully laying his guitar behind the front seats.

"What can I say, I'm not the most organized person in the world. Speaking of that. I think I have an extra sweatshirt somewhere in here." He leans into the backseat, digging under a blanket, and I steal a glance at his butt, his perfectly-fit jeans hugging it just enough to highlight its perfection.

When he turns around, I grin and nod to his shirt. "Yeah, going to school in yesterday's clothes will put you even more in the skank department than you already are."

"Excuse me?" He crosses his arms and looks down at me with those dark, soulful eyes. A smile twitches on his lips.

"Just sayin' . . . "

"I think showing up with you will do quite enough to put me in that category, thankyouverymuch."

"Ouch." I clutch a hand to my heart. "That hurts."

Grinning, he picks me up in a bear hug and spins me around, his lips tickling my neck. We make too much noise, but the houses stay dark. When he puts me down, I'm dizzy from so many things.

"Okay. I'm starving," I say, pulling my arms into my sleeves as I head for my side of the car. "I'm also freezing."

"All right, we'll stop for bagels. Let me just check the trunk for a shirt."

I slide into the front seat and open my visor while I dig in my purse for lip gloss. In the mirror, I see Vaughn, backing away from the trunk with a weird look on his face.

Like he's terrified.

I lean out my open door. "Vaughn? What's up?"

"Uh. I think you need to come back here."

My stomach fills with cement and I'm shaking before I even get out of the car. He's pale as ice, staring at the trunk like it's alive. The only part of him moving is his hair in the breeze.

Slowly, I follow his gaze.

Oh shit.

"Horse tails," I mutter. Three days, three horse tails. But here, there's only one, hanging from the back of the closed trunk.

"That's definitely not a horse tail." He steps toward the blond ponytail and squats down. *That* is human hair."

Our breath dissipates in the cold and I look around, sure someone is watching our discovery. The sun is almost up now, the sky a deep, inky blue. Across the street, lights are on in the upstairs windows of a small, clapboard house.

"Should we open it? You don't think—" I can't even bring myself to say the words. I can barely imagine it – that the ponytail is still attached to a person.

His eyes widen. "No. Can't be. But still. I should open this up, just to be sure what we're dealing with." With a deep breath, he hooks his fingers under the trunk's lid.

I look over my shoulder again, afraid of what this looks like.

Afraid of what we'll find.

The latch releases, the trunk popping up to hover above a mostly-empty trunk. The ponytail falls to the street.

"As if there was going to be someone in there." I shake my head. "I need to get my imagination under control."

But Vaughn doesn't answer. He uses a plastic grocery bag to pick up the ponytail, tying the handles in a knot and throwing the whole thing in the trunk.

"Come on," he says. "Let's go. This day is off to a shitty start. We gotta get our game plan together and figure out who the hell would cut off their hair for us."

32

DESPITE THE ANTICIPATION of going to Sharon's after school and the relentless pit in my stomach from the ponytail, the morning flies by, lunch coming faster than I expect. I pace in front of the cafeteria, waiting for Vaughn and feeling accomplished from the list of names and phone numbers in my pocket.

I managed to track down one Edith Sellers McRand, originally from Shady Springs, died 1962 at the age of 83. The online obituary listed surviving relatives, including two grandsons who still live in town, who are thankfully listed in the white pages. But I haven't called them yet.

I'm not even sure why I agreed to meet Vaughn here. He insisted we eat where we want to, and to hell with hiding from Stace, but this hardly seems the day to start taking a stand.

I hear Kelly's loud, contagious laugh before I see her. When she turns into the hall, I smile, trying to act natural.

"Hey!" She calls, waving.

The nervous bubbles settle a little. But then, as she gets closer, my mouth drops open.

"Oh my God! Where's your hair?"

She runs a hand against the blunt edge. "You like it?"

"It's nice, but what made you do that? You had the longest hair ever."

She shrugs. "Time for a change. Besides, Stace was cutting hers for Locks of Love and talked me into it."

"Really? Wow." My chest constricts, barely letting me breathe.

Chill out, Lange. It's a coincidence. No one would be that obvious. Not even pissed-off Stace.

"Didn't you see the announcements the past few weeks? The music department sponsored it. Yesterday after school there were some hairdressers here. Stace and some of the other music students ran it."

I look around and see what I didn't before. She's right. All around us, girls who yesterday had hair halfway down their backs, are sporting bobs and super short styles. They swarm like bees at a hive, taunting and dangerous.

It could have been any of them.

"So, what's up with you?" She smiles.

"Um, nothing really." Oh you know. Sort of fell in love with Vaughn. Oh and by the way, we were in love in our last life too. We've been chasing down my murderer while trying to find the person who's messing with us in this life.

I can barely keep up with my spinning mind. Where the hell is Vaughn? Three senior girls with fresh haircuts walk out of the cafeteria laughing.

It could have been anyone's hair. It could have been any of them.

Round and round the thoughts go. A carousel at a haunted circus.

"I'm sorry," I say. "I gotta run."

She looks at me sideways. "Are you sure you're all right?"

Deep breath. "I'm fine."

"Okay. I'll see you later then. You're meeting me during your free period, right? Down in the Costumes room?"

I am? Oh that's right, I totally made plans with her. "Sure," I croak, forcing another fake smile. "Definitely."

She looks at me like I've sprouted another head. "You really all right?"

176

"I'm fine. Seriously. I'll see you later. This afternoon."

Moving quickly, I walk with my head down. I can't get out of here fast enough. I'm nearly knocked off my feet when I slam right into someone. With a mumbled apology, I look up.

Stace grins down at me, her shoulders thrust back. Kelly was right, Stace chopped her hair off too, even shorter than Kelly's. It sticks out in spikes all over her head. My mind flashes to the ponytail in Vaughn's trunk. It could be the same color blond...

But it could be anyone. I have to get out of here.

When I try to step around her, she puts a hand on my shoulder.

"Looking for Vaughn? I just saw him in the stairwell." She smirks. "He's ready for you now. Since you like my leftovers."

"Whatever. Nice hair." My hands clench into fists.

"It was for a good cause!" She calls after me in that same sarcastic voice.

I finally find him near the main office, strolling along. I'm so wound up I could crack, yet here he is, loping along like he's got nowhere to be.

"I was waiting for you!"

"Whoa—what's wrong?" His eyes search mine.

"I just ran into Stace."

"What now?"

"Have you seen her today?"

"No. Why?"

"Come on." I pull him toward the stairs. "We are *not* going to the cafeteria."

We skip out on spending lunch hour in school, eating sandwiches in his car instead.

"It's too obvious," he says. "Who cuts off their hair and then uses the ponytail as a threat against someone? That's like wearing a neon sign of guilt."

I wipe my napkin across my lips. "Fine, it could have been anyone's. There were a ton of people with short hair today. But still. Stace was one of the ones running the event."

"So what? She stole someone's hair because she's jealous of us?"

"Sounds as reasonable as anything else. She *did* outright threaten me, remember?"

"I agree she's jealous. And I agree she's pissed off. But you can't force a solution just because you *want* it to fit."

"So what then?" I suppress an annoyed sigh.

"Just forget her for now. Let's get through this afternoon and get to Sharon's. Then, we need to call those Sellers guys. What are you gonna say to them?"

I stare at a pair of hummingbirds on a wire. "I'm not sure. I may just tell them the truth. Well, not the *truth* truth, but that I found the mirror in my attic, with Edith's name on it. Maybe it'll spark a conversation or some kind of clue."

Uncertainty crosses his face.

"What other option is there? Telling them I heard a voice during a séance that whispered their dead grandmother's name?"

He rubs his eyes. "I guess you're right."

"Whatever. We'll decide later. Right now, I have to meet Kelly."

BACK AT SCHOOL, I head down to the theater rooms with a head full of questions, but I try to erase the anxiety from my face and voice. All I have to do is fake a conversation with Kelly, get through one more period of school, and then Vaughn and I will be off to Sharon's, where I have no idea what to expect.

No one answers my knock on the Costumes door. Despite getting way distracted with Vaughn, I've still managed to get here a bit early. Screw it. I don't want to stand in the hallway alone. I'll wait inside.

It's as messy as I expect it to be, costumes and material flung all over the place. There's a sewing machine set up in the corner along with nearly life-size sketches of what she envisions for the costumes. I squat, looking through them. They're really good. I wonder how many other student designers are working on these with her.

I close the sketchpad and reach for the one beneath it, bumping into something when I slide down the wall to sit. From the corner of my eye, I see something colorful. A patchwork backpack.

Stace's bag.

I pause for only a second. Why would her bag be here of all places? But I don't have time to think about it. Working quickly, I pull the drawstring open, glancing every two seconds over my shoulder, even though the door is closed.

The bag is pretty packed. Books, notebooks, what appears to be reams of sheet music. I dig faster, listening intently for sounds in the hall.

I pull out an iPod case, a pair of sunglasses. At the bottom of the bag is a large mailer envelope. I work the metal clasp quickly, dumping the contents in my lap. Blank envelopes.

My chest tightens as I look through them, looking for a small, ivory envelope, one with a linen finish. There are so many, I can't be sure. Sizes, colors, finishes.

The knob turns.

Shit. I shove the envelopes to the bottom of the bag and toss the iPod on top.

I'm still cramming papers when the door opens. I turn, shoving it all behind my back, working fast to stuff the rest inside without looking, pulling the string and rearranging it behind me. In the doorway, Kelly's talking to someone in the hall. By the time she turns around, I'm all smiles and hopefully looking more normal than I feel.

I need to find Vaughn.

"Hey." I jump up and nod to the sketches. "I was just looking at your designs. Hope you don't mind."

"No, not at all," she says, moving toward the sewing machine.

"They're awesome. Do you have any done yet?" I stretch, blocking the view of Stace's bag. Like any guilty person, I'm convinced she'll see right through me if she notices the evidence.

One more class. That's all I have to get through. One more class.

33

VAUGHN GOES HEAVY on the gas.

I'm thrown back in my seat most of the way like I'm on a roller coaster. Even with our windows open, the air doesn't cool me.

"Slow down! Sharon's info is no use to us if we don't make it there alive."

When his eyes cut to me, I realize how inappropriate my word choice was.

"Sorry. Anyway. What about Stace?"

"I know, I know." His jaw clenches.

"Circumstantial or not, it all points to her."

"I already told you, I'll call her tonight. I'm not sure if she's even talking to me at this point, but I'll try." He frowns, igniting a fire in me.

"What's with the face? And why do you keep defending her?"

"I'm not. It's just that I've known her forever. She may be screwed up or jealous, but I'd like to think I could spot a psycho a little better than that."

Air rushes in from my open window and I take deep breaths of it until I calm down. As he veers off the exit, I decide to change the subject.

"What do you think Sharon's going to tell us?"

"We'll know soon enough," he says with a sad smile, making turns through the city streets. I watch people walking cluelessly, wishing I was anyone but me. Normal people don't have these kinds of problems. Normal people don't know about their past lives. They aren't being threatened by jilted ex-girlfriends or who knows who. Normal people aren't weighing common sense against a serious threat.

"I was thinking," I say, choosing my words carefully. "Regardless of the threat, I think we have to call the cops."

Confusion clouds his eyes. And fear.

My words come out in a rush. "I know, I know. The threat was clear and we don't know who we're dealing with or what they'll do if we tell. But, this is serious. And it's lining up so close to the threats Ginny got. And, well, neither of us wants a repeat of that." I rub my hands together, staring at my nail beds as if they have the answers.

He chews on his thumbnail for a while then finally turns to me. "Okay," he says. "You're right. Maybe it's time. Things are getting too dangerous."

As scary as the image of my mom in that photo and the warning scrawled on the back of it is, scarier still is what could happen if we don't get some real protection. It feels like a huge weight has been lifted.

I squeeze his hand. "Later then? We'll call tonight?"

Nodding, he pulls into a parking spot just down the block from Sharon's. We lean forward to look up at her building. Soft lights blaze in her place on the top floor. After a moment in silence, we get out of the car and close our doors quietly.

"Here we go," he mutters.

SHARON PEEKS INTO the hallway, looking quickly both ways. "Quick," she says. "Come in."

When we step inside, the apartment is warm, glowing with the light of a million candles. It smells like apples and cinnamon. It's a much warmer environment than I remember from last time. She's wearing a sweater dress today, with seamed stockings and heels. It amazes me that she dresses like this in her apartment. She's as flawless as last time, but there's something reckless about her today, less in control. After kissing us each on the cheek, she ushers us into the living room.

We settle onto the plush white couch, with Sharon across from us on the loveseat. On her lap is a large envelope which I assume contains the pictures. She places a palm on it, her face stretched with an excited grin.

"As I told Vaughn on the phone, I have never seen anything like this. I ran the developments three times to make sure I had it right. And each time, I got the same result." She closes her eyes and takes a deep breath. "If only my father was here to see this."

I lick my lips. Beside me, Vaughn holds his breath. Our hands are in a death grip while she unwinds the envelope's string for what seems the slowest, most painful stretch of time.

She pulls a stack of eight by ten photos from the envelope and rests them on her lap face down. "I read through Dad's notes all night, over and over. I found the pictures that supported his theory of reborn love, but . . . " She shakes her head, her eyes glistening. "I don't think even an old romantic like him could have dreamed up something like you two."

My heart jumps, expanding against the walls of my chest. I glance sideways at Vaughn, his lips drawn tight beneath a thin sheen of sweat.

She turns the first photo over and lays it on the table. She goes through them, one by one, setting them side by side for us to see.

"I believe I told you about Dad's theory after seeing the Travis photos with the couple's auras holding hands as a sign of reunited souls. Well, as you can see, that's quite simply, nothing. Comparatively speaking."

Sitting on the edge of the couch, Vaughn and I lean over the table. At first, I'm not sure where to focus. The photos she took of us are all messy, as if they've been double, triple or quadruple exposed. It's like someone has scribbled all over us. But then, shapes start to come into focus. Blurs at first, something that I might dismiss as nothing, but . . .

I pick up one of the pictures. It's one of the poses where Vaughn and I stood a few feet apart against the wall. Except we're holding hands. But not. I hold it close to my face.

"My God." I gasp.

Behind us are shadows that appear to be holding hands. There are at least three of them between us, all clasping fingers. On either side, other pairs of auras flit around us. Two sets press together on the left, and yet another pair hovers near the right edge of the print.

"I see them," I whisper, running my fingertips over the picture's surface.

Vaughn rests his chin on my shoulder, his eyes darting among the couples in the photo. "Wait, so you're saying these things in the picture are . . . "

It can't be.

"Is that Ginny? And Beau?"

But Sharon grins and points one of her perfectly manicured nails our way. "It's you all right. And whoever you were before. Ginny and Beau, and whoever else. Those, my dears, each and every one of them, are you. In your past lives. Apparently, the two of you have found each other many, many times before."

Thank God Vaughn's holding onto me, because Sharon swims like I'm looking through a fish-eye lens. The photo slips from my hand.

"I can't even begin to explain it," she says. "I'm not a romantic, but you may have changed my mind."

The crook of Vaughn's arm has never felt safer. I bury myself in him and wonder in how many lifetimes we've done this very thing.

"But I want to be upfront with you," she says, shifting in her seat.

"What?" It comes out sharper than I mean because I'm racing inside, everything knocking together as I try to convince myself that look on her face cannot mean something as bad as it seems.

Vaughn tightens his arm on my shoulder.

"Well," she says, frowning. "There's no proof of anything, of course. And my father, well, he had ideas that I honestly have always thought were a bit overboard. But, after you guys proved him right on at least one issue, I feel I really should tell you how my dad always said that love could come back and find each other again."

We nod. Obviously, we know that. When I open my mouth, she holds up a hand.

"But as I told you last time, he believed evil was just as strong as love. He believed it could come back again and again and while love can deepen over time, so can evil become stronger. He believed the two were closely attracted to each other, magnetic, if you will. Like opposite poles, say. In his opinion, the strongest love would attract the worst kind of evil."

We're silent.

Why does the good have to have the bad? Hadn't we suffered enough in our last life?

I look at the couples in the photo and wonder what we endured in each life.

"I'm only mentioning it because of how obviously resilient your love is." She gestures to the pictures. "I've been thinking about it a lot. And I know you said Ginny encountered a violent death in her last life. What happened to Beau, do you know?"

"We're still trying to find out. We've hit some dead ends." Vaughn sighs.

"But we're having other trouble now, too."

Her eyebrows arch high on her forehead. "Oh?"

I look at Vaughn and he motions for me to go on.

"Someone has been threatening us." My voice shakes as I explain the last few days with the rabbits and the notes, and the photos.

Sharon's face is tight with worry while she listens. When I'm done, she nods, scooting to the edge of her seat. "Okay. I didn't want to get into all this with you earlier, but it looks like you're both in a bit of trouble as it is."

What now? My stomach clenches.

"You have to promise you won't tell a soul. I promised my father I'd never reveal the secrets he left with me when he died. These are very dangerous people."

Her pause seems to go on forever.

"There's a group. Completely underground."

"The Society you mentioned last time?" My voice shakes.

She nods. "They call themselves Obitus. They know who we are. All of us. Who each and every person is and was in every life. They keep tabs, so to speak, on all the souls in the world."

What?

Finally Vaughn clears his throat. "Care to explain *how* this secret society does this?"

Secret Society. The words trip in my brain. My life has somehow become a series of unbelievable twists, like I'm living in a video game.

"Here's the thing. With the birth or death of any person, the soul emits what Obitus refers to as an echo. From what I understand, it's an imprint that is specific to our souls. This echo, or imprint, travels with the soul throughout its lifetimes even though it comes back in different people."

Even though my mouth hangs open, I can't speak.

"Like soul DNA?" Vaughn says in an incredulous tone.

"Exactly." She points at him. "Very good. Now, once the echo is released, Obitus captures the data in the atmosphere. They use a Vitagraph, an ancient device they invented centuries ago, which is set at the level the echo travels."

"Huh?" Vaughn scratches his head.

"Yeah. What he said."

She sighs. "Sorry. I know, it's complicated. Think of it like sonar, sending and capturing signals we can't hear. Only it's looking for soul echoes, not regular sound waves."

Vaughn nods slowly. "Okay. Then what?"

"Once the device captures a soul echo's information, which is pretty much always, considering how often people are born and die, it's cataloged in the Obitus system where it's cross refer- enced with matching echoes already in the system. Thus, they know who shares the echo over lifetimes."

I rub my temples and stare at the thick white carpet.

"From what I've heard, the ancient records are just names and soul echo information, just old-fashioned paper lists with minimal information. But as computerized data started gaining momentum, Obitus employed means of accessing all kinds of information like actual birth and death records, fingerprints and true DNA. You'd be surprised how infiltrated they are in our society."

"How big is the organization?" He asks, chewing his lip again.

"I'm not sure. They're a relatively large group, but what's more important, even, is that they have many *regular* people on staff. Mostly in jobs that could help their objectives. Like places where records are kept. Municipal jobs, town records type stuff, police departments, even detective agencies. Many are also staffed in laboratories and hospitals since scientific research is a top priority to them. Many of these people don't even know exactly who they're providing information to, and certainly not what it's being used for."

"So what you're saying is, if someone wanted to find someone based on who they were in their last life . . . "

She nods. "Obitus could definitely do it. Like that." She snaps her fingers.

Well.

"But, they wouldn't just do it for anyone. First of all, not many people know they even exist. So if someone is trying to find you based on who you were then, they'd have to have an in with someone pretty high up in Obitus who'd be willing to track you down."

I pace, finally stopping at the window. I exhale, my breath fogging the glass and then dissipating slowly.

"And how do you know so much about them, again?" Vaughn asks behind me.

Sharon's voice is sad when she answers. "My father," she says. "He worked for them for years. The organization is incredibly smart. They know what they're doing, and they keep a low profile. They've been around since at least the early 1800s, and that's only the records my father saw. For all we know, they have information even older than that. When he started researching his photo development ideas, they shunned him and eventually got rid of him. They thought he was too soft, wasting too much of their scientist resources on emotional research. But he never believed that was the real reason he was let go."

Sharon shakes her head sadly. "He saw a lot of corruption in Obitus in the few years he was there. It was slowly being infiltrated. He heard word of the most horrible souls reunited, evil people brought together again and again. He was snooping into this, trying to find out if the criminal souls of murderers and rapists and worse were being tracked more than others. That was when they began to cut off his access to the archived records.

He had no proof and neither do I. But as you've proven, coincidences very often spell out the truth."

"But why would they do that? Empower the evil souls more than the others?" I ask.

"Power. The same thing most of the world's problems come down to. The leaders of Obitus realized the power they had, tracking people over their lifetimes. They could find an evil, tortured soul who'd spent lifetimes honing his wicked tendencies and paired up with another misfit, they were practically bursting with the need to create chaos and evil. Obitus capitalized on that, started using them for their own means." She looks down. "Not only were they tracking and reuniting the worst souls, they were trying to influence where souls would actually end up. Instead of a soul choosing its own path, Obitus wanted to be able to force it a certain way, either for their own use or even for revenge. My father thought it was impossible, but they seemed to be inching their research toward that very thing."

"How?" I ask.

She gives us a worried glance. "I'm not sure exactly, but I do know that they were working on it when he left. Experimenting like crazy. From what I understand, as long as the person who dies is not a child, they were able to sometimes partially influence which direction the soul would go after death, or even if they could force the soul into a state of unrest. An in-between place, so to speak."

"But why not children?"

"I don't know the exact details, but I do know the soul of a child – anyone under sixteen, typically— is too close to the other side to be influenced. Until you've reached a certain age, your soul is still somewhat moored to your previous live, evolving-wise. The souls of children are nearly untouchable because of this and their purity. But once that soul has aged a little more and evolved more fully into its new life, it's much more likely to be influenced, and therefore a more attractive conquest for Obitus. They can do the most damage to a slightly older soul. Children are almost useless to them. Like I said, I don't know completely how they do it or what the Vitagraph told them. But my father was very scared about that research. He even thought Obitus was working on ways to groom souls during their life for this very purpose when they died. I just hope they haven't made much more progress with it. My biggest fear is not only that they can keep track of the evil souls in the world, but cause good ones to go that way as well."

The ticking clock is the only sound in the space until Vaughn finally speaks. "Is there any way for us to find out if someone has contacted these people about us?"

Sharon shifts on the couch. "There's no way."

She's lying. Vaughn slides me a look.

"Please Sharon." He leans across the table. "We're in real danger. We decided we'd call the cops for protection but even if we do, they obviously won't be able to track down the person if it's something like this."

She snaps her head toward us, her eyes wide. "No. Do *not* call the police. If someone is working with Obitus, it's possible they've got someone in your police station working with them. They're very thorough."

The bottom of my stomach drops out. "So what then? What are we supposed to do?" Panic races through me. It's like I'm on the very edge of a rooftop. One more setback and I'm afraid I'll go over the edge.

"Sharon." His voice is filled with authority, but underneath it, he's begging. "Help us. Please."

She stares at the window with her jaw set. When she looks back at us, her eyes shine.

"Anything you can do will help," I say in a meek voice. "If we can't call the police and we can't figure out who's doing this on our own, I don't want to think about what could happen. Look what happened to Ginny."

Vaughn's hand tightens around mine. *"That's* not going to happen."

She looks from Vaughn to me and back to him again. "Fine. I'll help. Because I like you. And because I know it's what my father would have done."

The first wings of hope start to beat in my chest. "What's our first step?"

She puts her hand up. "Slow down. The idea that this is your answer is still a huge long shot. I have a few friends with connections in Obitus. I'll try and call in a favor. It might take some time, though."

"Time is the one thing we don't have," Vaughn says, running a hand down his face, the other pulling me tightly against him.

34

DESPITE SOME CRAZY-ASS dreams, I sleep the sleep of the dead. Or at least the sleep of the heavily drugged. I'm sure it has something to do with the bright green glow of the alarm system lights which, as promised, had been activated by the time Vaughn brought me home from Sharon's. With the ponytail day behind us, and learning all about our history and the elusive Obitus, I was exhausted. Sleep came on fast and strong.

I wake feeling more rested than I have in a long time.

"Honey?" Mom knocks on my door, opening it a second later and leaning in. "I'm leaving in an hour. Want to come down for breakfast first?"

"Leaving?"

Sure enough, she's wearing black pants, a green sweater and black leather clogs. In other words, super dressed up for Mom.

"Photographers convention? Out in New York, remember?" She taps her nails on my door. "Just overnight. I know I told you about it." She examines me closely. "Are you okay? If you don't want me to go, I can stay—"

"No, it's fine. I'm sure you told me." I can't keep anything straight these days. Yawning loudly, I ask, "What's for breakfast?"

"I'm making omelets," she says. "See you downstairs in a few."

While brushing my teeth, I nearly burst into tears at the thought of Mom leaving. Which is ridiculous. I'll be fine. And at least Mom will be safe.

I need to call Vaughn ASAP. Until we hear from Sharon or I finally get in touch with either of the Sellers guys, I need to keep busy. Otherwise, I may just go crazy.

AFTER BREAKFAST, MOM heads out without a single lecture. After her comments about me and Vaughn the other night, I'd expected at least a warning about him not staying over, or God forbid, something about safe sex.

But she's out the door, toting enough camera equipment to require a few trips. I hum along to the kitchen radio while I clean up the breakfast dishes. Each time she makes a trip to her car, the melodic beep of the alarm system chimes to signal the door is being opened and closed and opened again.

Ding Ding. It's like a heartbeat, comforting and constant.

I wave to her as she pulls out of the driveway. She's always loved this stuff. Back when we lived in Jersey, she used to go to these things on a monthly basis.

And anyway, I'll be fine here. I'll just call Vaughn and he'll come over. With the dishes done, I head upstairs to shower.

I spend extra time washing my hair, relaxing beneath the spray. I even apply the Critical Repair conditioner sample Kelly gave me last week.

In my mind I can still see the photos at Sharon's. This apparently supersonic love that travels through the ages. Last night, I couldn't think of anything but who we were last time, and the time before, and probably the time before that. Walking down Market Street after we left Sharon's place, I wondered if we'd ever done that exact thing before, on that street or any other.

But what I realize now, is as amazing as all that is, it's just an extra bow on an already perfect gift. It's in this life I've fallen for him. Just the thought makes me break into a huge smile, my face in the hot spray while I scrub my shoulders and arms. He's made me believe in things I never thought possible, like happy endings and knowing the depth of a person's soul.

Soul.

Soul echo. Obitus.

Why does there have to be a downside?

My skin stings, streaked red from the hot water . I open the door to let out the steam while I towel off and finger brush my hair.

Ding Ding.

It doesn't register at first. But then I hear it again.

Ding Ding.

It's the alarm sensor. One of the doors has been opened.

Ding Ding.

And closed.

Breathe, Lange. Focus.

Slowly, I close the bathroom door until there's only enough space for me to peek into the hall.

Ding Ding.

I look around the bathroom. There's nothing even close to a weapon in here.

Lifting my foot cautiously, I gently step into the hallway. The wood creaks like a loud, out of tune instrument and I wince, turning my ear toward the kitchen stairs. I hear nothing. I look both ways, and eye the staircases on either end of the hall. The north stairs lead to the kitchen and the back door, the south stairs to the front of the house, where there are two exits within two rooms of the stairs. I wrap the towel around me tightly and press myself to the wall, skulking down the hall like an intruder in my own house.

Upstairs, something creaks. I stop and look at the ceiling, my heart slamming against my chest.

Calm down. It's probably the house settling. You hear that crap all the time.

I slink again down the hall, squatting when I reach the stairs. If anyone's in the house, going down the stairs will most definitely alert them. There's no way to be quiet on these things.

The hiss and bang of the radiator on the landing makes me jump so suddenly, I almost drop my towel. It takes me a minute to catch my breath, while I listen to the drip drop drip from my hair on the wood floor.

I take the first step and stop at the sound of a rustle, almost like an animal downstairs. Did I leave the window open? No. Any fans on? No. There should *not* be a breeze down there.

I creep as quietly as possible, which isn't quietly at all. There's a bang and then the soft pitter patter of feet. Running feet. Outside.

Pressing my towel to me, I stand on my toes to look out the window, but see nothing. No one running. No one anywhere. Just the trees swaying, dropping leaves like rain.

I slowly walk the rest of the way down the stairs. The back door is open halfway, caught in an air current which sucks it closed and then open again.

With a big exhale, I tsk. "You're an idiot," I mutter to myself. It wasn't closed right. Just the wind causing it to latch and un-latch again. I shake my head and click the lock into place.

The sun warms my face when I push the curtain to the side. But then I notice the small package on the top step.

My heart plummets as I squint, trying to make out exactly what it is.

I open the door to get a better look. Outside, it's funeral-home quiet. It's not a package at all, I see. It's something round and looks like straw.

195

A nest?

Despite being wrapped only in a towel, I take two steps across my porch, eyes darting across the yard. I squat near the object, reaching out to touch the side of it, rubbing the rough branches with my fingertips.

It *is* a nest. How weird. Inside are two tiny eggs. I know nothing about birds, but imagine this is the last place a nest should be. I look up at the trees and back down again. Maybe I should move it to the yard. I touch the side of it, with more force this time. The eggs move, but not in the way eggs normally move. They don't roll or slide.

They jiggle.

I step back, clutching my towel tighter around me. The cool air nearly freezes my hair but that's not the reason I shiver.

With my toe, I rock the nest again, and when it tilts, the eggs finally *do* roll, until they're staring up at me.

But they aren't eggs.

They're eyes.

35

BY THE TIME Vaughn arrives, I've somehow managed to get dressed. I pace the kitchen wildly, keeping my eyes off the back door. I'm refolding the kitchen towels for the millionth time when I hear his tires crunch on the gravel. When he bounds up the porch stairs, stopping briefly to look at our special delivery, my stomach tightens.

"Hey." He strides into the room, his face drawn with worry, and pulls me into a tight hug.

"Did you see it?" I say against his chest.

He nods.

"The message is obvious. They're watching. And there's two of them. Two eyes. Two days. The countdown continues." I look toward the back door. "Any word from Sharon?"

As I expect, he shakes his head. He pulls out a chair and falls into it, pulling me onto his lap.

"I *did* talk to Stace though."

"And?" I keep my eyes on his, refusing to look near the back window.

"I didn't give her details, of course, but I said you were getting some threats. I asked her about the ponytail charity thing and said someone left you something we thought came from there, along with some threatening notes."

I stop breathing. "And?"

"She flipped the hell out. Called me every name possible, accused me of cheating on her and a bunch of other things. It was weird. She jumped from one topic to the other. Me writing songs without her, me cheating on her, us meant to be together, her mom getting remarried soon and not loving her enough, her failing her latest English test. It was like she was on something, just spewing everything that was ever wrong in her life. And pinning it on me." He shakes his head solemnly. "I'd like to think she couldn't do this. But she was definitely not acting like the Stace I know, either."

"So what now?"

"Um, steer clear of her and keep our eyes open. Until we hear from Sharon, anyway. I'm not sure how Stace would be connected to those Obitus people though. If it has something to do with them, I'm guessing it doesn't have to do with her. Of course it could be neither, too."

Confusing.

"So we wait, I guess. Oh, and I finally left messages for both of the Sellers' grandsons last night," I say. "I kept it vague, just said I'd found something that had belonged to their grandmother and left my name and number. Until we hear from them or Sharon, we'll just do what we can here. I feel like we're running in circles."

He shifts under me to reach into his pocket, grinning to lighten the mood. "If we're going to be running in circles, we at least need some fuel, right?" He holds up a king-size Twinkie.

I burst out laughing, despite myself.

"Now *that* makes everything worth it." His hair tickles my cheek when he nuzzles my neck. He rips the wrapper open with his teeth and takes a bite.

I look over his shoulder to the back porch. "What kind of eyes do you think they are?"

He gulps and tightens a hand on me. "I have no idea, but they're small. A cat maybe?" He grimaces. "I really don't want to think about it. But I did notice something."

I raise my eyebrows. "There's more?"

He shoves the last bite of Twinkie in his mouth and chews. "The bottom of the nest was lined with hay. I didn't touch it, but there was enough of it to tell what it was. Let's go out to the barn and see if anything's disturbed."

"Sounds like a long shot."

"Worth a try, right?" He pats my leg. "Give me a bag and I'll get rid of that thing. You don't need to look at it."

He disposes of it quickly, washing his hands afterward in scalding water and almost the entire bottle of hand soap. On our way out to the barn, I grab my keys.

"Hold on. I'm gonna lock up." From behind me, he kisses my cheek with lips that are still sticky sweetness.

There's a bite in the air, just cold enough to wish I'd worn a jacket. I pull my hands into my sleeves and wrap my arms around myself. We walk in silence. We haven't been back to the barn since the night of the séance, but with the sunlight streaming through the rafters, it's hardly as spooky as I expect. I prop open the doors at the east end—the same doors that banged open wildly during the séance—and we step inside.

"What exactly are we looking for?" I toe the hay as we walk toward the stalls.

Vaughn shrugs. "Who knows. Probably nothing. I just saw hay and my mind immediately said, 'barn.' I'm getting desperate for clues at this point."

We walk in and out of the stalls, back and forth across the wide center aisle. Once we've covered every inch of the barn and find nothing, I sigh. "Well? That solves that. Nothing weird in here."

"I guess not," he says, kicking the hay. "This is driving me crazy."

I hug him tightly. His lips touch mine in a soft kiss, like feathers dusting my skin. When he pulls back, his eyes blaze with intensity. "Can we just forget everything for a while?"

"I wish."

He kisses me again. "You know I'd do anything for you."

"Hmmm."

"I'll keep you safe. Always. I know I couldn't do it last time, but I will this time around." The pain in his voice is mirrored in his expression. He looks at a spot over my shoulder, his jaw clenched. "I don't know what it did to him, losing her that way."

"Vaughn—"

"I know he wanted to solve it, I know he thought he could help before it was too late. And he failed. And I bet it killed him. Losing her like that."

I remember Ginny's words. How Beau was so adamant about figuring it out himself. About how she believed in him and yet how they weren't smart enough to stop it. Or quick enough.

"Let's get back to the house," I say, pulling him toward the door. "Being out here isn't helping anything." Outside, I tug on the barn doors until they slam closed.

"Fine, but let's do a quick walk first to make sure nothing's out of place," Vaughn says, leading with a nod toward the woods. "Like you said before, never can be too careful."

WE SEARCH ALL afternoon. We do in-depth tours of the yard, the stables and sheds, walk every inch of my woods. At home, we spend hours on Vaughn's computer, looking for every Beau in a hundred mile radius of Shady Springs in the last eighty years. By the time the sunset throws deep golden beams across my bed, our frustration is mounting.

"Dinner?" Vaughn lies next to me on the pillow, rubbing his eyes.

I prop up on one elbow. "Sure. What do you want?"

He grins, his smile lifting on one side.

I swat at him. "Perv!"

"Hey, you asked." He shrugs, feigning a sheepish smile.

"For dinner. What do you want for dinner?" Despite my utter exhaustion, I laugh.

He springs from the bed, reaching for his keys on my desk. "Come on, I'm taking you out. Enough sitting around and looking at this twisted stuff. Let's get away from it for a while, huh?"

I know we won't stop thinking about it, especially with the clock ticking down the way it is. But I'm willing to give it a try. His eyes meet mine in the mirror while I brush my hair.

"Italian?" I ask.

"Sure," he says, standing behind me with his chin on my shoulder. His fingers tap against my stomach.

"And cheesecake at Marty's?" I play on his sugar craving. I can't stand the thought of coming back here right away.

"Hmmm." He kisses my neck and instantly, I'm covered in goose bumps. "We'll worry about dessert later."

36

We wake late the next day, my room warm with the midmorning sun. I settle into Vaughn like a cat curled on a sunny spot of a comfortable couch. Lazy Sunday morning.

My eyes fly open. It's Sunday. The last day of the countdown. *The day before she was killed.*

I push the thought from my mind and roll halfway on top of Vaughn. He barely returns my kiss while I climb over him. I muss his hair and smirk when he doesn't even notice.

When I get back from the bathroom, he hasn't moved, his hair dragged across his face, his lips set in a semi-puckered state.

But much as I'd like to, I've got more things to do than watch him sleep. Sometime during the night, an idea came to me. I pull out a stack of scrap paper and scribble headings on the top of each sheet. *Clues. Presents. Timeline. Supernatural. Suspects.*

I doodle small pictures under each heading until my brain is relaxed enough to think. I start to fill out details on each sheet. Clues are things that could be connected: Ginny and Beau, Sweeney murders, Edith Sellers, Hank. Presents are the sick things we've received: the dead rabbits, pictures, ponytail, nest of eyes, the note, slashed tires, the pen, the knives.

Timeline starts with the séance, everything leading up to Mrs. McDermott's fire, and chronicles all the weird events between and since.

Supernatural is easy: my drawing, Vaughn's song, my visions, like the one in the attic or seeing and hearing Ginny's picture practically come to life.

Suspects takes a bit longer. I consider anyone that may dislike us. I start with the most obvious: Stace. I add Obitus and Edith Sellers. I'm still not sure where she fits in, but if she was important enough for the voice in the barn, she goes on the list. Last, I write Hank Griffin. It's stupid really, but if he killed Ginny last time, who's to say he's not back in this life and around somewhere now?

Satisfied, I lean back on my heels, looking over the clues. I quickly tape the pages together until they form a big square. I move my rug to the side and tape the whole thing to the floor. The wall would work best but I'm not about to have Mom walking in and seeing this. At the top I write the words from the barn.

Sell. Her. Sweeney.

I stand, pacing around the lists, racking my brain for a connection. It always looks so easy on those police shows. They draw a chart, look at it from different angles and BAM—they have the solution.

Not so easy in this case.

"Hmmm?" Vaughn rolls onto his side, facing my pseudo detective display in the center of the room. His eyes are still sleepy-soft when he smiles. "What's all this?"

"Ugh. Just my lame-ass attempt at looking at this from another angle. Literally."

He turns his head sideways. "Hmmm. Well, it looks like a good collection of all our info, in any case. It could help." He yawns, running a hand through his hair to tame it. "It's too early for thinking."

When I sit on the edge of the bed, he rests his cheek on my thigh. I rub his back absently, frowning at my lists.

"I know. It was a dumb idea, I guess. I just thought if we had it all laid out, it would magically make sense."

"Like on some detective show?" He looks at me with a mix of pity and amusement.

"No! I just, I don't know." My cheeks burn.

"It was a good idea." He nuzzles into me and yawns again. "And actually, it's a good record. Once we figure out who's doing this, we'll have a list of proof to fling at them when we turn them in. Besides, it may help us think." He stands, circling around the list a few times before heading into the hall.

"Did you make any coffee by chance?" He calls from outside my door. "Or are you sending your slave out for lattes again?"

"Oh, would you? Pretty please?" Even though he can't see me, I smile.

"You're lucky I love you," he growls before closing the bathroom door.

"Thank you!" I call.

I stare at the lists for a while longer, eventually pulling my rug on top of them.

37

No one died.

Nothing happened at all. The string of clues that's arrived for the last four days has abruptly stopped.

I'm not breathing easy yet, but still. It's a small relief. Sunday night, I go to sleep thinking maybe, just maybe, it'll be okay.

Yet I wake Monday morning with Ginny on my mind. Even though the dates are different, if we're following the timeline, today would be the day she was killed—five days after the clues started. But with yesterday's clue never arriving, I can't help but walk with my head a bit higher.

It's also Hunt day and school is insane. The student council even convinced the administration to cancel last period for people to go home and get ready. I shouldn't have even bothered to come in. Hearing about murder details does little to take my mind off Ginny.

After school, I dash home to change. Vaughn's been roped into helping with the community center music set up, so we're meeting there. Being my first year in Shady Springs, I'm not sure what to expect. I dress kind of emo, going with all black clothes and some dark eye shadow. Halloween's not until tomorrow, but I figure a fake murder hunt requires some kind of dark attire.

I'm on my third coat of mascara when Mom peeks into my room. She grimaces and steps back.

"Holy cow—what happened to you?"

"The Hunt thing is tonight, remember? I'm borrowing your car." I say through O-shaped lips as I finish the last of my mascara.

"That's right." She tilts her head to the side. "Oh, nice, you're wearing the comb."

I bring my hand to my hair. Of course I don't know for sure, but I like it to think the comb Mom found in the attic was Ginny's. "Yeah, I love it. As long as this wing doesn't stab me." I readjust the comb. "I guess accessories used to be a lot more dangerous than they are today."

She looks at me strangely. "If you say so. Oh, and before I forget, there was a message for you on the machine. Some guy. Ron Sellers? He said you left him a message."

My insides halt.

"Thanks," I mumble when she hands me the phone. What am I going to say to him?

"When did he leave the message?" I call down the hall. But she's already gone, dashing down the stairs. I sigh at myself in the mirror.

On Edith's original note card, I've scribbled Ron's and William's phone numbers. Sitting on the edge of my bed, I punch Ron's in and wait. It rings and rings. And rings.

Damn it.

"Hello?" A woman's voice.

"Is Mr. Sellers there?"

"No. I'm sorry. He's stepped out. May I ask who's calling?"

"Uh, sure. My name is Lange. I left him a message a few days ago and he called me back. I found something that belonged to his grandmother, from a bunch of years ago."

"Oh."

"It's this big heavy mirror. It's kinda cool. She'd left her name on it. Anyway, I thought maybe he knew something about it or that he'd want it or something."

I bite my lip to shut myself up.

"Oh. Well I'll have him call you as soon as he gets in." She's nice enough but I can tell she doesn't know what to make of me.

Think fast, Lange. You need this clue. If Sellers was important enough for the voice in the barn, you need *to know what he has to say.*

"Please," I stammer. "I think this was important to her. He may know something about it that can help me." My words are totally ambiguous but hopefully make a bigger impression than my *I found your junk in my attic* spiel.

"Very well dear. He'll be in touch."

"Great, Lange," I mutter when I hang up. "Drive away one of the last clues you may get. Not to mention probably one of the most important."

I throw the phone on my bed, completely not in the mood for this Hunt thing. I've had quite enough blood and guts the last few weeks. But at least tonight's mayhem will be fake.

My favorite dressy shoes, silver heels that shimmer when I walk, are the only color I've planned for tonight's outfit. When I tug them on, the left clasp snaps, metal dangling against my ankle.

Great. Tonight is feeling more and more doomed by the second. I search my closet floor for a replacement pair and find a pair of red platform-ish ones that would probably look just as fierce. They need a quick dusting. Easy enough.

My eye catches something white in the back of my closet and I inch forward for a closer look. A folded sheet of paper sticks out of the closet's secret door. One of Ginny's letters or notes must have come loose when I put them back.

When I pull it from the crevice between the wall and door, a chill washes through me. Sitting against the closet's molding, I open it, scanning to see which one it is. But the first few lines are unfamiliar.

August 13, 1934

He brought me the sweetest present I could ever imagine. I don't even know when he found time for shopping while on his trip, but my beau, he always surprises me.

He stood on my porch, all shy-faced with the package behind his back. He handed it to me when we were sure everyone was in the parlor with the radio. "It's an early wedding present," he whispered.

"Shhh." I looked behind me. God forbid Mother should know our plans.

And when I opened them, they were the loveliest pair of candlesticks I've ever seen. Solid, heavy. Pewter, he said. They have a pretty scroll pattern up and down their sides and I told him we'll use them for everything. Anniversaries, birthdays, holidays, too.

My lungs are threatening a full collapse but I read on. Of course I read on.

And, being the hopeless romantic he is, he even wrote my future initials on the bottom! Can you believe that? Oh I can't wait until September! Mother is going to flip, but I decide when I'm ready and that time is now. I want him and nothing else.

Oh that Hank. He will always surprise me, I think. That's what I told him.

"Every day of your life, Mrs. Griffin." He whispered in my ear, tickling my lobes the way he does with his lips. Anyway, I'm going to hide them, where we've hidden everything else we'll take with us, down in the root cellar where Mother will never look. He really finds the strangest things, not that any of us would ever bother with the barn the way he did. Anyway, not much longer now. The future is mine! Like he always says, our love is an abyss. Where we start and end and will always be. Deeper than the deepest depths. Soon my beau will be my husband!

The room contracts, my vision bowing like a funhouse mirror. My thoughts jumble as I read the words again and again, the letter shaking in my hand like a branch in a hurricane.

No. This can't be.

Beau is Hank. Hank is Ginny's love? Hank who killed her? And her family? What about Beau? Beau is really *a* beau? As in, a boyfriend?

The boyfriend is Hank. Hank Griffin the killer with the dark and twisted thoughts is her true love?

No.

I shake my head, trying to force the thoughts loose. I have to call Vaughn. This is crazy. This is—wait.

If Hank is the boyfriend then Vaughn is Hank and if Hank killed Ginny then Vaughn . . .

My lungs have fully collapsed now, the black edge of my vision closing in like a tightened belt.

This *has* to be a mistake. *Has* to be. There's no way Vaughn is dangerous.

But if Hank was dangerous to Ginny, does that mean Vaughn is dangerous to me? Quietly, I close my door, kicking back my rug to look at the list on the floor. This makes no sense. Vaughn is totally *not* involved in this.

He can't be.

So what if they both wanted to keep the cops out of it. It means nothing. And Vaughn did eventually agree…

The clues bend and blur in my vision. His song. The diary and letters. The pen. The ponytail in his trunk. But we're always together. It makes sense he's been there for so many aspects of it.

Out of the listed suspects, only one name makes sense, even if he's dead: Hank Griffin. Except he isn't really dead, is he? He's just Vaughn now. Isn't he?

I drag my rug back over the notes and reach for my jacket.

38

THE AIR IN the community center is thick with excitement and sweat. It's furnace hot in here, and packed wall to wall. Up on stage, Purgatory sets up, tuning their instruments and adjusting their mics. Feedback screeches from the speakers and I look over everyone's heads, in search of Vaughn. Black lights have been strung around the entire room and heavy drapes pulled across the windows.

A loud *woot* I recognize as Stace's travels from the front of the room. I squint, finding the cluster of them—Kelly, Ben and Stace—against the far wall, as close to the stage as possible. Stace stares at the stage, probably wishing for Kent Lee's attention, but only Mr. Murphy looks out at the crowd.

He taps the mic. "Hello! Is this thing on?"

Everyone groans.

"Welcome to the annual Hunt adventures! Tonight we are featuring one of your favorite local bands, PURGATORY!"

Yells and cheers fill the room. He clears his throat a few times until the excitement settles down. "But, before they play, let me go over The Hunt rules once and once only." A few hoots in the crowd make him raise his eyebrows. "First, The Hunt will start at eight, directly after the band plays a few opening songs. Second, the crime can be found within walking distance of the community center, all you have to do is follow the clues on your list. There are five sets of lists, so different groups will be going in different directions. But each set of clues will lead you to the final scene. Pay attention to what you see along each of your three stops. What you observe along the way will solve the crime once you find it.

Third, whoever is first to solve the crime will win bragging rights, a free day off and a parking spot in senior row. *Solve* people. You have to solve the crime, *not* just find its aftermath."

This is complicated. I bury my hands in my pockets. I'm not even sure where I put the clue list they gave me when I came in.

"All right, all right!" Someone yells.

Mr. Murphy points to quiet them down. "So, in a few more minutes, I'll turn it over to the band. Once the last song ends, the lights will flicker on, then off, then on again, at which point, I suggest you get outside and start The Hunt. Keep it safe. When you figure it out, meet back here for the judges to confirm. Good luck to you all!" More feedback screeches through the room when he returns the microphone to its stand.

Kelly spots me and waves wildly. She whispers to Ben and Stace and with a broad smile, pushes through the crowd toward me.

On stage, I finally see Vaughn. My stomach turns inside out and I force an exaggerated swallow for fear of throwing up. He moves swiftly, carrying a guitar case and a mic stand, shaking his hair from his face, his eyes gleaming with some joke to the band. His smile is bright, so pure and real and so utterly ingrained in me. So mine.

Your voice is resting in my ear, You're in my veins, you're crystal clear.

I'm not giving that up without a fight. There *has* to be an explanation.

I'll talk to him. It's a crowded place, right? What could possibly happen?

"Lange!" Kelly's halfway across the room, skirting the crowd near the back wall, pointing and laughing at the mob. She throws an imaginary rope and pretends to lasso me and pull me to her.

Purgatory's first notes ring from the speakers. When the lights dim, I grin at Kelly, trying to compose an expression that looks normal. Up on the stage, Kent Lee croons into the mic. A deep bass fills the air, a slow, rhythmic drumbeat. I stand on my toes, looking for Vaughn, but it's impossible to see with the lights this low.

By the time the second song starts, Kelly's nearly to me, inching through the last few people.

"Hey!" She says when she reaches me, her teeth and eyes glowing in the black light. She gives me a big hug and squeals. "Isn't this exciting?"

"Sure." I force a smile and look over her shoulder for Vaughn. He's nowhere to be seen. I spend two songs feverishly scanning the crowded room and stage crew area while Kelly dances and sings along beside me.

"Stace and Ben have different clues than me!" She yells over the music. "What about you?"

I shrug. Right now, I don't care about The Hunt.

"You want to go together then?" Huge grin.

"I guess," I say. "I wanted to find Vaughn first—"

The lights flicker, bright then dim to almost totally dark. Wait, didn't Mr. Murphy say that would happen *after* the show? They've only played three songs.

"Here we go!" Kelly jumps up and down, clapping her hands.

"Already?" I panic. I need to find Vaughn. I just want to talk to him, not go on this stupid murder hunt.

"Come on, Lange! Get excited!" She drags me by the arm toward the back door. I throw another look over my shoulder, skimming the crowd quickly. He's still not there, even though we had plans to meet. The stage is empty, Purgatory milling over by the speakers. But no Vaughn.

"Good luck, kids!" Mr. Murphy's voice rings out through the crowd. "Hurry back afterwards to crown the winner and hear more Purgatory!"

The crowd erupts in cheers, the voices swarming in my head. The room teeters and I have to close my eyes and breathe, wishing I could wake up tomorrow and have all of this be a dream.

Fat chance. Where the hell is Vaughn?

"You coming?" Kelly tugs my hand, pulling me outside, I look back once more, the mob closing in on us as everyone rushes out the door. There's really no choice. I can either stay behind, alone, and find him, or follow Kelly.

I let her lead me into the street.

"Okay," she says, her breath forming small clouds in the cold night air. She looks down at her paper. I don't even pretend to look for mine. I'll just follow. "Number one, Float like a butterfly, sting like a bee, find the men where the pole will be."

"Butterfly? Bee?" Kelly taps her chin as we stand side by side on the sidewalk. All around us groups huddle together, reading clues and brainstorming, shooting off in different directions, towards their various destinations.

"The park?" I mumble.

Kelly looks in that direction.

Behind us a group of boys talk loud enough for us to hear. "Float like a butterfly, sting like a bee. It was from that boxer. Mohammad Ali! I remember my grandpa always saying that quote."

Kelly's eyes meet mine. Her eyes sparkle and I nod. We take off, sprinting down the block.

We aren't the first ones to have figured it out. Mohammad Ali's, the Barber Shop on Main, is swarming. I take in everything I can about the scene. It's the first time I've been in Mohammad Ali's, but it's like any other barber shop, I guess. Three beat up leather barber chairs, long Formica counter, old linoleum floor.

But there is the air of a crime here and definitely clues to take notice of. The open register, no money inside. The barber tools tossed haphazardly on the ground. The broken hand mirror on the floor.

"A robbery?" I suggest.

Kelly shakes her head. "I think they're trying to throw us off. Open register, yes. No body though. No sign of one either. This isn't where the murder took place." She looks at the barber's tools and makes a note on her paper. "It does involve him though." She nods, bending down to examine the tools more closely. "Definitely. Something is missing from these. I'm not sure what yet."

I stare at our reflections in the window, the way everyone mills around in here, looking for a killer or victim. A chill passes through me. But then.

Wait.

He's gone. There was a guy standing against the glass, hands cupped for a better view. Light hair, stocky build. There was something vaguely familiar about him, but I can't pinpoint exactly what it was. And he disappeared almost as soon as I looked his way. Weird.

Beyond weird.

Kelly leads me toward the door, but now I can't get past the idea of someone watching. Was someone watching?

"Ready for the next one?" She pulls me out to the sidewalk again. I look up and down the sidewalk, and across the street. Groups of students move back and forth, lost to themselves and their clues. There's no one lurking. I don't see the light haired guy anywhere.

It's got to be in my head. Paranoid. Simply paranoid. Right?

"Number two," she says. "There was a song called Mack the knife, but at this place, the goulash is nice."

214

"Macky's" I say offhandendly and we start to move toward the diner. Everyone knows Macky's is famous for the goulash.

"Duh. Lame clue." Kelly pulls her hair back as we rush down the sidewalk. She's distracted, checking out her reflection in each window we pass. Not me though, my eyes are searching every face, every head bobbing through the crowd.

When we push through the doors at Macky's, it's packed. The lights are turned way low and I squint until my eyes adjust. I'm not even looking at the scene, though. I'm looking for the light haired guy I saw in the barber's window. And I'm looking for Vaughn.

"Coffee?" Kelly mutters, jotting something on her paper. "Tea? Hot chocolate?"

I blink, finally taking in the scene. Mackey's is your typical diner, albeit filled with old school décor, like puffy leather bench seats and mini jukeboxes in each booth. But despite how old it is, the owners always keep it immaculate.

Not tonight though. Tonight it's a mess, and it looks like they haven't cleared tables or done dishes in weeks. There are coffee cups everywhere. They cover every table, even the long bar. Some have spoons in them, some have saucers. But most are mugs.

"Mugs," I say. "Write it down."

Deliberate muddy footprints are tracked down the diner's center aisle. Kelly and I, along with a horde of people, follow them into the kitchen. They lead to the big freezer, the walk in kind. Kelly ducks her head in, taking notes feverishly. I'm too busy watching the back door for signs of the lurker and wondering where Vaughn is to pay attention to what she writes. I need to find Vaughn soon. I think of Ginny's letter. How could Hank have been her Beau? And how could he have killed her?

I'm pushed through the crowd, Kelly right behind me. I wipe a tear from my cheek without even realizing I'm crying.

How much does history repeat itself?

We're pushed back into the dining room, toward Macky's front entrance. The kitchen door has been propped open. Over the heads of what seems like a million people between us, I see Vaughn come in the back door.

He's alone, eyes wild. When they find mine, he seems to settle. "Lange!" He calls. I start to move toward him.

Kelly steps in front of me, blocking him from view. She waves her paper. "Got it, let's go!"

"Wait," I try and move around her, but the crowd is thick and I'm pushed into the dining room again. Vaughn may be somewhere in the mob, but I don't see him and Kelly's pulled me halfway down the block before I can even try and figure out which way he went.

"Wait," I say. "Vaughn was back there." I try and wrench away from her, but she keeps pulling.

"There's no time to wait. We'll see him at the end. Come on!"

Up ahead, I see a platinum blond figure turn into an alley. I blink, not sure if it's the same guy from the barber shop or if my mind is playing tricks on me. I look behind me for Vaughn. He's not there either.

How could Hank kill Ginny? *How how how?* He loved her. They had plans. They had a future. They were in love.

Like us. Like us. Like us.

"Summer nights and summer days, every flavor, sixty-two ways." Kelly reads from her paper.

"What are you talking about?" I snap.

She gives me a quizzical look. "The next clue?"

Deep breath. Deep breath.

"Which is obviously Scoops ice cream. Another easy one." She takes big strides, turning the corner toward Scoops, and I follow her, looking everywhere for Vaughn. And unable to shake the feeling of being watched.

Inside Scoops, we find blood everywhere. I gag, unable to look.

"Shhh," Kelly gives my arm a gentle squeeze. "It's fake, Lange."

But it doesn't feel fake. None of this does. The ice cream cases are smeared with red and the place is completely dark, lit only by the moon and the streetlights outside. It's enough light to see by, but it's eerie as hell. The back door is open, the aprons on the back hooks flapping in the breeze.

"The alley!" Kelly dashes for the door.

Outside, a huge crowd of students gathers in a circle. A body lies in the middle, and although I know it's just a dummy and it's all fake, it's too much. I can't look, I can't stand it. Kelly pushes her way through to the center, but I hang back. I can't be a part of this. I should have stayed home. Slowly, I back away from the crowd.

"Lange!" Vaughn is here and he's out of breath, but he grabs my hand and squeezes. "I couldn't find you," he says.

It's all happening so fast. The dead body with the black pants and rubber soled shoes and the people milling around it, making guesses right on top of the fake and splattered blood and Vaughn is here, just holding onto my hand, and then me, and my mind is flashing to the pictures I saw of Hank and the words Ginny wrote. And never got to write. I see our hands, held over and over through lifetimes and I see those candlesticks at Mrs. McDermott's. Ginny's candlesticks. And I'm just wondering over and over and over again how Hank could have killed her. How could he have done it?

"You're dangerous," I say. I don't mean it to come out the way it does, but there it is.

He grabs my other hand, swinging them between us, playful. His eyes dance. "Am I now?" He says.

I drop his hands and take a step back. He must see something in my expression because the humor leeches out of him like a drain has been opened inside.

His eyes flash. Angry, then confused. Then hurt.

"Dangerous?" He says, voice rising on the last syllable. "I've been running around like crazy, looking all over for you and when I find you, this is what you say?"

"Wait!" I say. This isn't how I wanted this to go. "This is all too much. Today... and Ginny, and this," I wave around the scene. "The bodies and blood and... I found another letter." I can barely get the words out.

Vaughn moves in to hear me, his head so close I can smell his sweat and musky shampoo.

"Hank," I say, cautiously releasing the word like I'm unwrapping something explosive.

Vaughn's eyes narrow.

"You," I say. "Hank. Hank was Beau. Beau *was* Hank. He's the one that killed her!"

Vaughn's jaw clenches. "What are you talking about?"

"They were one and the same. Hank and Beau! She meant *her* beau, not Beau like a name. And if you are him, which obviously you are, then you're Hank too. And if Hank killed Ginny . . . " I swallow the boulder of a lump in my throat, watching the dark clouds that have moved into his expression. My fingers tremble against my leg, mirroring the way my insides feel like they're rattling to pieces.

He grabs my hand roughly, his fingernails digging into the fleshy part of my palm. "There's no way you really believe that. About me?" he pulls me away from the crowd. "Let's go talk. Alone, where we can hear each other."

But I can't. As much as I hate to admit it, I'm terrified of him right now. I pull my hand away from his and plant my feet.

"No," I say.

"No?" His eyes are wild with emotion, anger and hurt at war there.

"I—I can't." I take another step backward. I need to be alone. To think this through. "I'm sorry. I don't think that about you. I don't. I just need to digest all this." I stutter.

His eyes are cold and dark, like marbles. *"Digest* it? You can't be serious. Well go on then, save yourself from me." He bites his lip and looks at the ground.

"Vaughn stop, this isn't like you."

"Really? Are you sure? You suddenly don't know who I am, do you?" He spits the words as he leans in. His breath is warm on my cheek. He's so right here and right now. He *can't* be like Hank, can he?

"I'm sorry." The words tumble out softly and I can't make myself look up at him. "I *do* know who you are. Just give me a little time . . . to think . . . " I have to work hard to keep my voice from crumbling.

He shakes his head, that quick flash of anger surfacing again. His mouth twists into a scowl. "That really stings, Lange. This is unbelievable." And then he's gone again. And I'm alone.

Tears burn behind my eyes. My heart sinks with the possibilities of loving Vaughn and fearing him at once. But I have to be careful.

I search the crowd anxiously until I see Kelly's head bobbing way up ahead. I run after her, pushing frantically through people.

Someone solved it, I guess, when I realize I'm in the middle of the mob and we're all running back to the community center, and I'm running along, listening to Kelly breathlessly explain it all. The dead barber, the missing shears. The spilled ice cream. Mugged by someone at the ice cream store.

I barely listen because twice on the way back, I swear I see the shady blond guy ducking into doorways, turning quickly away.

We push our way through the side doors of the community center, the roar of people moving like water through a broken dam.

Once we're inside, the crowd disperses a bit, everyone rushing this way and that. I'm completely confused and don't even understand how and where we're supposed to report solving the crime. I slink toward the back of the room, watching everyone rush around in their excitement about The Hunt findings. The back doors are open too and within minutes it seems like all of Preston Academy is stuffed into the room. On stage, Purgatory warms up for the next set, guitar riffs blaring through the speakers. I can't help it; I scan the stage, looking for Vaughn. Everything about tonight feels so wrong. It's like I'm completely disconnected from everything in this room. I decide to find Kelly and tell her I'm going home. There's really no reason to stick around.

But as soon as I turn, I run smack into Vaughn. He backs away quickly, not meeting my eyes. The crowd is roaring with excitement and I can barely hear myself think. I'm jostled by people moving toward the stage.

"Vaughn." Despite my common sense, I reach out for him but he takes another step back before my fingers can touch his sleeve. His eyes are flooded with the same darkness as before, emotion radiating off of him. His gaze darts to the floor, the door, the walls. Everywhere but me.

Feedback screeches through the speakers and Vaughn shoots a look over his shoulder. "That's my cue. Sound check time."

I just nod, feeling relief? Pissed? I don't even know, but the fact that we're not having a conversation right now feels like a very good thing.

I have to get out of here.

I look for Kelly. I just want this night to be over already.

A minute passes. Two. Who knows how many more.

It comes out of nowhere, really. The band is singing, Kelly's finally coming toward me, she's right by the back door. And then the room goes dark. Pitch black.

The music's out too, the band singing for a few seconds before realizing they've lost power.

I wrap my arms around myself, inching backward, into the throngs of people. There's laughter in the air, hoots and yells.

"What the hell?"

"We want music!"

"Come on, is this another murder!"

Bile rises in my throat.

I cover my mouth with my hand, shouldering into the person behind me, looking for some light.

A blood-curdling scream rings out, freezing time.

It's five days after the rabbits, just like Ginny. Five days of clues. Five days later. If the timeline is right, this is the day of her murder. Murder.

Shut up shut up shut up, keep moving.

Her killer is here.

No, he's not! Vaughn didn't kill anyone.

He couldn't have. He wouldn't.

The screaming is nearby. It's loud and getting louder. And I'm nearly trampled with people pushing all around me. I can't figure out if they're running to or from whatever is going on.

But I'm planted now. Planted to the floor in shock, listening to the wails.

Please make this be part of the charade. Part of The Hunt.

But the shiver running up and down my spine tells me I know better.

The lights flicker on and off again. They're dim, but bright as the noon sun to my unaccustomed eyes. Students press against the walls, confusion on their faces as they look at the scene in front of them, trying to figure out what it means.

"Someone call 9-1-1!"

Slowly, the faces in the room change. Confusion turns to fear as everyone realizes this isn't part of the game. This isn't fake.

And then I see her on the floor. Kelly. A bright red stain on her shirt. I move toward her, but someone pushes me back. It takes me a minute to realize it's Mr. Murphy. Horror has turned his face into a scared mask.

"Lange, you don't need to see this." He tries to turn me around.

But I can't just leave her there. That stain– my God, it's blood.

I break free from his arms, and run toward her, slipping at the last second and nearly falling. Her hand trembles in mine as I search her vacant gaze. When she sees me, she forces herself to focus. I can actually see the effort it takes for her to bring her eyes to mine.

"Vaughn," she whispers.

Then she closes her eyes and it's only me that screams.

39

I DON'T REMEMBER driving home, but here I am, forcing a shaky key in the back door.

After the ambulance rushed Kelly to the hospital, the police questioned everyone for what felt like days. Even though I had almost nothing helpful to add, they talked to me forever, and by the time I was done, I couldn't find Vaughn anywhere.

I tiptoe up the stairs, wondering if they got to question him before he disappeared.

In my room, moonlight provides the only light and I examine the things it touches—photographs, posters, my art supply box, a bottle of pear-scented lotion—as though I'm a stranger in my own house.

Something crackles beneath my feet and I reach for the light switch. The rug's been moved and my sheets of clues are torn down the middle, flapping with the air that stirs up as I glide across the floor.

Someone's been in here.

Was it him? Before the show? He was missing for quite a while . . .

I run through it in my mind but the timelines don't jibe. Is someone else involved?

Stunned, I sit on the edge of my bed. It's silent. No creaking footsteps upstairs. No hissing radiators. No lights in the hall. No shadows.

Mom!

Must find Mom.

Gathering the energy to stand is not easy. Pulling together enough courage to go looking through my house is even harder, but I grab an old tennis racket from the back of my closet and leave my room behind.

"Mom?" I call into the hallway. No answer. Not a single sound. When I flip on the hall light, a buzz and pop signals the end of the bulb's life. Sure enough, it burns out. Great.

She has to be here. I had her car tonight. My mind argues that she's probably in the attic, but I hear nothing.

What did he do to her? Whoever *he* is.

It's Vaughn. A voice inside me whispers. Kelly said his name. *Vaughn.*

Hank killed Ginny.

It's Vaughn.

Moving slowly through the second floor, I peer into all the dark bedrooms, then tiptoe quietly up the stairs, pausing for a breath on the landing.

The third floor has three bedrooms besides Mom's, all of which have been shut up since we moved in. I can't imagine the noise opening them will make, so I don't. With my back to the wall, I continue down the hall. At least the light up here works, though it's dim and fades in and out with the wind.

Mom's door looms like a shut-up tomb. My bracelet rattles against it as I push it open.

"Mom?" My voice is tiny, the word like hardened gum on my tongue.

I click on the side lamp, which throws light across this corner of the room. Everything looks normal. Her bed is made, her lavender cardigan hanging on the closet doorknob. My feet whisper on the rug as I cross the room, my moonlit reflection barely recognizable in the dresser mirror.

The door to her studio is closed. A tornado churns through my intestines as I press my ear to the door. Silence.

The churning nags at me, and I knock softly. "Mom?"

Oh God, where is she? What's happened to her?

I try the knob.

Locked.

In the glass bowl on her dresser, I find a bobby pin. Straightening it with my teeth, I kneel, digging it in the keyhole until the lock pops back. I straighten and take a huge, steadying breath before pulling the door open.

ME. VAUGHN. VAUGHN. Me. Vaughn and me. Me and Vaughn. In the barn, kissing. In my room. At the circle of ash that was Mrs. McDermott's house. Him cradling me on the city steps, after I saw the rabbits.

And more. Nearly every moment we've spent together, captured on film. The pictures hang like accusations, clipped side by side on the wire she's strung from one corner of the room to the other. I've been in here dozens of times, looking at her prints of still lifes. But now, it's all . . . me. And Vaughn. I pluck them down one by one and fall onto a stool, flipping through them in the light of the dim desk lamp.

Breathing isn't easy.

After I look through the stack a few more times, I drop them on the table.

What's going on? Has Mom been following me? Why would she do that if she trusts me?

But where my hand rests beside the photos, a different one catches my eye. It's a picture of me and Vaughn, on my porch the first night he'd sang me our song. But there's something different about this print. My stomach lurches as I pull the lamp toward the photo that shakes in my hand.

In it, me and Vaughn lounge on the porch swing, his guitar balanced comfortably on his knee, arm slung over the instrument's body. But behind us are smudges, blurry images all around us. It's not as strong as the effect in Sharon's, but it seems like the same process. I can tell by the way our outlines waver as they lead into the transposed image.

Everything goes out of focus: the picture, the light, my hands. The floor beneath me swells like a tidal wave.

Breathe, Lange.

Why did she take these pictures? Maybe all her crazy bullshit makes sense, after all. Maybe she is in tune with this stuff. Was she looking out for me? Does she know all the weird stuff I've been trying to hide from her?

But still. It's weird. How would Mom know about Sharon's development process? How involved is Mom in the very things I've been trying to figure out? And why hasn't she told me?

Where is she? Where is he?

My focusing problem soon becomes my breathing problem and in the stuffy closet, I realize how dangerous the situation truly is. Someone tried to kill Kelly. Someone could be coming after me next.

I have to get out of here. I have to go where no one expects me to be and think this through. I can't face her. I can't face anyone. Not yet. I have way too much to figure out first.

A loud creak, like the house itself is screaming, comes from down the hall. I turn off the light and tiptoe from the closet as silently as I can, but even the knob clicking into place sounds like it's over a PA system. Quietly, I rattle the knob, making sure I relocked it.

I listen again. Footsteps on the stairs.

My heart flips in my chest, a fish out of water. I move quickly, creeping down the hall. Somehow, I make it down the creaky stairs and my dark hallway. I head for my room.

Upstairs, her footsteps pause in the hall. "Lange? Is that you?"

"Yeah." I try and hide the tremor in my voice.

"Everything okay?" She sounds so worried I actually feel bad lying to her, but I'm in no shape to talk about any of this.

"I'm fine," I call upstairs. "Just tired."

After a few seconds, her footsteps move again, into her room. *Please don't let her notice I was in the studio.* I'm so not ready to talk about that yet. I'm creeped out by the pictures and the fact that she knows about Sharon's development process. I don't want to talk about my past life and all the things I've found out.

Besides, she's been *following* me. Totally invading my privacy. No matter what reason she had, it feels wrong. It doesn't make sense.

I feel like running, like just opening the back door and taking off, to somewhere very far away. And safe. I wonder what's happened to Kelly and can still see the pale, scared look on her face when she uttered that word to me. His name.

Vaughn.

What did he do to her?

I need a plan.

The clues on the floor stare up at me. If only they made sense!

Ginny's last letter still lies where I left it, on the seat of my desk chair. My eyes scan it again and I'm chilled:

Oh that Hank. He will always surprise me, I think. That's what I told him.

"Every day of your life, Mrs. Griffin." He whispered in my ear, tickling my lobes the way he does with his lips. Anyway, I'm going to hide them, where we've hidden everything else we'll take with us, down in the root cellar where Mother will never look. He really finds the strangest things, not that any of us would ever bother with the barn the way he did.

And then, it jumps out at me. Words that are familiar. Root cellar. Cellar. *Sell. Her.*

On the floor, written across the top of my scroll of clues are the words that started it all. *Sell. Her. Sweeney.*

Oh my God. Root cellar. Sell Her. Christ—it's all making sense now. Root cellar. It wasn't Edith *Sellers.* It was *the* cellar. Where they hid things. A place Hank found.

In the barn.

40

IT TAKES FOREVER to find it.

I use a broom, sweeping the hay to the back of the stalls, up against the walls. It's not until I nearly give up, walking back into the grass, that I think about checking along the outside. When that turns up nothing, I'm sure it doesn't exist. But then I remember. That old stack of wood and pallets in the far stall.

The pallets are heavier than they look and they tear into my fingers. But I'm numb and don't care. After those, I drag heavy pieces of plywood out of the stall, one after another. Sweat burns my eyes and runs down my neck and back. I lean against the wall, breathing in the night air that wafts in from the stall's broken window.

Back to work. It goes on and on until I finally reach the last piece of plywood. No amount of dragging or kicking helps to budge it. It simply won't move.

"Shit." I run my dirty hands through my hair, tilting my head sideways to consider it from another angle. I grab the right edge and with a loud groan, pull as hard as I can.

And like magic, it opens. As easily as if it were on hinges.

It's a door.

I shine my light down the staircase. It's dusty and narrow and exactly, I realize, sinking onto my knees right there in the hay, exactly where I saw Vaughn in my vision.

Find me. Before it's too late.

~   ~   ~

I'M LIKE A marionette puppet, my body limp and shaky as I walk down the crumbling stairs.

When I reach the bottom, I have to duck through a doorway into a tight space the size of a small room. I shine my light into the dusty, cobwebbed corners, and force myself to keep moving, trying not to think of what bugs are possibly lurking here.

Against the far wall, a cloth lies across a small mound on the floor.

Do I want to know?

I shine my light back the way I've come, up the stairs into air that's cool and sweet. Breathable. The stars wink at me through the stall window, beckoning me.

But I've come this far. Right?

Squatting, I lift a corner of the cloth. A centipede, at least eight inches long, slides out from under it, squirming quickly away from the light.

"Ewww." Holding my breath, I lift the cloth completely.

At first, it looks mostly like junk. But then I see it's not. It's pieces of who they were. Ginny and Beau.

A small box filled with toiletries; a cracked hairbrush, a crumbling toothbrush, its bristles dirty and splayed. A bottle of perfume. I bring my nose to it, not surprised at all when it's the same scent I smelled in the attic. A leather bag bursts with clothes, folded shirts and skirts, musty and soured with time. Under that are two record albums, vinyl with the labels scratched off, their paper sleeves disintegrating when I touch them. I bring them to my nose, inhaling their dusty scent, wondering what songs were special to them. A checkered linen tablecloth sits on top of four stacked plates, each painted with a pale pink floral design. Beneath it all, I find a framed eight by ten photo. It's Ginny and Hank, smiling into the camera, shielding their eyes from the sun. They lean into each other, looking half at the photographer and half at one another.

Tears prick my eyes as I look through her collection, the things she planned to bring into her married life. The things that mattered so much to her.

Find me.

I hold the picture to my chest. *I have found you, Hank. But, what have you done? How could you have killed her?*

With my eyes squeezed shut, I listen to the sound of blood in my ears, the heavy breathing I can barely manage in the thick air.

"Lange?"

I switch off my flashlight. Sweat drips down my neck. *Think fast, Lange. What excuse do you have to be down here?* But this is Mom. Hopefully, she won't question the craziness.

"Yeah, Mom?" As if it's normal to be in the root cellar, *underneath* the barn.

"Are you okay? What *are* you doing down there?"

Footsteps on the stairs. Mom's concerned face. Warmth floods me, comfort trying to make its way into the situation. Mom's here. It's going to be okay.

Then more footsteps. Behind her.

It's like seeing a ghost.

Breath gone.

Picture tumbles to the ground.

A new light shines on the wall in front of me, a bright, wide beam like a train is running me down. I don't turn around. I just bite my lip and taste my salty tears.

"Look at you! All holed up down here." Her voice sounds normal, but if she's with *him,* nothing is normal. "Can you believe this?"

"Hell no, I can't," he says. It's a voice I know well. A voice I didn't expect to hear again. Not tonight. Not ever.

Bodies shift behind me, coming closer. I can't move, can't look. All I can do is stand and tremble.

What is she doing? How is this even happening?

And then an arm hooks around my neck, pulling me backward. I tumble, falling with a thud against the ground. My head cracks against something hard. Sharp pain explodes in my skull, warmth oozing in my hair. But I don't think about that, because I'm staring, making out the details of the serpent tattoo I'd forgotten, the way it curves around his forearm, the snake's head against his wrist, mouth open beneath his thumb.

And I blink, staring up at my parents' faces.

41

MY EYES ARE barely open when I realize there're no longer stars up the narrow shaft of stairs. No hay or barn stall visible. Just the bare, unfinished underside of the wood door. My parents sit on the bottom step, looking at me fondly, as a pair of lions would their newborn cub.

"What the hell?" Sitting only brings on a wave of dizziness. I bring my fingers to the tender spot on the back of my scalp and feel the stickiness there.

"Yeah, honey, you hit yourself real good." His voice is just as I remember it, like gravel and whiskey. I close my eyes.

Behind me, something moves, making me turn with a start.

Vaughn's against the wall, passed out and wrists bound. His hands hang limply at his side. But he's here. Beat up and bruised, but here.

And they're over there. My mom. And my *dad*. And he's grinning now, elbowing Mom. "The moment we've been waiting for, huh?" he says. His hair glints, much grayer than it used to be, almost platinum white in the dim light. The man from the barber shop window. Same build. Light hair.

Mom keeps her eyes on the ground but a strange smile creeps across her face. Distant, and . . . utterly demented. Like her dazed and brainwashed look, but a million times worse.

"Miss me honey?" Dad asks, grinning as he drops to crawl across the floor toward me.

Recoiling from his presence, I scoot as far away from him as I can, inching toward Vaughn, willing him to wake up.

"Damn, it always is the same, ain't it? People just never like us for some reason." He looks over his shoulder at Mom.

Vaughn stirs beside me. I nudge him with the slightest lean, to let him know where I am.

And then I realize something. *My* arms aren't tied. *I'm* not the threat.

I make my hands shake even more. If I'm scared, they may discount me doing anything at all.

"What is this?" I motion around the room.

"This," Mom says in a condescending voice. "Is where old Ginny stashed the things she and her loving Hank planned to take with them when they eloped." A soft laugh floats from her. Her eyes are blank, almost looking through me. Sweat darkens the hair at her temples.

I shiver uncontrollably. Who *is* she?

"Unfortunately for them, Hank had a real interest in investigating murders," she says.

"All murders," Dad adds, cracking his knuckles.

"Right. All murders. He was quite nosy," she slides into an easy routine with my father, their banter natural as if they're discussing dinner plans, not past lives and murders. They look at each other knowingly. I use the second their attention is away from me to inch in front of Vaughn, partially blocking him from their view.

"It was convenient though," Dad says. "When it was time to blame someone. Plenty of people knew about Hank's obsession with the murders. It was easy to say he'd gone a bit mad."

"Wait, what?"

"Lange." Mom shakes her head. "I always gave you credit for being smarter than you are."

Dad smirks. "Your poor, poor Hank. He couldn't live without his Ginny. Especially when he knew they should have reported what was going on. He totally blamed himself. And so, he very willingly, very efficiently, hung himself in her barn, just feet from where his true love lay in bloody pieces." He sticks out his bottom lip in mock sadness.

"Stop it." Mom swats him and scoots down to the floor. "Don't talk like that. You know Lange's always been sensitive about blood."

I ignore them, trying to work it out in my head.

"Wasn't there a suicide note with a confession?" I barely croak the words out of my dry throat. God, I've been so wrong about everything.

"It isn't so hard to forge a suicide note," Dad says.

Against the waistband of my pants, Vaughn's fingers move, brushing my belt loop.

He's awake. Play it cool. He wants them to think he's still out of it.

"Then again," Dad says. "He was a smart boy. Much smarter than Ginny, anyway. That damn theory he came up with, based on the locations of the bodies. Well, that's what led them to us, eventually. You guys were already gone, but it didn't matter. The cops were on the right track because of him."

Mom's eyes narrow when she shakes her head, resting her hand on Dad's tattooed arm. "I bet we had a lot left in us, don't you?"

He grins at her, his teeth like broken gravestones. "But we can still make up for it now, you know. Lost time and all that."

She gives him a look of total adoration. Their words roll around in my head like balls on a pool table.

Wait.

My face must show the recognition. "Ahhh," Mom says, wagging a finger at me. "Now you finally see, huh?"

Sweeney. Sweeneys. Sweeney murders. It's them. Hank led to their capture. They killed themselves.

Knocked down by the information, I fall back on the dirt floor. Vaughn's fingers touch mine again, stronger this time. Nearly grasping. He's definitely awake.

"Thanks to him," she nods to Vaughn. "We had to end our lives before we were done. Hank was so concerned about figuring things out and solving our crimes, all the while planning the perfect, successful life for him and his Ginny. It was pretty sickening. Greedy. Hank had to have it all. Both of you did. Greedy, materialistic, self-serving people."

Dad nods, but when he opens his mouth, Mom keeps talking. She's on a roll now.

"It's not a normal way to be, Lange. Caring only about your own ambitions. It's creates a dirty, tainted spirit, not giving back to the world." She's staring into space again, totally dazed.

Does she even hear herself? Does she honestly believe *she's* giving back to the world?

"And this time, we figured we'd bring you two together again, one last time. Turns out not much had changed, only this time it was both of you playing detective, determined to be smarter and better than those around you. All while your precious love grew." She sticks a finger in her mouth as if to gag herself, the mean and distant look flashing in her eyes again.

Dad nods. "We went back and forth for years about you two meeting up, and with the house sitting here empty, we figured why not? Meant to be, I guess. Not that you were easy to find in the first place. Tracking souls is not the easiest thing in the world. But we waited it out. It's doubtful your real parents ever knew what a pure, long-standing soul they rebirthed."

My real parents?

"You don't still think you're actually ours, do you?" Mom says. "Look at your face. Oh no, Lange. There were hundreds of

236

missing children the year you were born. You were merely one more unsolved case.

This is not happening. They're insane. I need to buy time, while I figure out what to do. "How?" I ask. "How do you find souls when they come back?"

"Ah, come on, the best of the best don't kill and tell now," Dad says. "But you don't go from life to life killing unless you pick up some tricks along the way. It's in our bones. It's who we are." He winks.

"You could tell her *something*. It's not like she'll be around much longer to tell anyone."

The room tenses again, the walls shifting in my vision. The cut on my head throbs.

"Very true," Dad says, weighing his words. "Well, do you really think your precious Sharon is the only person who's tapped into people like us?"

His question and his condescending tone stop me from speaking. How do they know about Sharon? Did they hurt her too?

"Put it this way, while Sharon has been wasting time developing photos, there are others, more advanced than her, who have been cataloging lives, following them through generations. Rebirth genealogy type stuff. DNA. It's a real science. With *big* plans for the future." He grins.

I shake my head slowly, pretending to be ignorant. He's talking about Obitus. We're in way over our heads.

"They keep impeccable records, especially of those most interesting to them. Some of us, like me and Cheryl here, have been helping them through the ages." He squeezes her hand. "We helped rid the world of people who didn't deserve to live. The greedy, the selfish. Those unwilling to live by the right set of rules. I've never been so proud as when we recovered those memories."

"Recovered memories of past lives? I thought that was impossible?"

He shrugs. "Not on their own, of course. But there's all kinds of hypnosis to pull out where your soul has lived and what it's done. Like I said, there are experts out there doing big things, Lange. Huge things! These are exciting times for us. And getting bigger and better. I miss that last life though. We had a real purpose. Before *he* came along." He sneers in Vaughn's direction.

Mom looks at me as if she's explaining the way to bake a cake, not trace souls across lifetimes. "A bit of research from our friends, and they tracked you both down."

"But why? Why bring Vaughn and me together again? What can you possibly get from us?"

"What else?" Dad says. "Revenge."

But the way her eyes cut behind him, I know there's something else, something even worse that they aren't saying. Her gaze rests on a metal suitcase behind him and my heart plummets. There *is* something else going on. What is it?

"So why wait?" I stammer. "Why now? I've been with you for years."

They exchange a glance and a small smile pulls the corner of dad's lips up. "The truth? We have plans for you. Tonight is only the beginning."

Plans?

"Revenge aside," he says. "There's something much bigger going on here. Much more important to your fate. To the fate of many souls." He drags the suitcase toward him, clicking it open. He nods to Mom and together, they push it against the wall. Inside is a machine, all gears and antennas and wires and shiny metal surfaces.

Oh. My. God.

Sharon's worst fears were right. It's exactly what she was talking about. The research about forcing souls a certain way after death. That has to be it. I was their experiment. They kept me around simply to mess with my life *and* my soul's destiny. I'm old enough now. That's why she's kept me alive all these years. They've been grooming me, getting my soul ready. I'm nothing but a lab rat to the Obitus research.

Vaughn's fingers brush mine again. I have to buy more time.

"Well, why didn't you just kill us when we first got together? Why try to throw us off the trail so many times?"

"It wouldn't have been the same unless you were absolutely falling for each other," Mom says. "Plus it was fun to watch you scramble around playing detective to try and figure it out."

Trying hard to control the urge to lash out, I look at Dad. "It's true," he says. "But she wanted to go ahead and get it over with last week. She was chickening out on making it count."

Anger flares in her eyes. "Oh come on! That isn't fair. It's not that I didn't want to make it count, it's just that—" she looks down, a small frown forming on her lips. Could it be . . . regret? Does she have any qualms about all of this?

He waves a hand, pulling a cloth pouch from the bottom step toward him. "Please, Cheryl. You wanted to do it in her sleep. Where's the fun in *that?* And with him not even there to witness it?"

The urge to scream boils in me. I inch closer to Vaughn.

Dad looks at me again. "I was afraid for a while there. Thought she'd lost her touch. Or started to actually care about you."

She scoffs, but her lip trembles. She puffs out her chest as if to prove her conviction. "Please. I've always liked torturing her. It was my idea to pretend to kill you off all those years ago, if you remember."

He frowns. "True. But it made sense. I was busy. Being with you guys was dragging me down."

"Yeah, before he left for good, he'd come visit for a few days and go and kill someone and we'd have to up and move again. And again. It got annoying." Mom's eyes twinkle with the memory as if she's remembering cozy Thanksgiving dinners. "Daddy's in town!" Her voice pitches. "Someone gets stabbed, let's move!"

I swallow bile. All those moves. Multiple murders. No wonder reading about the Sweeny murders felt so familiar. I'd been living alongside something way too similar, in the next life.

"Dying was the cleanest exit I could make. And adding a good dose of Daddy issues did make it interesting."

"Added bonus," Mom agrees. "Dragging you to Dr. Ramirez and watching you cry and go on and on? It *was* amusing."

My heart hurts with the memories. Has everything she's done been a lie?

"What about your photo sessions? In the attic and all that? How is that related?"

"That's a whole other story that is none of your business," she says. "Let's just say we were doing some research for some friends. Returning a favor, so to speak." Like a witch's cackle, her laugh breaks into the space, making me flinch. Dad gives her a knowing wink.

Friends? It has to be Obitus. The photographs were research for them. Payback for them finding us.

I steal a glance at the machine in the corner. What exactly is going to happen to us?

Dad unfolds the cloth. Inside, silver glints. I close my eyes.

"Not quite as many as we had with your last family, but they'll do."

At the sound of metal, I open my eyes and watch him rub the blades of two long knives against each other. He grins at me, offering Mom the one with a thick, bowed handle.

I focus on the blades, the way they glitter in the dim flashlight beams.

Mom—I can't help but still think of them as Mom and Dad—crawls over to me. Her makeup is smudged, and she looks at me with raccoon eyes I don't recognize, because somewhere deep inside, the light has gone out. It isn't her anymore, just that weird gaze like she's on some kind of mission. Which, judging by the way she keeps looking at the machine in the corner, I guess she is. She drags the tip of the knife slowly up my arm, slitting my sleeve. When she rests the tip against my throat, I swallow against it.

And then there's pain. Sharp pain like a needle, but deeper. More angry. A slice against my neck, just above my collarbone. She pulls back immediately, but I feel the blood surface on my skin. It runs down my chest, soaking my shirt against my skin. She rests the knife on her chin, the bloody tip against her lips.

Behind her, Dad kneels on the floor, knives spread on a blanket like a street vendor selling belts. A flashlight next to him shines up toward the ceiling, throwing weird shadows across his face.

I don't see how I can overpower them.

Closing my eyes, I breathe through my nose. Dust. Sweat. The remnants of Ginny's perfume.

Behind me, Vaughn shifts again, gripping my fingers as he groans and settles, pretending he's still out of it.

Mom takes my other hand in hers, her fingers long and thin, dry like I've always known them. She pulls me forward, until our faces are only inches apart, her eyes somehow flooded simultaneously with sorrow and violence.

"You're so sweet, believing, just like last time, in the power of true love." She runs the tip of the knife against the inside of my wrist, applying enough pressure to draw blood, but not enough to end it.

Not yet.

I search her face frantically, racking my brain for a solution. Behind her, Dad hums an old fashioned lullaby as he sharpens knives with a sharpener I've seen in our kitchen. Every one of my nerve endings protest at the sound of metal on metal.

"Don't," I whisper, hating the pleading tone in my voice but seeing no other option.

She flinches, regret briefly lighting on her features again. Dad clears his throat. When she looks up at him, he nods toward me. With a deep breath, she drags the blade across my palm, gently tracing the lines there as if with a feather.

I whimper.

"You know, I loved giving you Ginny's old things," she says. "The candlesticks, perfume bottles, hair combs," she pauses to rip the comb from my hair. It clatters to the ground, taking a chunk of my hair with it. She watches it for a second with a crazed expression, as if the comb itself is alive. "Each object sparked something in you. Not enough to reveal the truth, but enough to drive you a bit crazy."

She cuts deeper against my palm, drawing more blood. "Ah, the lifeline." Her eyes flash. "Did your meddling psychic friend say anything about that?"

Wincing at the fresh sting in my hand, I grit my teeth and refuse to answer. There's no way I can win against them. Even if one of them drops their guard, there will still be the other to take down. Plus, I'm getting lightheaded. I watch the blood drip from my hand to the dusty floor, the gashes burning like fire on my skin.

Behind me, I can sense Vaughn is fully awake, the even way he breathes I know is fake. I can only hope he has a plan and knows exactly when to strike.

Dad has put down the sharpener. He works with a gray cloth, shining the blades of each knife, giving every one a disturbing amount of attention.

Come on, Vaughn.

As if on cue, he shifts further down the wall.

"Hmmm," Dad says, looking at Vaughn's slumped form. "He's supposed to be awake for this."

"Why not wait then?" Mom drops my hand and scoots back the few feet to where Dad still kneels over his knife collection. I hold my fingers up, squinting at the blood she's smeared across my palm. I wiggle them, watching the pattern of red as it changes, morphing into different shapes like an inkblot test.

Dad shakes his head. "From the looks of her, she'll pass out soon. You've always been a little over exuberant with drawing early blood."

Mom pouts. "I've been waiting sixteen years, holding down the fort without killing *anyone*. Sorry if I got a little excited."

"Suffering, my dear. Haven't you learned? Isn't the suffering worth so much more than the kill?"

The kill.

My stomach rolls, bile burning the back of my throat.

She huffs. "You do it your way, I'll do it mine."

He gives her a sideways glance, eyes dancing. "I can't stop wondering if you've gotten soft in this life."

With a growl, she leans forward to slash the air with her knife, cutting through my leg, just above the ankle. When I cry out in pain, she lunges for me, all the while watching for his approval. Blood quickly soaks through my pants.

He stops her with a hand on her arm. "Tsk. Patience."

And then I'm dry heaving, bent sideways at the waist and trying to will myself to keep it together.

It's just blood. It's just blood. I repeat the mantra, but it doesn't help. Each place I'm cut—my arms, wrist, palm, head, neck and leg, pulse with the blood oozing out. I squeeze my eyes shut.

It's just blood.

If I pass out, I know this will be it. They won't let me wake again. And who knows what will happen to my soul.

"Stay calm," he tells her. "Let's get this set up. And then, we can rouse the boy and get started."

This time it's not dry heaves but real vomit that comes, passing over my trembling lips while I try and drag myself as far away from them as possible. But sheer terror has me rooted in place. Everything in the cellar looks soft, as if the edges of things have faded away.

Mom's eyes never leave mine, though even she comes in and out of focus.

Stay awake, Lange.

Everything wavers, but I know this may be my only chance. With the tiny bit of energy I have left, I throw my shoulder against Vaughn, then roll away from him. It's the only signal I can manage.

He takes it.

He springs into action with a roll that brings him to his knees, then to standing. His hands are tied, but he's managed to loosen them enough to maneuver his arms.

He's a shadow to me, my vision so dulled I can't make out his features. He's barely got limbs now, moving like a blob in my weakened sight. It reminds me of one of our past-life blurs in Sharon's photos.

Summoning one last burst of movement, I roll, grabbing the framed picture of Ginny and Hank and smashing it against the wall.

Mom and Dad move toward us in the split second I manage to grab the largest piece of glass. It slips in my blood-coated fingers. Since Mom still grips the knife, I go for her first.

Behind her, Dad and Vaughn tumble in a mess of grunts and flailing limbs. I slice at the air around her. I see two of her—no three. Frantically, I push forward, stumbling over nothing, into the wall. And then I strike something. It's soft and warm, with little resistance. Mom hisses near my ear before falling back on her heels.

I fall to the floor, my skull bouncing again with a loud crack against the cellar wall. A dark cloud descends over me, and through it I watch Dad push Vaughn against the wall.

"You ready to watch her die? Last time you only saw the aftermath. This time, I'll let you live until the last drop of life has drained from her." His hand presses Vaughn's neck to the wall, the serpent tattoo opening its mouth against Vaughn's Adam's apple.

Vaughn's eyes dart between Dad and Mom and me. My head throbs from where it hit the wall a second time, even more blood gushing down the back of my neck. Panic rises in me, buoyed on the reality of the circumstance. We are going to die. And that's not the worst part. They are going to force our souls somewhere horrible.

Mom's on her knees, blood soaking her shirt. Her hands clutch the knife by my feet. She crawls toward me, the knife in her outstretched hand so out of proportion to my addled brain it looks like a sword.

"Do it, Cheryl!" Dad's scream fills the root cellar.

She looks between us, biting her lower lip.

"Now!"

She moves forward, the knife trembling. Something sharp digs into my knee. A quick glance down reveals the gilded, antique bird's wing. With my left hand, I scoop up Ginny's comb.

With the glass still clutched in my right, I attack the air with both hands as the room goes dark, the panic and blood loss finally just too much. Grunts and the sound of pounding flesh fill the space, and the smell of blood is everywhere. Something clangs against the glass, the force vibrating up my arm. I'm shoved right, then left, nearly falling backward. A burning pain cuts at my shoulder as the knife slices through my flesh. I push back with everything I've got, digging as deep as I can.

A blunt, heavy object hits my temple. Pain shrouds me like a white-hot wave.

42

WHEN I OPEN my eyes, I see something I don't expect.

Stace.

And Ben.

They sit at the foot of my bed. Overhead there's the sound of an intercom, behind me the beep of machines.

Hospital noises.

Rhythmic pounding fills my head. My body burns and aches, my mouth so dry even the idea of speaking seems impossible.

"Hey," I manage.

"Don't move!" Ben's immediately at my side, fingers with his neatly trimmed nails lined up against the metal rail. "I'll get the nurse."

Once he's in the hall, Stace stands, leaning against the doorframe. Her black eyeliner is heavy under her eyes, smudged, and her hair is in some kind of fancy bun. "You're going to be okay," she says, looking down at her feet. "Kelly will be, too. Apparently, Vaughn saved her."

A nurse pushes a cart into the room. She shoos Stace from the room and leans over me. She has a blood pressure cuff on my arm and motions for me to open my mouth. She places a thermometer under my tongue.

"Well, how are you feeling, darlin'?"

"Hmmm."

"It's okay. No need to talk. You had an ordeal. There's some officers here to talk to you. You up for it?"

Officers?

Oh.

Flashes start to come back. The Hunt. Kelly. Home. Mom's pictures. The letter.

The root cellar.

Vaughn.

My father. My mother. Except they weren't.

The knives.

Vaughn.

I choke on the thermometer, spitting it against the blanket.

He was fighting my dad. I squeeze my eyes shut and imagine him as he usually is, lazy smile and tender eyes. I ignore the memory of the tattooed serpent around his throat. The knives glistening in the dim light.

"Vaughn?" I ask in a sandpaper voice. Behind me, one of the monitors beeps like crazy. The nurse places her hand on mine but I can't feel her. I look down and see how many bandages are on my arms. I look like a mummy girl.

"Just relax now. You don't have to talk to them if you don't want to. It's only been a few hours. I'll tell them to come back tomorrow."

A few hours? That explains Stace's eyeliner and hair. The Hunt was only last night, just a few hours ago? What time is it? The clock across from my bed tells me it's only four. Four o'clock in the morning?

"When did I get here? Where is Vaughn?"

The nurse continues to bustle by the foot of the bed. "Shhh. It's been a long night. Everything will be okay. I'll tell the officers to come back. You just rest and feel better, honey."

It's like she's purposely ignoring my question about Vaughn. My throat is too tight with fear to ask anything else. She wheels a tray next to me, placing a pitcher with ice water and a cup on its surface. I wrack my brain, trying to remember what happened last night.

"Breakfast is in a few hours," the nurse says in a soothing voice. "Any requests?"

I shake my head. "I don't want food." What I want is Vaughn.

She looks at me with a sad expression and smoothes my hair back. She turns the bedside fluorescent light off and tucks the blanket around my legs. I close my eyes and let the exhaustion drag me back into sleep.

43

I WAKE TO the sound of crinkling plastic. With my eyes still closed, I imagine plastic grocery bags, crumpling in the wind. The beeping still goes on.

I'm still alive.

I open my eyes, just slits at first, trying out the real world to see what it has to offer.

I see his bruised face and blink.

Don't let this be a dream.

But when I open my eyes again, wider this time, he's closer. Beside me, he smells like sweat and the root cellar dirt still caked on him, his hand like pure heat on my shoulder. My face stings when hot tears slide down the scratches on my cheeks and into the corners of my mouth.

"Hey you," he says close to my ear. Gently, so gently, he lets his lips stray from my lobe to my temple. I turn my face to his. Even with the bandages, the sheets aggravate the cuts on my body and head, but I can't stop moving toward him. He stops me by leaning closer, with his lips hovering against mine.

"You saved us," he says.

THE NURSES LET him use the shower in my room. His mother brings him clothes. No one asks him to leave. They know he won't.

But what really matters is that I know it. He sits in the chair by my bed and I fall asleep with my bandaged hand nestled comfortably in his. The nurses keep the blinds closed tight so even when the sun rises, it feels almost like night.

For hours, nightmares wake me. But each time my eyes open, I see our clasped hands. Sometimes he's awake, ready to calm me with the brush of his lips or the pure, simple look in his eyes. Sometimes he's slumped over in his chair, snoring. But his hand never leaves mine.

After a particularly violent dream I wake with a start. When the cold air sneaks beneath the gauze to chill my fingers, I realize he's gone. I half sit, the pain ricocheting in my bones. It skates across every exposed surface of me. But worse than the pain, is the fear of losing him again.

"Shhh," Vaughn says from behind me. His arm curls around my stomach. He's crawled into my bed.

It hurts so bad to turn toward him, but I do. I wrap my leg around his and his arms circle me like all the stars in the universe.

He mumbles sleepy words against my lips. I mumble some too. And then the hospital bed is filled with half-asleep kisses and the taste of him is the best medicine I could ask for.

44

By lunchtime I'm up and showered and I nibble on my grilled cheese and stare at the TV, which plays some soap opera on mute. Vaughn watches too, feasting on a Twinkie and a cup of coffee.

"Okay," I say. "Just tell me everything. The cops are coming back soon and I don't even have a clue what happened."

"What *do* you remember?"

"I don't know. My mom." I swallow. "I can't even call her that, can I? This is so weird. What happened to her down there?"

Vaughn spins his coffee cup in his hands. His eyes don't meet mine.

"She's gone, Lange."

"Gone?" My voice lilts in question. But I already know the answer. "I did it, didn't I?"

He nods. "But you had to. And it saved us."

The pit in my stomach lurches, threatens to come up. I push my lunch tray away. "How?" I whisper.

"You had that glass in your hand, that comb thing," he says quietly. "You attacked her, somehow. She fell, she was gone, I think . . . soon . . . after that. And you were lying nearby. You were passed out but I didn't know. Didn't know if... you were okay. It took Gerard's attention for a second, when she slumped down that way. It was all I needed. My hands were tied, but I put them, somehow, around his neck. He struggled, but eventually I broke my hands out of the rope. We were too evenly matched at that point. He grabbed his suitcase and took off."

"Did they catch him?"

Vaughn's silence is answer enough.

I close my eyes and take a deep breath. "What else?"

"Your parents. The police are looking for your real parents. After I called them from your house, we were brought here but I wasn't really hurt, so they questioned me for a while. I told them everything I remembered hearing down in that cellar, well everything that wasn't Obitus or rebirth related. They know you were kidnapped as a kid. They'll find your real parents . . . "

My real parents.

"How is this possible? I found the letter and went looking for that cellar. I found Ginny's stuff, our stuff. But then, when I saw them . . . *him*. And then after that . . . you, knocked out like that. God, it's all a blur, really. How . . . "

"It was weird," he says. "At the community center, I saw this creepy guy. He had this white blond hair, but like punk dyed. And he looked older, yet familiar. He was dressed young, like he didn't want to stand out. After my argument with you—"

"Oh my God, I am so sorry about all that. How could I—"

He waves my worries away. "After our argument," he says again, "I was up on the stage and I saw the guy again sort of in the backstage area, near the power lines and setup. He looked so familiar and then I remembered those pictures on your dresser. It was him, but different. And it was freaky because—"

"He was supposed to be dead."

"Exactly. So I watched him closely, not believing what I was seeing."

I lean forward, rapt with Vaughn's story.

"The lights went out and I didn't think it at the time, but when I went over it with the cops, I'm sure it was him. He somehow tripped the power and then took off across the room.

I wasn't far behind him but he moved quickly. I knew where you were and I knew, right then, that he knew it too. I reached out and spun him around. There was too much confusion for many people to notice, I guess. It was so dark. But Kelly was there, like right there somehow, by the door, I think. It's kind of a blur, but she said my name, and I knew her voice. The next thing I knew, she was on the floor and I was being dragged outside. There was a scream. But everything was still so dark in there. I knew the scream wasn't you, and that is the only thing that kept me going when he dragged me away from that place. I felt like I knew you, at least, were safe in that moment. Even if nothing else made sense."

"I'm so sorry," I whisper. I don't want to picture it, but I can't help it from playing out in my mind like some horror movie. "Stace said Kelly is okay, at least?"

"Yeah, she'll be fine. She's just downstairs but going home today."

"That's good," I say, still replaying the scene in my mind. "When do I get to leave? Any idea?"

Vaughn shifts in his chair. "I don't know. Your injuries aren't all that bad, really. Just some cuts and stuff. But they want you to talk to some therapists and they have to find your real parents." He looks at a spot over my head and I realize what he's not saying.

"I can't leave because I have nowhere to go. That's it, isn't it? I literally have no family and no home."

The truth is like a punch in the stomach and I fall back, deflated, against the pillow.

Vaughn rubs his thumb against my cheek, wiping at the tears. He pulls my hand to his chest, taps it against his ratty old Zeppelin tee shirt.

My eyes meet his and I understand exactly what he's saying. He's my person. He's my home.

45

BY THE END of the week, I'm feeling fine physically and I'm antsy to get out of the hospital. I'm tired of the doctors and nurses and psychologists fussing over me. But they still won't let me leave.

As usual, Vaughn visits in the afternoon.

I close my sketchpad and push it aside. I haven't really been able to draw anything anyway.

"How was school?" I ask, scooting over so he can lie beside me.

"Good, I guess. It's school, you know? Everyone says hi." He rolls onto his side to face me.

"Everyone, huh?"

"Pretty much. It seems like every single person I pass stops to ask how you are. Even Stace was happy when I told her how well you're doing."

"Yeah?" Things really *are* changing. Stace has visited with everyone a few times. It's not like we'll ever be best friends, but after all the violence we've all gone through, she seems to have mellowed considerably. I don't know if she still has feelings for him, but she seems to have accepted me and Vaughn together.

"Yeah, she was downright bubbly today about her mom's wedding plans. Apparently she volunteered to make the hand-made invitations." He nudges me. "Hence the envelopes, by the way."

"Ahhh." I cringe. "Oops."

"Yeah. Oh, and it's official: The Hunt is done for good. Everyone agrees after what happened, a fake murder isn't exactly something anyone wants to do anymore."

"End of an era, huh?"

"I guess." He shrugs and kisses my forehead. "You look tired."

"Nightmares," I say. "They won't stop."

The details of Monday night are still torturing me. It's unraveling in my mind, years of lies and deceit that culminated in the scariest night of my life. I keep seeing Gerard out there somewhere. The police haven't found him, but I try not to dwell. Not now. Not while I'm healing, anyway.

And as much as I'm sick of sitting around this hospital room, it has given me time to think about some stuff. Like how Cheryl's death is hard for me. Knowing I took a life is not easy, even if it had come down to my survival. I can't fathom the lie my life has been, the way she plotted against me, waiting all this time to kill me and mess with my soul. I can't fully accept that my life has been fake, some evil Obitus experiment. And even though her last moments were crazed and evil, I saw enough uncertainty and regret to believe she wasn't fully in control of herself. She didn't want to do it. Or maybe that's just what I want to believe. I can't face it otherwise.

Or that I almost died.

And I'm especially not ready for what's coming next. So yeah, my nights are filled with nightmares.

Vaughn brushes my hair back. "Want to talk about it?"

"No. I'm reliving it enough when I'm asleep. Tell me something else. Something about school. I feel like I'm missing everything."

"Nah. It's all bland without you there."

Neither of us say what we're obviously thinking; that this is how it will be from now on. That I'm not coming back to Preston.

"Draw anything today?" He asks, lips flitting in my hair as he pulls me against him.

I look at the closed sketchpad on the bedside table. "Not really. Not yet. Scribbles."

The smell of Vaughn—simple soap and that unmistakable guy scent—surrounds me as I bury my face in his shirt, trying to etch every part of this moment to my memory. The rumble of his voice against my cheek, the way the soft, over-washed cotton bunches under my chin.

"Any music?" He laughs gently against me, referring to the iPod he bought and loaded up for me, determined to get me up to technology and music speed. My favorite track is his recording of the song he wrote. *Abyss.* Our song.

I nod, swallowing around the lump in my throat that's swelling by the second. Vaughn rubs my back, gentle strokes like letters, like he's spelling out a secret. Somehow, he pulls me even tighter.

"They coming back tonight?"

I nod. "Around seven."

Tonight's agenda: Another awkward visit from my real parents.

Stewart and Annie Cambridge were located a few days after my ordeal. A nice couple who live in North Carolina with my sister, in the town where I was abducted and filed as a missing child sixteen years ago.

"Want me to stay and hang out with you guys?"

"Nah. I have to get used to them. And they're nice. It's just…"

"Weird?"

"Yeah. I mean, I have to move in with strangers. Nice strangers, but strangers, you know? I'll be hours away from the only friends I have. Hours away from you." I trace the line of Vaughn's jaw with my fingers, realizing how something as simple as two-day-old stubble is going to be a memory soon.

But it's only a year and a half apart. Right?

"Can you sing to me?" I whisper, nodding to the guitar he left against the wall so that even when I wake alone, it's like he's here.

"Of course." Vaughn pulls himself to sit beside me. He lets his fingers linger on my shoulders, on my cheeks and lips, and finally in my hair and I wonder if he's feeling the ache of what's to come. But then he picks up his guitar and he sings to me, like he always, always does.

Acknowledgments

When I think about all the people who were instrumental to *Second Verse* becoming a real book, I'm overwhelmed and amazed and filled with heaps of gratitude. It really does take a village.

Major kudos to Tracy Blanton, my first reader, the one who read the earliest, ugliest, messiest drafts—and every draft thereafter. (And there were many!)

Huge, huge thanks to all my critique partners and beta readers who pointed out the gazillion things I missed and needed and didn't catch myself: Steve Cordero, Debra Driza, Sarah Fine, Melanie Kramer, Tracey Martin, Dawn Rae Miller, Jaime Reed, Angie Spartz, Jenn Wood and the extra wonderful Shveta Thakrar.

And to all those who helped me navigate the publishing details: Kell Andrews, Emily Kokie, Stephanie Kuehn, Alice Loweecey, Gretchen McNeil, Jan O'Hara and LynDee Walker: thank you, thank you, thank you!

Of course that also extends to all members of all my various writing groups: The Purgies, The LBs, The Writer Nighters and the Divorcees—you people kept me sane at times, helped stoke the insanity at others, but always kept me laughing, no matter what. I never met more knowledgeable, smart, witty, and downright hilarious people as all the writers in my life.

Thanks also to my wonderful editor, Tracy Richardson, for her keen eye and insight and for being such an amazingly nice person to work with. Working with you is a dream!

Rachel Marks, thank you for making my book so pretty with your awesome pixy magic!

Barbara Schutzman who let me read every single book on her shelf, some even two or three times. You helped me fall in love with books.

And to my parents and brother, who have always been excited, supportive, and there for me with encouragement, no matter how far away the dream, I love you.

To all my extended family and friends for being there and always listening to me go on and on about writing and publishing way more often than you likely wanted to hear it, a million thanks.

To my wonderful boys—Love you much, more, most! To the moon and back.